WISH FOR

THE CRAVE SERIES
BOOK 3

J.L. STRAY

Cover by: Y'all That Graphic
Edited by: Word of Advice

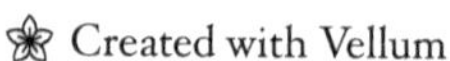 Created with Vellum

J.L. STRAY MOST RECENT RELEASES

The Crave Series

Lust For ~ *November 2023*

Lust For is a Brother's Best Friend, Rockstar Romance. There is no third breakup, however the slow burn is just perfection in this tale of sizzling chemistry.

Long For ~ *February 2024*

Long For is a Best Friend's Brother, Rockstar Romance. This book features an accidental pregnancy, with so much steam and spice thanks to the forced proximity.

Sinning with You ~ *June 2023*

Sinning with You is a Single Mom, Second Chance at Love Romance. This book includes found family and a FMC who isn't afraid to run a friends with benefits situation when the MMC can't get it together.

IMPORTANT NOTE

This book contains descriptions of abuse that may be upsetting for some readers. Skimming or skipping over does not in anyway take away from the story.

Please read however is best for you, and thank you for reading.

WISH FOR PLAYLIST

Interested in hearing what Crave Sounds like?

Scars - *Papa Roach*
Your Betrayal - *Bullet for My Valentine*
Broken - *Seether & Amy Lee*
Remember Everything - *Five Finger Death Punch*
Last Resort- *Papa Roach*
Break - *Three Days Grace*
One Step Closer - *Linkin Park*
What I've Done - *Linkin Park*
It's Not Over - *Daughtry*
I'll Follow You- *Shinedown*

CHAPTER ONE

The bright sunshine coming through the curtain gives me the impression that I've slept in. And I have.

"Fuck!" I cry out, looking at the time on my phone. I'm supposed to be on set with the band in twenty minutes. Showing up late is not going to be a good first impression. I fly out of bed and somehow manage to stub my toe on the corner of my bedframe. "Son of a..." The words die on my lips as I grab for my toe.

The path to the bathroom is mostly clear, and I switch on the water, readying it for a shower. There's no time to wash my long, thick red hair, but I can rinse off and wash my face. With a cold shower, I realize, as there is no steam rising from my water.

"Come on. Please, please warm up," I beg the shower as it refuses to listen. I guess I'll have to put a ticket in with maintenance. Not that it will do a whole lot. The maintenance men aren't the most dependable, and they don't always care when I call and complain about my lack of hot water. Especially when I'm late on my rent—again.

After the fastest cold shower of my life, I'm throwing on clothes and rushing out my door, the liquid caffeine of Red Bull and a granola bar in hand.

"This is just perfect," I say as I throw the car into drive and rush toward the job that will hopefully lead to bigger and better things. That is...if I can survive it. I'm pretty sure once the band's drummer gets a look at me, he will say, "Absolutely not." I'm an idiot for even accepting the audition. But I need the money, and a lack of it in my bank account has certainly had me doing stupider things. I'm behind on my rent, have no full-time job, and haven't had any dancing jobs for weeks.

I'm worried, though, that as soon as Brent gets his eyes on me, I'll be history. When I booked the job, I told the band's manager, Dale, that I knew Brent and that he wasn't going to like me being in the video. Dale assured me he would make sure I was hired. He said with my red hair, long legs, and chocolate eyes, I'm a perfect fit. Being on set today won't be like other jobs I've booked. It will be full of run-throughs, I think, and downtime while things are perfected on both my side and the band's. Once the run-throughs take place, the guys will watch it to make sure it matches the look they are going for—drummer be damned.

I haven't seen Brent since I was eighteen years old. I had it rough as a child, but he was my protector. I would run to his tree house whenever I was in trouble, and he would keep me safe until morning. His parents even helped pay for my dance lessons when my father wouldn't. They became like a second family to me, and how did I repay them? I ran away the first chance I got. I try to comfort myself by saying that they would understand. That they knew how hard it was for me. That they would be happy I was free and made it out alive. I knew, however, that Brent would never forgive me for it.

The man is now a drummer in a rock band, looking a lot like the boy I knew. The one who always promised to slay dragons for me. To make sure that the princess in the tower was forever protected. But who's going to protect me from him?

On my way out the door, I send Dale a text.

Blair: Please don't be mad, but I'm running a
little late. I'll be there as soon as I can.

I hit send, then do my best to get my beat-up Jetta through the busy LA streets. This black Volkswagen is the same one Brent and I found when we were fifteen. He spent so much time and money fixing it up for me, even teaching me how to drive. I worked in a diner so that I could buy it. It always cost more to fix than I had, but somehow, he always made it work. She's been a loyal car and the only thing I've ever had to remind me of home—and Brent.

My phone chirps, drawing me out of my thoughts.

Dale: No problem. Just get here, okay? I don't
want to have oversold you.

I sigh. Yeah, there's no pressure in that sentence.

Blair: I won't let you down.

I hurry to the studio as fast as the little Jetta can get me there, and parking is easy to find, thank God. Giving myself a quick once-over in the mirror, I take in my wild red hair and brown eyes, which look tired from all the sleep I'm losing over the lack of rent money.

"You can do this kiddo," I tell myself. I've been my own personal hype squad since I left that little town in Georgia where Brent and I grew up. I'm glad to see he got out, but I'm not so sure that he'll be glad to see that I'm here entering his life again after having run away so abruptly when we were teens.

CHAPTER TWO

I barrel onto the set, not bothering to look around too much. The video is being shot in a studio I've been to before. It's a giant open building that is sectioned off with dividers and what look like sound barriers to keep the music from echoing too much. Lighting equipment and cameras direct me to where I need to go for the shoot. There's a line of chairs in front of the green screen, where they have the band's instruments set up. There's a space right off to the side—the only space large enough for me to dance in. And it's right next to the drums.

I search for someone who looks like they're in charge so that I can announce my arrival, and when I spot Dale, I hurry over to him.

"I'm so sorry I'm late," I call out to him.

"Blair!" he says, rushing over to me. "For someone who needed this job, I thought you would be a little more punctual." He shoots me a teasing wink.

"Ugh I'm so sorry. Do the guys know yet?" I ask him, my stomach flipping at the thought of seeing Brent in person. I've Googled him over the years. I've kept watch on him on social media, through the band's page. I never wanted to actually look at his personal one. I never wanted to see the girlfriend or family he might have. More importunity, I didn't want to accidentally 'like' one of his posts and let him know that I've been checking up on him. It's a little embarrassing how much I've online stalked someone whose life I so easily shattered and could have been a part of had I not left him high and dry.

"No one has said anything yet. Everyone is waiting for you, so let's go over to them." Taking my elbow, Dale guides me through the various makeshift rooms that don't reach the ceiling.

It almost reminds me of an office, with the bland tan walls, but there's no office work happening here with all the lighting and camera crew running about. I note a makeup and hair area off to my right as he hurries me past.

"I think they are in this room over here," he says. Dale's hand is on the small of my back, as he leads me around the set. Steering me towards a destination that he has in mind. He stops and pushes open a door that wasn't quite latched. It's where most of the band is hanging out. There's a nice spread of some drinks and light snacks in there. No one is eating though. Their all talking in quiet voices. But I don't get the impression that we are intruding or interrupting anything. All eyes snap in the direction of the open door, as Dale says, "Guys, this is Blair."

Derek steps forward and shakes my hand. Aiden, the base player, does the same thing.

"This is my wife, Emma," Aiden says. "And my sister and Derek's girlfriend, Audrey."

I've seen pictures of both of these women. The media has a done a really nice job of getting those photographs of both of them. Audrey when she was sneaking around with Derek and Emma while she was pregnant. They are beautiful woman. I notice that about them immediately. But there's also a warmth in the way they smile, they're eyes are kind. Neither one of them looks at me with any type of malice.

Audrey is Aiden's twin. There's no doubt about that. Their

facial features, brown hair and hazel eyes are matching. She's long and lean, even though what I know of her it's her job to look a certain way, you can see by looking at the two of them it's genetic in some ways. Her warm features are a nice compliment to Derek's darker ones. Emma is pure sunshine. I've read, like the stalker of the band that I've become since Brent joined the band, that Aiden calls her Sunshine. It's a very fitting nickname. Emma's blonde hair, blue eyes just exude warmth. Her smile is warm and welcoming. Not guarded like I would have expected from women. Instantly decide that I like these women.

"Hi, it's so nice to meet all of you," I say, doing my best to keep my voice from shaking. I stand tall in front of them, keep my spine ram-rod straight, letting them know I'm a dancer who has grace and poise and isn't going to bend under the pressure. "Thank you for giving me a chance to do this. I really appreciate it."

Dale smiles. "Well, you were the best one for the job, and your style will fit in perfectly with the band."

The door pushes open. There he stands, all six foot four of him, looking as dangerously handsome as I always remembered. He no longer looks like the boy I fell in love with. No, Brent looks every bit like the man I've seen on social media and entertainment sites.

"What is she doing here?" There's no greeting. He looks completely infuriated by my presence.

Keeping my breathing under control, I do my best not to buckle under his scrutiny and anger.

"Brent, you seem to already know this, but this is Blair, and she's here to do the music video," Derek tells him. He leaves Audrey's side and comes over to Brent, placing a hand on his shoulder. "Is that going to be a problem?"

"Yeah, it will be. I don't want to work with her."

Fuck. His reaction doesn't surprise me, but it sure as shit does sting.

Dale sighs and pinches the bridge of his nose. "Look, I'm not sure what's happening here, but I'd like her to dance in your video. She was the best one for the job."

Ha. He knows exactly what's going on here, but I guess since he needs to appear to be on the band's side, he has to act like he doesn't. So much for thinking that Dale might be an ally.

"Dale...please," he says.

Emma is pleading with her eyes for Aiden to reason with Brent or Dale. She's tightly cradling her adorable baby as she shifts from foot to foot.

"Sorry, dude, no cigar," Dale says, trying to defuse the situation quickly. "She's who we signed the contract with. She will be dancing. All you have to do is play the drums. It'll be fine."

"I'm sorry, Brent," I reply. "I would have warned you, had I known how. But I'm here to do this job, and I promise I won't screw it up. I'm not going." I jut my chin out with a hint of defiance.

"You better go somewhere," he says. "Anywhere but here."

Nothing could have prepared me for how ice-cold his tone is. He must really hate me. I mean, I hadn't expected a warm reception, but this is worse than I thought it might be.

"No one is going anywhere." Dale stands in the middle of them, hands outstretched like he's holding them back, even though they aren't moving toward each other. Well, not yet anyway.

"Brent, can we talk to you?" Aiden asks. He gestures for Brent to follow him.

Brent just shakes his head. "No, I'm good. I'm not going anywhere. She is."

"I can go," I finally relent, throwing my hands up. He's not leaving me any other choice, and I highly doubt the band will side with me over their bandmate.

"Please don't go," Dale says.

"Go," Brent insists.

"Brent, over here now," Aiden roars so loud he causes the baby to cry.

Audrey and Emma work to calm her down while the boys walk away and talk to Brent. And I stand there, waiting awkwardly.

"Why doesn't he want you to hear?" Dale asks.

I sigh. Seeing Brent feels like there's a shard of glass in my chest; no matter how I move, it hurts. "Because I was almost his wife. Many, many moons ago."

Dale's jaw hits the floor, and I look over to see Brent glaring at me. But after some quick words from the boys, everyone makes their way back over.

"The show must go on, Brent," Dale says. "Suck it up and let's do this video." He walks away and talks to the other crew members, no doubt to get everything put together.

"Brent..." Aiden says. He seems to be at a loss for words.

Brent's face is pale as he runs a shaky hand from the back of his head to the front. He stares at me like I'm the one thing he's spent his life trying to outrun. Now I've found him here, and no one is helping him send me away.

I wring my hands, fidgeting from one heeled bootie to the other. Is it a million degrees in here? My palms are starting to sweat, and my face feels flushed. I'm sure everyone can see the embarrassment written all over my face.

"I can go..." I offer again, my eyes attempting to meet his, but I don't feel like I have the courage to do it. There's no sense in fighting it; if he doesn't want me here, why stay?

"Good. Go," Brent says, turning and storming away.

"No one is going anywhere!" Aiden booms, and the baby makes a whining sound again. "Sorry, honey."

Emma just winks at him. I want to smile at their adorable interaction, but the pit in my stomach is growing.

"You're already under a contract with us or something, right?" Aiden asks, his attention directed at me.

"Well, technically—" I begin to say.

"She is," Dale says, jumping in and shooting me a sharp look.

"Then there you have it," Aiden says. "There doesn't appear to be anything we can do about it, Brent. God knows I don't want to make you uncomfortable, but we need to do this. The dates are all booked out for the press, and we have the studio time."

"Which is expensive," Dale chimes in.

"I don't want to cause any trouble..." I say, the rest of my sentence dying on my lips. I want to tell him that I don't want to cause any *more* trouble, but I can't.

"Well, then you'd better go," Brent says to me.

"You're not," Derek butts in, trying to sound reassuring.

Aiden pinches the bridge of his nose. "We're not gonna get this done today, are we?"

"We are," Dale replies, coming over and standing beside Brent. "Look, I want to help you out. You are the one member of this band who keeps things running on the straight and narrow. But I need her to do this. And frankly, she is the only dancer we interviewed who didn't have spikes coming out of her nose."

He's exaggerating. There were plenty of normal-looking dancers in that room, but it looks like he might be breaking Brent's resolve. His shoulders shrink forward and his brow furrows. He's relenting and it's killing him to do it. The pain in his brown eyes is clear even from here.

"What the fuck ever," he says, and he walks away from all of us.

"Dude, what did you do?" Aiden asks me with a smirk.

"Don't answer that," Emma says, shaking her hand in Aiden's direction.

I can't help but smile at her fierceness. She's just a little bit of a blonde thing, but clearly, she's the boss of him. I was up so late last night googling and trying to see if I could find out about the guys. Mostly Brent. I wanted to know if I was going to walk in on him with some fabulous, leggy wife, while I'm circling the drain and almost on my way back to Georgia.

"We better get started," Brent grits out from the other side of the room. "Blair doesn't like to hang around long. Let's this done while we can."

He drops the insults and goes back into the main part of the set.

The rest of the guys wordlessly follow him. The girls scurry after them, and I'm left standing with Dale.

"At least he's not protesting anymore," Dale says, shaking his head.

"Yeah, expect that he would rather have anyone here other than me."

"He might, but this is your chance. Go in there and perform your ass off. Show him what he's missing and that you're worth hiring."

Dale means it as a pep talk, but damn if my feet do not want to move.

"Did I hire the wrong girl?" Dale asks.

I shake my head, blowing out a heavy breath. "No," I state with a confidence I'm not sure I feel. But let's fake it until I can make it real. "I can do this."

"Yes, you can," he says and turns face the stage area. "Now let's go do this."

We walk in the direction of the stage, where the band is warming up. "Guess I should get to stretching," I say to really no one, because no one cares what I need to do to get ready. They just want me ready when they call action.

I can't help but notice that Brent hasn't bothered to look in my direction, even though my eyes drift to him all the way through my stretches.

When I finish up, I just stand there watching them work through the song "Love Drunk." It has a nice beat to it that is perfect for belly dancing, which is where I come in. Once the band completes a run through of the song, Derek comes over to me.

"Hi. I'd like to officially thank you for doing this for us. I'm sure it's not easy for you, considering…"

"It's not a problem. I'm looking forward to it," I say.

"Seeing Brent or shooting the video?" he asks me with a wink.

I grimace. "I need the work. I won't be any trouble—"

"That's not at all what I'm worried about." He raises his arms to defend his words. "I just want to make sure you're going to be okay here. This isn't going to be easy, but we appreciate you being here."

I nod. "Well, thanks for the work and the chance," I say lamely. I'm not sure what else to say to him.

Derek nods. "It was nice to meet you, Blair. Thanks again."

With that, he disappears. Emma and Audrey are staring at me. How long it will be before they come over and ask questions? The guys seem like the type to respect Brent and leave it all be, but the girls look like they want to know more.

"Let's do a take," the director says. "Is everyone ready?" He's staring at all of us, holding his hands out like he's hoping to hold back whatever blowup may be bubbling up.

"I think we can," Dale says.

I nod my head and so do some of the band members. Breathing in and out slowly, I decide it's time to show the guys why I was hired to do this. I was the best choice, and old drama or not, I can do this.

The band begins to play, and I find the beat. I don't come in until they hit the bridge. My dance doesn't last for the whole song, only portions of it. The rest of the video will be made up of the guys playing, but I will be featured in about half of it.

Derek begins to sing. "Drunk on your love. Drunk on all the promises we once made to each other."

The lyrics strike me as coincidence that this is what brought me back into Brent's life. But I ignore all of that for now and move my hips to the beat. Step up and do the job I'm getting paid for. With a snap and a whip of my hips, I'm off and dancing. The small black bra top bares my flat stomach, and the black biker shorts with attached silver and black flowy skirt accent my movements. I hear a hoot and holler, but I block it all out and keep dancing. When the song ends, the lights drop, but the applause remains.

I flush and wipe a bit of sweat from my brow; the lights are hot. I take a deep breath and steal a glance over to see that Brent is staring at me.

I want to nod or acknowledge it in some way, but instead, my eyes bore right back into his. He has the ghost of a smile on his face, but he looks away, his frown a surefire sign that he didn't like being caught watching me. I look up to see the rest of the band looking at the monitors with Dale, commenting and nodding. I did the performance as instructed, so hopefully it was enough.

Soon, Dale makes his way in my direction. "You did a hell of a job. Your piece of this is iron tight."

"Good." I smile big. I guess getting it in one take means I'll be leaving the set and disappearing yet again from Brent's life. I should be happy about that, but something about seeing him again makes me want to hang around a bit longer. "So does that mean I'm done for the day?" I ask.

His response fills me with relief. "No, we need to run this another time or two, and then you can head out. I'm not sure if they'll run it more tomorrow or not. I guess it all depends on these next few takes."

I nod. "Okay."

"You doing okay?" Dale asks me. His expression is full of concern, his brows furrowed as he leans in toward me.

"I'm fine."

"Okay, good. You're doing awesome, Blair. This could really lead to some bigger things." He taps my shoulder and hurries back over to the rest of the band.

The director announces that we have a few more takes before we can wrap it for the day. We go through them time and time again. I'm exhausted and dripping with sweat when it's all over. The skirt is sticking to my slick skin. I chug some water, really wanting to douse myself in it, but I'm not trying to make it look like it's some type of wet T-shirt contest.

"We're gonna wrap for the day," a voice says.

Shocked, I look up into a familiar pair of brown eyes.

CHAPTER THREE

"**D**id you know I would be here?"

Brent's tone is cold and distant. This is the moment he's going to erupt. I've been preparing myself for the full force of his anger since I signed on for this project.

There's no point in lying to him. "Yeah, I did. I knew this was your band. I just really needed the job." I instinctively wrap my arms around my waist, hiding my toned stomach. Not that he is looking at me that way.

"Why?" he asks.

"Because I need the money," I admit with a shrug. "The jobs aren't always steady."

I watch his eyes, spying a hint of pity in them.

"I would have rather you picked a different job."

I swallow, the sound audible between us, as he steps closer to me. I want to step back, but I don't. It's been a long time since we've been this close to each other. There's a heat radiating off his body that I long to lean into. It would feel as comfortable and safe as I used to when he held me. But he's not mine anymore.

"I'm sure," I say. "But I would rather pay rent."

I know what I need to do. What I need to say. It's what I've always thought I would say since the day I left him. I've practiced this moment, thought over and over again about what it would be like and how I would win him over. But this doesn't even come close to how I thought it would be. The anger is there, sure, because I know Brent well enough to know that he won't let my betrayal go easily. He'll make sure to hold it against me every chance he gets, and I can't blame him for that. He was the sun in my life for so many years. When there wasn't a glimmer of hope or happiness, Brent was there. Then I just left him one day without explanation, and I took more from him than anyone else ever had.

"I..." I falter at the words I need to say, but I don't have to worry about it because Brent swoops in and speaks over my silence.

"I just wanna know why. Why would you accept this job? I'm not buying the starving-artist rap. There's gotta be another reason." He glares down at me, and I want to shrink back.

I wish I had more to say than that I'm starving and close to being sent packing from LA back to Georgia. "Brent, that's it. Believe me, if I had any other way to make ends meet, then I would have. But I didn't. I needed this job. It was a saving grace."

"You mean *I* was a saving grace to you yet again. I don't want to protect you or help you anymore, Blair. I've done that enough in my life, and a fuck lot of good that did for me. I could have gone so many more months and years without seeing your face again, and I would have gotten a good night's sleep."

I sigh and close my eyes, turning my face up to the heavens for any type of salvation, but I know it's not coming. An old habit from my childhood. When I needed to escape the horrors of what was happening around me, closing my eyes and finding my happy place was always my coping mechanism. Brent was always the face I pictured when I needed to escape and get away. But his angry face is right in front of me, and it won't help me now.

"I'm sure you would have." My voice shakes as the words come out. I tell myself that I need to say what I've rehearsed since the day I left him. Except in my head, it always ended with him forgiving me. But now I realize that was only a childish fantasy. "And if I could go back in time and undo my actions, I would. It just got to be too much. The burden of it all. You constantly needing to take care of me, be my safe place. I couldn't do it anymore. I needed to live in a world where there was no need for a safe place."

"And how is that working out for you?"

"The monsters are still lurking, but at least now I'm better at spotting them."

He watches me, nodding. Have I softened him at all? I doubt it. He carries too much resentment toward me.

"You've done really well for yourself," I remark, hoping that moving onto safer topics will help smooth things over.

"Don't do that. You don't get to just change the subject and compliment me and expect everything to be okay again. You left me. You abandoned me. I gave up so much for you. I stayed there when I wanted to run, and you ran without ever looking back, you selfish bitch."

I take a step back, looking at my feet and wringing my hands as I try to gather the courage to meet his eyes again.

"So how do you know Brent?" a sweet voice asks from behind me.

"Aud, don't." Brent is tense beside me, his posture rigid. "Please, I'm asking you not to."

Audrey's brown eyes look up at him with warmth and understanding. "I'm not trying to push or start anything, but I thought you two could use some supervision."

Brent nods at her and pulls her into a side hug. "Well, I appreciate that. But we're okay."

Audrey laughs and shakes her head. "You do many things well, Brent, but lying is not one of them. Everything is certainly not okay over here. I thought I would come over before someone said something they were going to regret." She bumps his hip with hers, and he looks down at her with admiration.

He cares for her. She's like family to him. I know that because I've seen that look before. It's the way he used to look at me.

Brent chuckles. "Thanks, Audrey, but there's nothing going on over here. Blair isn't anyone you need to be worrying yourself over."

My shoulders immediately slump forward like I'm protecting myself from his words. I wrap my arms tighter around my waist as they sink in. *Blair isn't anyone you need to be worrying yourself over.* Translation: I'm no one to him.

"That's not exactly accurate. You have never flipped out like this over just any random person Crave has hired before."

"Let it be," he tells her. His tone is stern, and she smiles even wider.

Their banter and body language are that of siblings, and a flame of jealousy fires up inside me. I hate that she's so familiar with him and knows him so well. It's what I've always wanted for him. It used to comfort me at night the first few years that I left him, imagining him with a family or with friends. The family part stung, but it allowed me to think that he could move on and be loved and fulfilled. That maybe one day when we ran into each other his life would be so full that my lack of presence still wouldn't be affecting him.

"You were amazing, Blair. I wish I was as coordinated as you are and could move like that," Audrey says, her brown eyes dancing as she speaks.

I flush, my eyes not meeting hers as she gushes at my performance. "Thank you."

I love the warmth of her brown eyes and the way she's trying to make me feel at ease, when in reality, all I want to do is leave. I want to flee the studio and hide out in my apartment. Eat my ramen and cry. But right now, they're both blocking my exit, and I can't leave without Audrey thinking poorly of me. Brent already does, so it wouldn't matter for him. But there's something so sweet and nurturing about her, and I don't want her to hate me too.

Emma soon joins us, baby securely in her arms. I smile warmly at her, wondering what she thinks of me. Clearly, they're very protective of Brent, so I'm not sure what their feelings on me are. Emma is small, but she has *mama bear* written all over her. She studies me carefully.

"I'm Emma," she says matter-of-factly, looking me up and down.

"It's so nice to meet you," I say, grinning at her.

I like how protective the women in his life are. Is there a girlfriend waiting to pop in and rip my head off?

"You were really great," Emma says.

"Thank you." I steal a glance at Brent. His eyes are boring into me.

"What's going on here, ladies?" Brent asks. The warmth returns to his eyes when he looks at them. I wish some of that was reserved for me.

"Just wanted to come over and say hello, probably the same as Aud," she says, winking in Audrey's direction.

"Uh-huh," Brent says. "What's really going on here?"

I smile at him, but he doesn't return it, and it quickly fades from my face.

"Are you sure you aren't just here for the dirt?" he continues. "Is that what you're looking for?"

Both girls flush and look at each other. That's it. That's why they're here.

"Can you blame us?" Audrey says with a giggle. "You're so secretive about everything. Even the bus bunnies get nothing more than a name."

Emma glares at her, and Audrey's hand flies to her mouth.

Brent chuckles, almost like he's enjoying my assumed discomfort over the mention of bus bunnies. I'm not one hundred percent sure what that term refers to, but I'm thinking it's some kind of hookup.

He shakes his head. "We're not talking about anything that would interest you, so you can stop trying to spy on me."

I guess it's expected that they're curious about us. Honestly, this little found family that Brent has makes me happy for him and sad for me. I don't have anything like this. I've made friends at dance classes and my old job. I don't typically spend holidays alone, but there's no closeness with me and my friends.

"But can you ladies give us a minute?" he asks. "I just want to ask her something."

My stomach twists into knots. What could he possibly want to ask me?

"It was nice to meet you," Audrey says.

"Yeah, I hope we get to see you again sometime," Emma agrees, passing me a towel like the rest of the guys had been handed. "You were amazing out there."

I don't miss the way they both touch Brent before walking away.

When they're a safe distance away, he speaks again. "You took this job because you had to? Because you needed the money? You weren't trying to see me again? Get another peak into my life?"

"I honestly didn't. I knew you were in the band. I knew I would see you. Hell, Dale even knew I was worried about seeing you because of how you would react. But I needed the money, and Dale said I was the best one for the job."

Brent pinches the bridge of his nose. "Did a part of you want to see me?"

I stare at him for a moment. He's getting at something, angling for a piece of information, but I have no idea what that is. "Just tell me what you want to know, and I'll say it."

He sighs. "I wanna know why."

I open my mouth to say something, but nothing comes out. All the reasons, all the things I've practiced saying over and over again, won't fall from my lips. I thought I would be able to give him this. It should be the easiest thing in the world, but the words are failing me.

"It was just time to go." It's a half truth. It was time to go; that much is true. But the rest of it...doesn't matter anymore.

"Was I even a factor in your decision? Are you really that selfish? I thought I knew you, but I didn't, did I?"

"I'm sorry," I manage, but it's not enough. His hollowed expression tells me as much. Though I knew it wouldn't be enough the minute the words left my mouth, it's all I've got.

"I see." With that, Brent turns on his heel and walks away.

I sigh and wipe myself down with my towel and prepare to exit the set. I just need to check in with the director to make sure I'm no longer needed, and then it's time to add some salty tears to my ramen noodles.

CHAPTER FOUR

Just as I think I've made my way to safety; Dale stops me and tells me that I have to join him and the band for a quick chat.

"What have you got up your sleeve?" I ask him as he leads me into a space set up like a conference room. The guys are already seated, along with Audrey and Emma. The conversation is light until they spot me, and then everyone falls silent.

Awesome. The only bright spot is that the conversation was too light for them to be talking about me. There was too much laughter and enjoyment. They're probably waiting until I'm not in the building before grilling Brent on exactly who I am. It doesn't surprise me, though, that no one knows about me. Brent was always a private man. It was almost like having my own private vault that kept all my secrets and many of his own.

"Please sit," Dale says, gesturing toward an empty chair, one that just happens to be next to Brent.

I lower myself into it. It's on wheels, so I do my best to shift it over so that I'm as far from Brent as I can be without sitting on top of Dale.

"Did we get everything we needed today?" Aiden asks.

"We did. In fact, the video is absolutely perfect. I love it. It's going to be some great publicity for "Love Drunk" and the tour that will begin next summer." He makes a point to look at Aiden when he says this.

Aiden reaches over and touches his baby daughter.

"What I really want to do is capitalize on the video and make a press tour out of it," Dale continues.

I don't miss the way he stares at each of the boys, like he's gauging their reactions. Emma and Aiden don't look too thrilled.

"I thought I was getting time at home." Aiden is staring daggers at Dale.

"It wouldn't be you doing the touring, and it also wouldn't be Derek. I was thinking of sending these two," he says, gesturing toward me and Brent. The wide smile on Dale's face is growing by the second. He either knows what he's doing, or he actually thinks this is a good idea.

"I don't think so," Brent says. "This doesn't seem smart. I mean, I like the idea of a press tour, but why me and her? It doesn't make any sense to me." Brent shakes his head.

"Is it because I'm sending you on tour or because I'm sending you and *Blair* on tour?" Dale asks him.

All heads have swiveled in Brent's direction.

He laughs nervously. "You're going to make me say it, aren't you?"

"I am," Dale challenges.

"Can you give us some background on why you chose Brent and Blair for this?" Derek chimes in, looking feverishly between Dale and Brent.

"It's a great choice because Blair is the dancer in your video and is dancing to Brent's drum break," Dale says. "It makes perfect sense. I'm a little surprised you're so against it, Brent."

I have a feeling he's being a little manipulative, but I don't say a word. I just let the boys fight it out with him.

"So, who would pay for her travel?" Brent asks.

"Well, we would." Dale points to himself, though I'm sure he means this is coming out of the band's funds. And maybe they can afford it, but I get the feeling Brent doesn't like that I'm taking more money from them.

"I see," Brent replies.

"Do you not agree that you and she make the most sense?" Dale continues probing. "Plus, this lets Aiden get some more time with the baby. Sending Derek doesn't really make sense with just the two of you. Who wants to see that? But, sending the two who are the main focus of our video…"

"I'm not the focus of anything," Brent denies.

"Your drumbeats are," Dale points out.

Brent shakes his head, his eyes cast down at the floor. "I don't think we need a press tour for this."

"We already talked about this, and we decided we're going to do one for the video," Derek reminds him.

"Well, that was before I thought it was going to be me and her traveling together," Brent says, laying it out on the table.

I cringe, wanting to slink so far down in my seat that I'm under the table and crawling out of the room. Everyone but Brent keeps stealing glances at me like they want to see how I'm reacting to all of this. What they don't realize is that all of this information was given to me before.

"I'm sorry, I thought you all knew about this. Dale and I talked about it when I signed the contract," I say lamely.

A hand smacks the table. I jump and my head snaps in Brent's direction. A hint of remorse flashes in Brent's eyes, like he knows he startled me.

"This is for the big ramp up for the Video Music Awards," Dale tells him. "Trust me, you want to do this. It will be great. It's not that many cities, either. I have you set to go to New York, then there's some press stuff in LA, and then I'm thinking about a stop in Miami. What do you think of that?"

Brent sighs and pinches the bridge of his nose. "Band meeting," Brent growls out.

"What? No!" Aiden exclaims.

"We didn't hold a meeting when I wanted one," Derek points out.

"You are not calling a band meeting right now," Dale says, shaking his head. "This really shouldn't be this devastating. Come on, Brent. Just do this for me."

"I hate to say this, buddy, but you kind of gotta do this." Derek gives him an apologetic look. "I had to do things I didn't want to do with Serena, and everyone was on board with that. It worked out well for us. This video is your chance to take one for the team."

Brent groans loudly like he knows he has no choice.

"I'm sorry, man, but you know he's right," Aiden adds.

"I do," Brent clips. "I just don't like it."

"I don't have to go, if it's going to be a whole thing," I finally manage to speak up. I'm trying to be polite, but I'm tired of being talked about like I'm not even here.

I don't miss the apologetic looks that cross Audrey's and Emma's faces.

"No, you're going," Dale insists. "Brent is going to be a big boy and put on his big boy panties and do this. Because right now, I'm asking nicely. Don't make me demand it, Brent."

"Fine." He sounds so defeated, and the pain twists on his face as he looks at his band members. "I'll do this, but I'm not happy about it."

"I get it," Derek replies. "But I think you'll have an easier time with this little assignment than I did with mine."

Brent shoots him a look. "It's not the same, dude. Trust me, it's not the same. And what you had to deal with isn't any worse than what I did. We're not going tit for tat here. This will be difficult in a different way."

If today wasn't hard enough, hearing his words makes it that much harder. I hate that I'm hurting him by being here. I hate it even more that I'm going on this press tour. Yes, it will be great for me—more exposure and more paid work. God knows I can use the money.

"Blair has made this video pretty special. You'll all get to see it tomorrow before the performance. We'll have Blair there as well so that she can perform live with all of you." Dale goes into explaining some additional details about tomorrow.

The only words I'm focusing on are "she can perform live with all of you." *Fuck.* I hadn't realized I would be doing that too. I thought maybe the video would be played or the band would perform live, but not that I'd have to. My stomach churns and I consider leaving to throw up. But fleeing would really only help make Brent's case. So, I sit there and stare at the table, trying to remember how to breathe in and out.

"You okay, Blair?" Audrey asks quietly from where she's sitting beside me.

"Sure, I'm great." I try to sound more convincing than I feel.

"Which part is more unnerving, that they're fighting about you being on the press tour like you're not even here or that you're performing live?"

I scoff quietly. "Well, both were surprises to me, so take your pick."

"I'm sorry Brent reacted that way to you," she says.

"He has every right," I say with a shrug. "Trust me."

"Even still, that couldn't have been comfortable."

"It wasn't. But it's okay."

She reaches over and squeezes my hand. "You're going to be great."

"Thank you."

I'm not sure what else is being discussed, because I'm too busy trying to keep from breaking in front of them, but I tune in just as Dale says something about emailing out schedules. I hope that means for me too. The guys get up and file out. Brent is the first one out the door. I swear I've never seen him move so quickly. Derek tells him this will be a piece of cake. I wish I felt that way too.

I walk over to Dale. "He doesn't want to spend this much time with me."

He shrugs. "He'll adjust."

"What if he doesn't?"

He sighs and looks at me. "Don't tell me we have to talk you into this too. Because remember, I am paying you to do this. All expenses paid."

I nod, hating that Dale is using my situation against me right now. I wish I'd had the guts to stand up there and say I wouldn't do it. That if it made Brent feel this way, I wouldn't do it. But I couldn't. I need the money, plain and simple.

"All of this is in your contract," he continues. "There's a clause that if we do press tours, you'll be a part of them."

"Yeah, but I thought that hadn't been decided on yet."

"I saw the footage from your rehearsal, and I knew before you even got here that it was the right move." Dale sighs, and I can't be sure if he's annoyed or starting to feel sorry for me too. "It couldn't have been easy to hear everything Brent said, and I'm not trying to paint you into a corner, but this is going to be good. For your career too. Think about it?"

He's right. "I guess. I just feel bad for Brent."

"He'll come around. Don't worry about it. Brent is going to come to realize how great the video turned out, and that it's the best decision for the band. He's always been great like that."

I know what he means. Brent always was the levelheaded one of the two of us. "I'm sure you're right. I just..."

"Blair, it's going to be great. You'll see. All of this will work out."

"Yeah," I agree. "Oh, and thanks for letting me know that the performance for the band was a live one for me too. That felt great to learn."

Dale chuckles. "You'll be fine with that too. I have faith in all of this. And I really *need* it to work, okay? There is a lot riding on this. The band really wants that VMA award, and it would be a perfect way to kick off the tour." His voice drops low. "It's the perfect way to ensure that we sell out those stadiums. No more small venues, just stadiums and world tours for them."

"He's always wanted that," I say lowly.

He grins like he knows he has me onboard. "See, all of this will work out."

"Yeah, I hope so."

"Who knows, this could be fun. Wearing all the fancy, fun things the stylist will send over for you. Traveling the world a little bit and hearing how much people love what you've done. Could be the start of something new for you."

I beam brightly at him. "That does sound pretty awesome. And if it helps Brent, then I'll play ball."

"Good. Thank you."

Dale pats my shoulder and then leaves the room. I sigh and begin gathering my things.

"Thank you for doing this for us," a voice calls as I'm leaving the room.

I look over to find Derek. I smile, getting ready to flee, but he comes over.

"I don't know all of what went down with you two. He's pretty private about it," he says, gesturing toward Brent. "But you meant a lot to him. He doesn't get worked up over girls easily."

"Well, he means a lot to me too." I don't miss the way his eyes light up at my statement. "But I don't want to hurt him unnecessarily. So, if it's best for me to sit out the press tour, I will do that."

Derek just shakes his head. "You heard Dale—that's not an option. And he'll adjust to it."

"I hope so." I feel like an ass causing all of these problems for these men, and I hate it. I just want to go home and curl up in my bed and cry the day away. Sure, there are moments I want to remember—the dancing in the video and the way it felt to nail it so quickly. Those moves were pure poetry with the song. I want to remember that. But it's been soured more than I would like with the new obligations from Dale.

"Don't worry, these boys get all caught up in their heads, but they come around quickly," Audrey says, sidling up to Derek. She shoots me a wink before adding, "Brent's bark is bigger than his bite. Go on home and get some rest. You have a performance to kill the day after tomorrow."

"Ugh," I groan.

"You were great, and the live show is going to be great too. You've got this. Plus, the way I see it, if you keep knocking it out of the park like this, you'll make all his dreams come true, and he'll have no choice but to forgive you."

"Maybe," I reply. "I want to be the one to help make his dreams come true. Whether he wants me to or not, I'd still do anything for him."

Derek and Audrey beam at me before she says, "I knew I liked you."

"Have a good night," Derek throws in, dragging his girl away from me.

"Night," I call after them, then I quickly make out the way I came in, thankfully without being noticed. Looks like I'll be getting my wish; it's ramen and bedtime for me.

CHAPTER FIVE

I run into my friend Angie as I'm heading up to my apartment. She's also a dancer and has been struggling too.

"Hi, Blair. Where are you coming from?" she asks when I bounce past her. "You sure are in a good mood tonight."

"I just came from a job, and it was amazing. I'm kinda on cloud nine right now."

"What was the job?" She looks excited to hear my news, so I spill.

"I was in a music video for the band Crave. It was so awesome. The band's manager said I nailed it. So much so that he's sending me on a press tour with one of the band members." I squeal with delight.

"Oh, well…that's great," Angie stammers out, a tight smile on her lips. "I'm glad you're working again."

And there it is, the backhanded compliment.

"Well," I say slowly, "I'm gonna go upstairs. Shower and get some rest. I'm beat."

"Yeah, I'm sure. Set must have been really tough." Angie rolls her eyes.

"Headed out tonight?" I ask, switching the topic. She's dressed in a silver top and skintight black pants. "You look hot."

"Thanks!" she says, smiling genuinely at me. Hopefully that means there won't be any more talk about the job I'd booked. "I'm really excited. I have a date tonight."

"Nice! He's going to love the outfit."

"Thanks," she says again. "I could see if he has any friends who we could set you up with."

I shake my head. "No, thanks. I'd rather just hit the hay."

"You haven't really dated anyone since you moved to LA. Come on, Blair, the guys in LA are way better than those in Georgia. I promise you."

"I'm good, Angie. But you have fun."

"One of these days, girl, I'm gonna get you to come with me," she says as she heads down the stairs.

"Be safe," I call after her before heading upstairs.

Making ramen doesn't appeal to me, so I just lie in bed, staring at the ceiling while thinking of how great it is that I got to be on the set of a music video and how it's translating into more work. This has to help me get another job, and hopefully another one after that. I squeal with delight into the empty room and wish I had someone to call who would actually be happy for me. Back when I was a teenager, I could have called Brent and told him all about it.

I think back to what Angie said about wanting to set me up. "Fat chance," I mutter. She was right, I haven't dated anyone since I came to LA. No one measures up to Brent. I'm always comparing every guy to him. They're never tall enough. It would be hard to be as tall as Brent, though. No guy ever has eyes quite like his. Sure, they're just brown, but I swear they remind me of a river of chocolate. One that I could swim in for hours.

I still remember the way his voice sounded when he was lying beside me at night. When we were kids, it was all innocent fun and his mother never minded that I stayed over so much. When we were older, she liked it less, but she knew my home situation wasn't the best. There were warnings to be careful and whispers into the night of promises that he would always be there for me. That he wasn't going anywhere.

But I was.

I roll over onto my side and pull out a picture from the drawer of the bedside table. It was taken at a barbecue his parents had thrown for his birthday. We were sixteen. Mine was two months prior, but they still included me. In the picture, I'm sitting on the swing with my feet on the ground, keeping me from moving. Brent is standing behind me, pulling me into him. His head is resting on my shoulder. We're both grinning wildly at the camera.

His mom was taking forever to take the picture, and he muttered in my ear, "Please take the freaking picture, Mom. Oh my god, she can never work the camera." He even asked my thoughts on launching me forward so I could knock her over.

I knew he wouldn't send me in his mom's direction. He loved her too much for that. He was a mama's boy through and through. But still, the words vibrating in my ear were enough to have me in stitches. His mom took the picture and gave it to me in a frame later that week. The same frame it remains in. It's always been at my bedside. Even when I left him, it was a little comfort from home I couldn't let go of.

We met when we were in grade school. It was the fourth grade, and we were paired together for a science project. The teacher assigned the partners, and I hated that I was paired with a boy. Girls, I understood; I was one. The only male I had ever really known wasn't very nice to me, so why would I want to be paired with one?

But the second Brent sat down beside me, I knew he was different. He was so sweet. He talked to me like I was just another kid. I didn't talk to a lot of kids in my class. I spent most of lunch and recess alone. Sometimes I would play hopscotch or hide-and-seek with the other girls. They didn't always remember to find me when we played, but I never minded. I liked the solitude it provided.

I kept mostly to myself by design. I couldn't invite anyone over to my house for fear they would figure out what was going on. Going to someone's house wouldn't work either; what if they saw the bruises? Keeping to myself seemed to be the best solution. The problem was it made me a social pariah. No one wanted to be associated with me because I was the "weird girl." The one who would certainly dance—I even won talent shows. But I wasn't invited anywhere, and if anyone tried to get too close to me, the popular girls would fill them in on just how weird I was. It kept people away, and it almost kept Brent away.

I brush my fingertips across his smiling face in the picture. Sighing, I lie back to stare at the ceiling and remember the first time I saw him. Even as a fourth grader, he was one of the tallest boys in our class. He made sure that no one teased me by doing a bit of bullying to some of those boys or even girls who thought it was okay to make rude comments to me or steal my lunch or lunch money from me. They thought I wouldn't say anything, and they were right. Or maybe they just enjoyed making my life harder. Either way, I hated it. But I never did a thing about it. And once I had Brent in my corner, I didn't have to. Because he took care of all of it for me. He made sure they stayed away and kept their teasing to a minimum and didn't let them steal the little lunch I had. In fact, he would even pack some extra in his own lunch to make sure I got enough to eat.

I also remembering feeling instantly safe around him. He just had that way about him. It was why whenever something was wrong, I ran to Brent. My dad would hit me or hurt me, and I went to Brent. Because at Brent's house, nothing ever hurt, and he would help me bandage myself up if I needed it. That happened a lot more than I wished it had.

His mother was great too. She always let me stay there and didn't say much about it. It wasn't until we were almost seventeen years old that she realized we were sweet on each other. Then she lectured us about being safe and not creating any little lives we weren't prepared to take care of. She watched us a little closer after that.

He was my knight in shining armor, the man who saved me in more ways than one, but I left him. I felt like I had no choice. He wouldn't have come with me, and I needed out. Staying permanently with him wouldn't have worked. My dad would have come over there, and I was afraid he would lay hands on Brent. So, I left, leaving behind the boy who was my first real friend, my first kiss, and my first everything.

It was a shitty thing to do, reasons be damned, and now I'm being damned by paying for it. I should have just told Dale that I couldn't work on the video as soon as I knew it was for Brent's band.

I look at the picture on the table again. "I'm sorry," I whisper. Then I cry myself to sleep thinking about the boy who saved me.

CHAPTER SIX

My nerves propel me forward through the large steel doors. It's heavier than I expected. I stumble a bit as I find my footing in my heels. The cool air hits me right as I enter, causing goose bumps to travel across my body. It's a small bar I've never been to before. I don't really go out much, though, so it doesn't surprise me. It's a swanky place called The Black and Blue Bar. True to its name, it has all-black furniture with silver accents, and the lighting in some areas has a blue hue. It's still empty, but the guys are up on the blue-lit stage, which has a blue curtain around the bottom of it.

I notice Dale off to the side, watching the whole thing take shape, so I make my way over. "Hey, Dale."

"Blair! Hello, my dear." Dale's eyes are shining brightly at me; he's got a nervous energy about him that seems to be making it hard for him to stand still. "I'm so glad you could make it."

"Of course! Thanks for sending the car for me." I smooth down my short black dress. I have on my black-and-white snake-print pumps, making me even taller than I currently am, although I'm sure the boys will still tower over me. I splurged on these shoes when I moved to the city. I wanted to make sure I could look the part when I needed to.

"You look great," Dale tells me. "Thanks for coming."

"You're welcome. I'm not sure why I'm here, though," I confess. He told me I wouldn't be dancing and could dress to impress, so I'm not sure what I'm needed for.

"The guys are going to play "Love Drunk," and as they play, a video of you dancing will play on the screen behind them. It's genius, really."

I giggle. If there's one thing I know about Dale, it's that he's not shy and is never short on compliments for himself. "Great."

"It's a pity we can't have you dance. That would really set the stage for all of this."

"Yeah, it's a real shame," I say lamely.

"You just get to cool your heels, enjoy the show, and prepare for those interviews." He notices the way I bite my lip when he mentions interviews. "Relax, this will be good practice for when you're on the road."

I nod. "Yeah, are you sure that's such a good idea? I mean, Brent doesn't even want me to be here, let alone on the press tour."

"Well, he's not the only one with a say," Dale explains. "Brent will come around."

I roll my eyes. "How you can be so sure? He's glaring at me right now." I gesture toward Brent, where he's standing with Derek and Aiden. He's clearly not paying attention to anything they're saying. "See, he can't stand that I'm here."

Dale chuckles. "Brent always does what I need him to do. He's not as strong-willed as the other two because he understands the importance of what we're working toward here. He's very good at the business end of things. Brent gets it. You'll be fine."

I wish I could be as sure as Dale is, but looking at Brent, I don't think he's budging. Finally, Derek looks my way. He gives me a small wave and shoves Brent's shoulder, saying something that looks like "Knock it off."

Aiden makes his way over to Dale. "Our boy is in a mood," he jokes.

Dale shakes his head. "He'll snap out of it."

"I wouldn't be so sure about that," I mutter, but Aiden hears me.

"I'm with the redhead. He's going to hold onto this one for a while," Aiden tells him, then he turns to me. "He's told me a little bit about you. Only talks about you when he's really drunk.

He sure does get around, though. There have been a lot of girls since you."

Aiden watches me closely, but I keep my features schooled. I refuse to let him get a rise out of me.

"He does it to get over you," Aiden adds. "They're never redheads. That he makes sure of."

"Stop it," Dale commands him. "She doesn't need to hear this."

I shake my head. "It's fine."

"He needs to sack up." Dale reaches over and grabs a glass of beer from a passing waitress. Raising it when she turns, he thanks her. "Look, this isn't the most convenient of situations, but sometimes in life we all have to do some shit we don't like. And this is what Brent has to do. End of story." He takes a long drink of his beer.

"This might be why we all think you're an asshole some-times." Aiden shakes his head, staring pointedly at him.

Derek joins us, but Dale hurries over to take care of some-thing related to the event. Brent stays exactly where he is.

"Dude, just come over here. We need to have a little band meeting before we go on, and you need to be a part of it," Derek says. "Hey, Blair. Thanks for coming out. This isn't easy on any of you, but we'll all get through it, and hopefully everyone will be all the better for it."

"Thanks, I hope so too," I say and smile at him. I don't know what it is, but I instantly liked Derek. He's a charming guy—I've read that much about him online. But in person, he is genuinely nice. Hell, he has to be a little nice or Aiden wouldn't let him date his sister.

"Brent, get your ass over here," Aiden calls, motioning for him to join them.

Brent looks like he mutters something, but he trudges over. "What?"

Derek chuckles. "Sweetheart, could you please stop being so mopey and just play nice? When the fans watch "Love Drunk," they need to see us happy. Got it?"

Brent nods. "Fine, I can do that. But not a minute sooner."

"Come on, bro, just be a decent person and stop looking at her like you'd like to kill her," Derek continues in a condescending tone. "You never know if the waitstaff or bartenders are watching."

Brent flips him the bird.

"I'm gonna give the two of you a minute," Derek says, dragging Aiden away. "Play nice."

"I'm sorry," I rush to say. "I wish I could leave. I wish I never would have said yes. I knew this would be hard for you. I guess I just didn't imagine how hard it would be."

"You never do think of those things, do you? Too busy thinking about you and what *you* need. Not really worrying about how all of this would affect me."

"No, I did. I was just made an offer I couldn't refuse." I'm so ashamed for not being well enough off to turn down a paying job. Even if I had a part-time one right now, I could have said no. But I'm so fucking broke that when Dale showed me the salary and all the terms, I just fucking said yes. "I'm sorry, okay? I'm sorry I'm not a better person than this. I'm sorry I wasn't a better person back then. I was only worried about getting out of there. I knew you wouldn't leave. I knew you couldn't leave your mom. But I couldn't live like that anymore." My eyes well up with tears, and his jaw tics, but he's not showing any ounce of emotion. "I couldn't handle the beatings. I couldn't do it, Brent. So, if this is the price I have to pay for a little bit of freedom, well, then I guess I have no choice but to pay it."

Brent just stares at me. He has no tells—that much hasn't changed about him. I watch him and wait for a verdict that may never come. Will he forgive me, allow us to be civil? Or is he going to keep on hating me?

I don't get my answer because the doors are opening, and people are rushing in.

"Get up here at the VIP table and stay with Dale." His hand comes out and gently takes me by the forearm, leading me to where he was speaking of. "Stay here, okay?" he says before jumping up on stage with the guys.

He watches me a bit longer, a softness to his brown eyes. I flash him a weak smile, which he doesn't return. Instead, he goes and prepares for the performance. Dale is at my side before I realize it, and the venue is filled to the hilt.

"We sold out on tickets," Dale exclaims excitedly as he sidles up beside me. "See, I told you this would be a good idea."

His energy is contagious. I wink at him and grin back. I'm so proud of Brent.

Before long, the band keys up the song and plays an instrumental version while they wait for everyone to get ready. This does the trick; the crowd lines up at the stage and screams their names.

Derek walks up to the stage as the band's spokesperson, like he's done this a million times.

"Hello you beautiful, wonderful people!" he exclaims. The crowd cheers loudly for him. "Thank you so much for coming out tonight. We're so happy that you could be here to hear our new song 'Love Drunk' and watch the amazing dancing of this young lady here."

Derek gestures toward me, and a blue-hued spotlight falls on me as the crowd cheers. I give them a little wave.

"Isn't she gorgeous?" he continues, to which he earns more

cheers. "How about we play you all a song?" More cheers erupt and the instrumental of "Love Drunk" begins to play.

"We are Crave and this is 'Love Drunk'!" Derek shouts and the band launches into their song.

I watch in awe as the video is pulled up on the screen behind them. It's different than the one I've seen. This time there's no band; it's only me and my dancing. I can't help but be mesmerized by the movements. I look around and see that the crowd is enjoying it. A few of them steal glances at me and then immediately look back at the band.

The song wraps and a long stream of applause follows as the band comes to the front of the stage. Aiden surprises me by hopping down and grabbing my hand. He pulls me with him and instructs me with his eyes to hop up onto the stage. Derek grabs my hand and helps me get up there. I'm stuck in between Derek and Brent. Derek moves closer, which causes me to move closer to Brent. An arm comes around my shoulders, and I look to see that Derek is also holding onto Aiden too. I reach up and put my arms around both of the guys.

Brent's eyes lock on mine. For a brief moment, I think he's happy, but then the trance is broken when the crowd yells my name loudly. I look over and laugh out loud. I couldn't in all of my wildest dreams imagined this. This is amazing, and I don't want it to end.

CHAPTER SEVEN

Once we're all led off the stage by security, we're moved up to the front of the bar, where there's a table and a line of chairs behind it, with little name tags in front of each spot. I don't miss the fact that I am again sandwiched between Brent and Derek. Did Dale do this on purpose or did the boys? My money is on Dale because I can't get a read on Derek or Aiden. They obviously want Brent to be professional, but when push comes to shove, I'm sure they're going to back their boy.

We all file into the chairs. Dale busies himself with making sure we're all comfortable and have water. He hunches down in front, motioning for us to get closer.

When we lean in, he says, "Listen up. They're going to come in and ask a few questions. The fans may yell out some questions even though we've told them not to. You don't have to answer any of them. Just focus on the ones from the press if you'd like. Okay?"

I look over to see the guys nodding, so I nod along with them.

"Everyone relax and have fun." He looks over at me and winks. "You've got this, girl."

He walks away, a sea of photographers coming toward us.

"They only look scary," Derek leans in and says. "Most of them are nice. Don't worry about it."

"Thanks, I'll try."

Brent surprises me by adding, "Most of the questions will be for us, and we'll do our best to keep the hard ones away from you."

I just turn and stare at him, dumbfounded. Why is he being so nice to me?

"Now, please look straight head." He winks at me and my stomach flips.

I try not to read anything into the wink and focus on the questions at hand. The guys are right, most of the questions are for them. They're talking to Aiden about the baby. There is nothing so wonderful as watching his face light up as he talks about his daughter. I keep peaking down at see him and his wide smile. Derek and Brent keep doing the same. Then a question is asked for Derek.

"When will you and Audrey be popping out some kids?" the reporter asks with a smile.

There are a few giggles from other reporters, and a few of the fans hoot and holler. I look over in time to see a blush covering his face.

"Yeah, that's not happening right now." He chuckles and shakes his head. "Next question, please."

The questions continue on and on, until someone asks me something I wasn't prepared for but should have been.

"Blair, what made you want to do this video?" a woman in the front row asks. "This is a special video and a special band."

My mouth opens and closes, and did she just answer her own question? What could I possibly say to it? "Um, well, like you said, this is a special band with a special song. I was so happy to be able to work with these guys. It's really been a dream." I lie so easily, though it really hasn't. There's been so much self-doubt and so much conflict that it's made it hard to enjoy this experience.

"I'm sure. Thanks so much," she says. "Brent, you have an amazing drum solo. Talk to me about what it was like to create that."

"Of course. When I was laying down the beat for this song, it just seemed to fit. I came up with it all in the moment. That's kinda how my process works. I heard the song coming together in my head, and I knew there would be this break from the guitars and the base, so why not give myself a solo?" He chuckles and she laughs along with him.

He's so sweet and charming. It's hard to imagine him glaring at me when he acts like this. I just wish he could act like this with me, that it was easy for him to be nice to me. Will it ever be?

The next question is asked of me. This time, it's about dancing and how I'm trained. I rattle off the answer that every dancer would give. "I've been classically trained for years. I take classes locally here in LA so that I can stay in shape and stay current. It's a labor of love."

More smiles and thank-yous. Everyone is pleased with my answer. I look over to see Dale giving me a thumbs-up. I'm doing well by his standards, too. I give him a smile and work on focusing on the wall of photographers and reporters that are watching us.

The questions continue for another half hour, then we're all led off the stage and it's time for pictures.

"Let's put Blair here in the middle," one of them is saying.

But Dale comes over and begins setting us up how he would like to see us. He brings over a chair and instructs Brent to sit on it. Aiden and Derek are placed on either side of him. "Blair, come sit on his lap, please." He looks over at Brent, as if shooting him a warning glance.

I can see the displeasure on Brent's face, but he nods. I move over to where Dale wants me and sit tentatively on his lap. Brent tenses when I perch on his lap.

"Hold onto her just a bit," Dale instructs.

Brent's arms come up on either side of my hips. I turn my attention to the photographers as Dale suggests, and that's how we take a few pictures. Then I'm instructed to look him in the eye. I do just that.

There's fire in those eyes. When his hands found my hips as I sat down, they relaxed. He may hate what I did, but his body remembers my body. It likes me being pressed up against him. To be honest, I like it too. More than I should. Because I doubt it will ever happen again.

The photographers are too busy giving us compliments to realize what's happening as we're staring at each other, but I see it. All of it. The moment when his guard is let down and his eyes soften. A ghost of a smile plays on his lips, which makes me break out into a full one.

"Perfect," a photographer says. "Oh, guys, I love it."

"Aren't they great? Look at that chemistry," Dale replies, feeding the narrative that the reporters are going to start spinning.

We're instructed to stand, so Brent gets off the chair and we take some pictures just the four of us, where we're just lined up. Thankfully, I'm eventually able to step out. I enjoy the chance to breathe and not be in the spotlight, but it's short-lived when they ask that we take pictures of just Brent and me. Then there's some more pictures of just me.

This is exhausting. I thought there would be a few questions, but I wasn't prepared for the large-scale photoshoot. And from the looks of the guys, I don't think they were either.

"Okay, all, thank you so much for all the pictures and questions, and for coming tonight. We're going to give the guys and Blair a breather."

Everyone murmurs their thanks. A few come up and shake hands. Some of the bolder ones even ask the guys for an autograph, which of course they oblige. I'm even asked for one too, which surprises me just as much as it does Brent. I can see the shock on this face when a paper is thrust in my face. I sign it and thank her for asking for it.

"See, kids, wasn't that fun?" Dale asks.

"I had no idea it was going to be this huge," I say when it's clear that no one else is going to say a word.

"Oh, did I neglect to mention all of that?" he teases. "Well, you all did so well. We got a lot of good content here. You were great in the interviews. Blair, I wouldn't have guessed this was your first run with the press. Really, a top-notch job."

I nod and say thank you. There's a seat just to the left, the very chair where I sat on Brent's lap. I sit there rubbing my hand on the edge of the seat and think back to that moment. I look over and see that Brent is watching me. I look away as soon as the eye contact gets to be just a bit too much for me.

The press is leaving and so are the fans. I'm surprised they're leaving so quietly. None of them got the opportunity to pose for pictures with the band. I could have sworn that was coming next after we did our little photoshoot for Dale.

"What are we doing tonight?" Aiden asks, looking around when it's just us left. "We talked about grabbing some dinner. Who still wants to?"

I shake my head, rising up on my feet. "I should get going." I'm not sure if they were thinking of including me, but I don't want to intervene in Brent's time with his friends.

"No, you should really come along," Dale says. "We're all going and I'm buying. Aiden and Derek, did you tell the girls about this dinner? They're welcome to come along too."

"Yeah, I'll let Emma know we're wrapping up," Aiden replies.

"Already on it," Derek says with a smile a mile wide.

"Come on, Blair, you can't bail on us," Dale says. "I'll make it a working dinner, so you don't feel guilty about it or something. Their plus-ones will be there, too. Make it less awkward for you."

I just nod. It would be nice to hang out with Audrey and Emma. I've only met them a handful of times, but I already like them. They're both so sweet, down-to-earth, and welcoming. It really helps with my comfort level around the band.

"Maybe just for a little bit," I reply.

"Great, it's all settled." Dale gathers his things. "Let's get ready for dinner."

We all file out of The Black and Blue, but not before thanking the staff for their hospitality. Dale also gave instructions for a couple of the roadies to grab the boys instrument sand get them back in the studio. I thought for sure Aiden and Derek would take their base and guitars with them. But I guess it's only in the movies that artists travel with their gear.

There are drumsticks hanging out of the back of Brent's dark jeans. I smile when he catches me watching him. He falters for a moment before continuing to follow the band. When we were young, he always had a pair of drumsticks with him. Some things never change.

CHAPTER EIGHT

We all file into the restaurant, and the girls greet me with hugs and hellos. Even Aiden and Derek say hello and give me a hug, but Brent just stares at me stone-faced. Dale is up at the hostess stand. He mentions something about a back room so we can all have some privacy. Which honestly sounds great with the amount of stares the guys are getting.

"I like that he's taking us somewhere nice to eat," Audrey says, "but damn it, does it always have to be somewhere they'll be recognized? Look at all the people who are staring."

She's not wrong. There are so many people looking, and a few have gotten out their phones to take pictures, but no one has approached them for an autograph.

"I'm just happy to have a sitter," Emma says, twisting her wedding ring around and around on her finger.

"Finally found someone you trust, huh?" Audrey asks her.

"Yeah, it was who Dale recommended, believe it or not. She's wonderful—British. Makes me feel like Mary Poppins herself is watching her."

Audrey laughs but hisses out, "You can't say that."

"I sure can. That was my favorite movie when I was a kid. That ride those kids went on was so trippy." She chuckles.

"I remember," Audrey says with a roll of her eyes. "I thought you were going to break that VHS."

"How was that trippy?" Aiden asks her.

Emma throws her head back laughing, not seeming to care that people are looking. "Oh, honey, spoon full of sugar? Did you really think that was just sugar?" When he just stares at her blankly, she adds, "Those kids jumped into a painting, rode horses, and chased foxes. Like seriously, how could that be sugar?"

Everyone stares at her dumbfounded, like she just figured something out for them. I've never seen it, so I have no idea what she's talking about. But I don't say anything. I just enjoy the looks on their faces as if lightbulbs are going off in their heads.

"You better believe we are sharing that movie experience with our daughter," Emma tells Aiden.

"What did I miss?" Dale asks when he joins us again.

"Oh, Emma was just ruining all of the positive memories we have of Mary Poppins," Derek says.

Dale blinks at us and says, "Cool." He doesn't even bother to ask what that was all about. "They'll be ready for us soon."

We all nod.

A woman walks over, and I notice that, immediately, Aiden and Derek step in front of Emma and Audrey. It's cute how protective they are of them. Brent, however, makes no moves toward me. But why would he? He hasn't stopped glaring at me since we got into the restaurant.

"Hi, could I get an autograph from you guys?" She's all bubbly and bouncy, excited to see the guys in the restaurant.

"Um, sure," Derek says, stepping forward and taking a notepad from her hand. Her fingers obviously brush over his hands when he takes the paper from her, but he plays it cool and doesn't say anything to her about it. He just signs the paper and hands it to the next one. "What's your favorite Crave song?"

She beams as she says "Forever" is her favorite. She looks at each of the boys up and down as they sign for her, biting her lip like she wants to ask for more.

"Would you mind taking a picture with me?" Her voice is shaky.

Aiden and Derek both hesitate, while Brent stands there looking at Dale, like he'll tell them exactly what do to.

"I'm sorry, not right now. We're about to head to our table." Dale snaps his fingers, and the hostess comes right over.

"Let's get you guys back," she says, motioning for all of us to follow her.

"I do hope you'll come and get tickets to an upcoming show," Dale says to the fan. "If you get a meet-and-greet option, you'll definitely get that picture."

I expect her to look disappointed, but she just nods eagerly and begins taking cell phone pictures of them as they follow the hostess. To their credit, none of them look annoyed. Although if I were them, I would be.

"Of course, she just took pictures anyway," Brent grits out.

"So did half the restaurant. I swear, some people's kids," Audrey says.

"Guys, it's okay," Dale says. "We're out here to celebrate and they put us in the back. It'll be fine from here on out. Now take your seats at the table." He directs them to their seats, ensuring that he sits me beside Brent like I'm on some kind of a date with him.

"Wanna switch?" Brent says to Audrey. That would put me beside Derek and her in between Brent and Derek.

"Nope." She grins like she's enjoying his discomfort.

"But I don't want to sit beside her." He sounds like a child when he says it.

"I don't bite," I joke with him, trying to lighten the mood.

"But you sure don't stay, so why would I sit beside you? I could end up alone before the meal even finishes," he spits out.

"Brent," Audrey warns.

"Come on man, don't," Derek adds.

I just sit there and stare down at the table. "No, he's fine. He has a right to be angry."

"I don't need your fucking permission," Brent replies.

"I knew this was going too well," Aiden says, shaking his head.

"This was going well?" Derek says.

"Can we just get through the meal?" Dale says.

"We aren't some weird little family," Brent spits out.

"Well, some of us are," Aiden reminds him.

"Uh-huh" is all he says about that.

I stiffen, unsure what to say or do. I start to push back from the table.

"No, stop," Audrey pleads with me. "Please stay here and hang out with us. I don't want you to go."

"Does anyone care what I want?" Brent asks.

"No, not really. She's staying," Dale says. He glares in Brent's direction. "Come on, man. You usually do everything I say, and I feel like all I owe you for that is a thank-you. But right now, I need more than that. I need you to just do what I say, okay?"

Brent just looks at him, and then his eyes go back to his menu. The waitress comes over.

"Hello, everyone. My name is Marie, and I'll be taking care of you tonight. May I start you off with something to drink?"

Dale takes the reins and orders some bottles of wine for the table. Marie leaves and explains to us that she'll be back to take our dinner and appetizer orders if we want any.

I don't miss the way she winks at Brent before she bounces away.

"Great," I mumble under my breath.

"What? Are you worried we're getting appetizers?" Brent spits in my direction. "That means you'll have to hang around for a while, and we both know you're not good at that."

"Enough!" Dale roars at him. "Just fucking stop it, Brent."

Looks are exchanged between the band and the girls, and has Dale ever talked to them like this before? I'm not sure what to do, so I keep staring at my menu. I hate that I'm the source of all of this tension at the table.

"I'm going to go use the bathroom," Brent says, pushing back from the table.

"There's one back there. Don't go out into the front," Dale instructs him.

Brent just nods and he's off.

"Hey, it's going to be okay," Audrey says, reaching over and touching my arm.

"I don't want to cause any problems. What if he can't keep his cool while we're on the road?"

"Nope, it'll be fine," Emma chimes in. "Okay? Brent is a good guy, and honestly, he always does what he's told. He's one of the good ones."

"Yeah," I reply, but I don't sound convinced, and I can see that none of the rest of the table seems to believe me either.

Brent returns, and thankfully, the waitress is back with the wine. She pours us each a glass and takes our orders.

"She's so nice," Aiden says. "Leaving us be and letting us enjoy our time together."

Emma scoffs mid-sip and looks at him. "Are you not paying attention to this dinner? The waitress is the least of our worries right now. Your drummer looks like he wants to kill the dancer."

"So, I'm just the drummer, huh?" Brent asks her, shooting a wink.

"Come on, Brent, just play nice," she replies.

"I'm being as nice as I know how to be," Brent says, looking at Dale. "And I would think that because I make it so easy for Dale that he would just cut me a little slack, but apparently I don't warrant that."

Dale sighs and pinches the bridge of his nose. "That's it. Both of you get up and follow me over here."

Dale doesn't even wait for us to answer. He walks over to the entryway of the bathrooms and waits for us to join him. I rise slowly and walk over there. Brent does the same.

"I need the two of you to listen to me very carefully, got it?" In the dim lighting, he actually looks intimidating, so I do as he asks. "Stop the bickering. Just stop it. I don't care what she did. I don't care what he did. I don't give a fucking shit why anyone left or what the reasons were, good or bad. I just want this to go well."

Brent goes to say something, but Dale holds up his hand. "We hired her to do a job. She's doing that job, and part of that is doing press. So, you will be doing exactly what I say. You will remember that you are a decent person and that you need this job. Act accordingly." He looks between both of us and adds in a menacingly low tone, "You do not screw this up and you do not make this into a story that the two of you are anything other than a dancer and drummer. You can be friendly and hang out together, but I swear to God, no fucking fighting. Tell me you both understand." Dale says the last sentence in a very slow cadence.

"Dale, I'm not seven," Brent says.

"Then stop fucking acting like it," he says, glaring at Brent.

We return to the table and finish our dinner. It's a little tense at first, but once the drinks are flowing and the food arrives, we're all happy.

A comfortable silence has fallen over the table while everyone is eating, and Emma turns to me and asks, "What other kind of work have you done as a dancer?"

I smile warmly at her. I've heard her called Sunshine a time or two, and I'd say that's an accurate description of her. "I've had a few jobs working as a dancer in the Macy's Thanksgiving Day Parade. That gig was so much fun. I got thrown on a last-minute flight when a dancer who was supposed to perform with Cher fell and broke a bone. My manager just happened to be connected to the right people and got me a job." I shrug, smiling widely at them all. "It was such a great time. I really hope to go back one day."

"That is so awesome!" Emma squeals. "I can't believe you danced with Cher. Was she nice? Did you get to meet her or get an autograph?"

Aiden places a hand on her shoulder. "Sweetheart, one question at a time." He chuckles and we all laugh along with him. "Are you ever going to get to dance for Cher again?"

"I'm not sure. I would love to. It was just last year. I picked up quick and she was so sweet."

"I can't believe you met Cher," Audrey chimes in. "I think it's really brave that you dance for a living—"

"Yeah, and it's not on a pole," Derek teases me. Audrey smacks him.

I shake my head, laughing. "Yeah, I try to keep away from the pole. But I do enjoy some aerial classes. Those are fun and help me with my flexibility."

"I've always wanted to take those." Emma is practically bouncing up and down in her chair with excitement. "We should totally go together sometime."

"We absolutely should. I'll let you know the next time I go."

I take a sip of my wine and another bite of my dinner. It's actually turned into a nice night.

"What is an aerial class?" Brent mumbles.

I look over at him and beam brightly, which I think might bug him more, but I don't care. I'm sitting here hanging out with these wonderful people who could have easily picked his side but didn't. They are being just as nice and welcoming to me.

"An aerial class is where there's an aerial hammock hung from the ceiling, and you do all those neat tricks and moves above the ground."

"That sounds like it takes some strength," Audrey chimes in.

"That's right, you're a fitness instructor. You would probably love it. It's amazing for building strength. You should come with us."

She nods vigorously at me. "I would love that."

"Great," I say, beaming back at her.

The conversation flows so easily from there, and I feel like I've picked up two new girlfriends.

CHAPTER NINE

I climb into bed after taking some Advil, knowing I may have a small wine headache in the morning. I don't drink much, and the calories are only a small part of why. My family's alcohol problem isn't something I want to be inheriting, so I try to stay away from it.

I sigh and roll over in the bed. I have got to go to sleep. I have an early class in the morning, and I don't want to be tired for it. Plus, there's more press that we have to do. More seeing Brent and hoping he doesn't hate me. *Ugh, what did I agree to?* is my last thought before I fall asleep.

I'm lying in my bed. Back in my childhood home. It's so confusing because I don't live here anymore. I should be in LA. I should be in my small, crappy apartment nursing a wine headache, not back in my childhood home.

That's when I see him.

The man who is supposed to be taking care of me. The man who is supposed to love me. But he doesn't. Ever since Mommy left, the only thing he has done is hurt me. And from the looks of it, he's back to do it again.

"Where have you been?" he growls.

This is always the first question he asks me. Every time I flee the house to go to Brent's, he gets angry. He has no intention of following me; he just wants to yell at me when I return. And hurt me. He knows just how to do that, too. He's gotten good at minimizing the bruises but not the pain.

He hauls me off the bed, grabbing me by my throat and slamming me against the wall. I shake and scream. I wish he would just let me go, but he's not going to. And now that I've cried and screamed, he's going to keep on doing it.

The smile on his face is pure evil. I've seen it one too many times. The pressure on my neck increases, and I know that soon, I won't be able to swallow. I wonder if this time he'll stop or if he'll just keep going until I pass out or he kills me.

Looks like he's in the taunting mood tonight.

"If you think for one second that you were hanging out with a boy who loves you, you are wrong. No one will ever love you. That's why your mother left us. That's why you're stuck here with me. It's why you will always be stuck here with me. So, get over yourself and stop running away from me. Got it?"

I don't reply. I never reply. I just try to avoid those cold eyes and try not to smell the alcohol and body odor coming off him. I shudder and attempt to keep conscious while he squeezes the life out of my throat.

As quickly as he grabbed me, he lets go and throws me to the ground. I hit it with a thud and begin coughing, trying to force the air back into my lungs, but it only makes me cough more. It's then that he lands a swift kick to my stomach, making me grunt and almost throw up the food Brent's family fed me. I cough and hack.

He makes a grab for my head and slams it against the wall. "Bitch, make sure you stay here."

He walks away like he's gotten the win on this one. I curl into myself and hope I can get to my room and not be noticed for the rest of the night. He slams the front door, and I hear the starting of an engine. Maybe he will end up in an accident and never come back. It's an awful thought and I know that, but I can't help it. Nothing makes him stop. Not the amount of alcohol he ingests, not therapy, not going to prison. Not the counseling that the probation officer makes him show up to.

If the man who is supposed to be supervising my father ever bothered to do half of his job, he would see that the man is beating me, but he doesn't seem to care. My father went away for petty theft charges and an assault. Apparently, not enough to warrant serious time. But those few years he was gone wasn't a reprieve from all of this. The apple didn't fall far from the tree, and his mother wasn't much better to me. And it wasn't a frequent thing, so I never knew when she was going to strike.

I carry myself back to my bedroom and curl up on the bed. I think about fleeing to Brent's, but that would only give him a new reason to be angry when he returns. So, I don't. I curl up in my bed and cry, thinking of the bruises I might have tomorrow from this latest outburst. I attempt to swallow, but I just end up coughing some more.

I go to the kitchen and get a glass of water to take to my room, hoping it will help my dry, burning throat. I lie back on my bed and cry some more. I want out of this life. I want away from him before I die at his hands.

I jerk awake and immediately reach for my throat. "It was just a dream," I keep repeating to myself over and over again. But I'm not even sure I believe it. I rub my throat, reminding myself it wasn't real. It hasn't happened again. He's not here and I'm alone in my apartment in LA.

"It was only a nightmare, girl. You've got this. You're okay."

I thought the nightmares would go away with time. That the longer I'm away from him, the less nightmares I'd have. But they creep up on me when I least expect it. They make me question my choices and wonder if I made the right call. Not about fleeing but fleeing without Brent. That's the kicker. That's what keeps me up late at night. And now that he's around so much and he's so angry, I don't know what to do about it.

CHAPTER TEN

I arrive at the press event early. I don't see Brent there yet, but Derek is. I walk over and wave lamely at him. I always feel so uncomfortable around the band, wondering if they're judging me because of what I did to Brent.

"Hey, how you are doing, Blair?" he says.

"I'm good," I mumble.

"You look like shit. Did you not sleep well last night?" He pushes a strand of my hair back so that my weary eyes are visible to him.

I just shrug in way of answer.

Derek pulls me into a side hug. "It's going be okay. Just relax. There are some beverages over there, so go help yourself. Brent is going to come in with a totally different attitude today, you'll see."

I stare at him for a moment like I'm not sure whether or not I should believe him.

"Just go," he says with a laugh.

I smile and head over to the table. I pick up a Red Bull and sip on it slowly. It's going to have to get me through the day and keep my awake.

The rest of the guys arrive not too much later. We're all

matching in black shirts and dark jeans, which is how Dale wanted us to dress. This is another press event here in LA. The press have been invited to ask us questions and see a preview of the video. This time, the guys aren't playing, though there's going to be a showing of the video on the large screen in the front. I never had any idea this is how things work. I just assumed when you release a video, it's sent out into the world and if they play it, they play it. But clearly, Dale is gearing toward getting them nominated for a VMA, so there is a lot of push.

Brent keeps his distance from me, but I do get a small wave. There's a lot of preparation to get things set up. Mics are placed on each of us, and sound checks are performed. They have us lined up like we're some kind of Comic-Con panel. Unfortunately, they've stuck me beside Brent. They should know that he wants me to keep my distance. And this makes it hard.

Dale says we're supposed to be getting ready for the interviews on the road, and because he wrote the beat that I dance to, it's a good move. I trust him for the most part. I just feel like he's forcing something. From what I remember of Brent, you don't force that boy. He'll come around on his own.

"Is Audrey not coming to this one?" I ask him.

"Nope," he replies. "But she's coming to dinner. You're coming to dinner, right?"

I shrug. "No one mentioned dinner to me."

He chuckles. "Well, I'm mentioning it now, so you're going."

I swallow, not really sure what to say to him. Derek's been the welcoming, friendly one of the group. I appreciate that he wants me to feel like I'm a part of this little family they've created. "Thanks for including me," I reply lamely.

"The girls will be there too, and I'm sure Audrey would like to see you. It'll be fun."

Brent clears his throat, drawing my attention over to him. "It'll really be fine," he says with a hint of annoyance. "Just come to dinner."

"You really got chewed out last night or this morning, huh?" I ask, winking at him.

"Something like that. Derek had some words with me, so..." His voice trails off, and I snicker. "We should talk later or something. I can take you to the dinner and bring you back here or something like that."

I look over into his pleading eyes. He's trying. So, I take the olive branch he's extending and go with it. "Okay, that would be nice."

"I have the bike," he says. "I'm sure you'll be fine on that, though."

"Okay," I mumble. I don't miss the fact that Derek was staring at us as we were talking. There's a knowing smile on his face, like we've finally figured out the secret he's known all along.

I don't say any more to either of them. I stare at the red tablecloth and focus on breathing in and out. These things are always so nerve-racking. Thankfully, all five of us are on the panel, so they have more of us to ask questions to. I get some questions about dance and the guys get more of the music questions. Sometimes personal questions come in for Aiden about the baby, or Derek gets asked about Audrey, which I'm not sure he likes, based on the way his smile twists at the mention of her name. He's always polite when he answers them. I'm not sure why the press thinks they have a right to ask questions about his personal life, but he does his job and answers, otherwise Dale might have his ass for it.

"Okay," Dale says, coming into the center of the room. "We are going to let the press in here in a few moments. I need you all to be smiling and happy. Can we do that?" He looks at all of us but doesn't wait for anyone to answer. "And we're smiling in three, two, one."

Dale motions for someone at the door to open it. They do and reporters and cameramen file in. Dale goes right up to one in particular and starts talking. I notice they appear to have video equipment, and he gives them a prime spot in front of everything.

My palms begin to sweat, and I rub them on my jeans.

"It's going to be okay," Brent says in a low voice. "You'll survive this. I promise."

I look over at Brent and smile wide. There's a flash out of the corner of my eye. We turn back to the cameras, and Dale is grinning. He seems happy the press caught that moment. I am less than thrilled, but I guess that's what happens when you let them into a room. No moments are private.

"It's fine," he says quietly to me.

I just nod slightly, hoping he caught it but not wanting to look in his direction to give the press any more ammunition or pictures to splash all over the place.

The questions begin to start. Most of them are for the band about the upcoming tour and asking about the VMA nominations. I notice that Derek is in business mode again, taking most of those questions, though Aiden takes one or two. Probably the way the band wants it. Brent doesn't appear too thrilled to talk to them.

"Brent, can you tell us about the inspiration for the beats for this music?" one of them asks him.

He gives her a flirtatious smile. "That's not really how my writing process works. There was no inspiration in writing out the beat. I was just messing around with sounds on the drums and came up with what she dances to." He points to me. "And I made a whole song out of it."

"How does it feel to work with the hottest boys of rock?" a reporter asks me.

"It's great. They are amazingly talented musicians, and I'm just glad I was chosen to bring their vision to life."

The reporter grins and adds, "It doesn't hurt that they're easy on the eyes, now does it?"

I giggle. "Sure doesn't."

Brent reaches under the table and pats my thigh. Thankfully, there's a tablecloth, so the reporters can't see, and I keep my features schooled. I try to take his touch as a good sign and listen to the question Derek is being asked.

"She's doing great. Not here with me today, though. You know she has a job of her own," he jokes.

The woman laughs and another one asks a question to Aiden about the baby. I tune it out for a bit because it's not for me to hear or answer. There really aren't many questions for me. I'm not sure if it's because the majority of them are women and they really want to talk to the guys, or they just don't know what to ask me.

Finally, it's time to watch the video. We turn our attention to the screens beside us and get ready to see it live. It's been a bit since I've seen it. And I swear every time I do, I pick up something different. The special effects, like the light show when I dance, are really awesome. The flashes of light match my dancing and Brent's drumming. It's incredible.

The lights are up once it ends, and the press and cameramen stand up and cheer.

"Aren't they wonderful?" Dale exclaims as he holds his hands out like he's presenting us all to the press. "Really put your hands together for Crave and Blair."

There is more cheering, whooping, and hollering. It lasts for a long time. The boys are grinning. They move quickly to get together for a group picture.

"Come on, Blair, get in here," Brent calls.

I move into the picture, and he places me in between Aiden and Derek. Brent kneels down in front them and has his drumsticks in his hand so that they're pressed against his shoulder. I look down and smile at his bald head before being called to "look here."

It's not long before Dale is clapping and says, "Thank you, everyone. Please head on out."

And they do just that.

"Dinnertime!" Derek says and claps his hands together.

"Emma and Audrey are already on their way to the restaurant, so let's go."

"You gonna follow us, Blair?" Aiden asks me.

"I'm gonna take her," Brent says.

"Oh, and on the bike. Nice!" Aiden says.

I smile and follow them all out of the back of the building with my head down. The press exited from the front, so no one sees us leave.

"Blair, come on!" Audrey yells.

"I thought you were heading to the restaurant?" Derek asks, looking down at his phone.

"Since when do I ever listen?" Audrey calls. "Now let's go!"

I laugh and run over to Audrey's car, hop in, and we pull out of the parking lot.

CHAPTER ELEVEN

The Mexican restaurant we pull up to is a smaller spot than we were at last night. It's nicer, quainter. Kind of feels more like them, too. No flashy menus or large wine listing. A small staff of people, small tables, and only room for one large party, which is us.

"The guys will be here soon," Audrey tells us as we're gathering around the table. She looks around and motions for one of the waitresses to come over.

"Oh, Miss Audrey," the woman says, hugging her tightly.

"Hola, Gloria. Thank you so much for holding this table for us." Audrey beams at her.

"Of course. I'm always happy to take care of you all. Shall I start a pitcher of margaritas for you?"

"Yes, please," Emma answers for her.

"Of course, ladies. I'll get one started. An original and a strawberry," she recites before hurrying off to the bar area.

"We come here a lot, as you can probably see," Emma says. "But it's a great little place and no one bothers us. We're able to just be us. I like it that way. Not that fancy shit that Dale is always trying to drag us to."

"At lease he pays," Audrey adds with a laugh.

"Yeah, there's that," Emma says. "He should, though, with all the shit he orders."

Brent and the guys come into the restaurant, saying hello to the staff as they make their way back. I love how personable they are with each one. It strikes me when Brent manages to lean down and give one of the small older women a kiss. She hugs him back tightly as they talk quietly.

Audrey notices that I'm watching her. "Brent really loves the little old lady. She's like a grandma to him. She fell and broke her hip once, and he made sure she had meals and was well taken care of while the family was at the restaurant."

I smile. "That sounds like the Brent I know."

Emma smiles knowingly at me. "He took care of you when you were younger, huh?"

"Yeah, he did. He kind of had to. I was a pain in the ass who never really went away. And he was a good guy who didn't mind taking care of me."

"He's a good man," Emma agrees.

"That he is," I reply. What I don't say is how much I regret leaving him. I left him all alone and now we're in this weird limbo where he's nice to me or he's very quiet. There aren't many traces of my Brent there. I just get to see glimpses of him. And right now, the way he is leaning down and talking to the woman is big glimpse of it.

Too bad that's not directed at me.

When everyone is at the table, having our margaritas and munching on chips and salsa, they start giving me recommendations.

"The fish tacos are to die for." Emma gestures toward the spot where I can find them on the menu.

"I would go with the enchiladas," Derek chimes in. "But the fish tacos are a lock. What do you always get, Brent?" Derek asks, trying to bring him into the conversation. He's been quiet since we all sat down, not really participating in conversation, just grunting every now and then.

"I get the fajitas," he grumbles.

"Yeah, those are good too," Aiden replies. "I get those sometimes."

I nod and look over the menu and decide on something vegetarian. I don't indulge in too much of the chips and salsa, but they sure are chowing down. I look around and smile at them. This little family Brent has is sweet and welcoming. I'm glad he found this. This is what I had hoped I could have when I was in LA. Too bad I never really put myself out there to talk to anyone or made a lot of friends. Now it feels like I'm being forced into this one, and it's kind of wonderful. They are all wonderful. No one makes me feel like an outsider, and there is always a warm smile coming from one of them.

I take a small sip of margarita and watch the couples around the table talking quietly to each other. I'm not sure what they're going over, whether it be the menu or filling them in on how the interview went. But it's sweet to see Aiden leaning and quietly talking with Emma. The moment feels so intimate between all of them, so I look away. My attention turns to Brent so that I can see what he's doing, but he's on his phone.

"What are you getting?" I ask him. I figure it's easier to just keep it to safe topics, but he must not be in the mood for talking, because his eyes stay trained on his phone, not even acknowledging the fact that I'm speaking.

"Those vegetarian enchiladas look really good," I say a little louder. "I was thinking of getting them." Nothing. No words or even a nod in my direction.

Unfortunately, even though he didn't answer me, Emma must have heard me.

"That's a really good choice." She then turns to Brent. "Blair was talking to you, Brent."

"Yeah, I heard her."

"Don't you think you should respond to her when she talks to you?" Emma asks him, speaking slowly like he's a child.

"No, I don't really see the need to respond to that question.

She'll be fine if she has to wait until I give the waitress my order," Brent replies curtly.

"Brent," Emma warns.

"It's fine. He doesn't need to talk to me if he doesn't want to," I tell her.

"See, she gets it." But he doesn't even smile or look in my direction, just keeps staring down at his phone.

"Stop being an ass," Emma says with a sigh and a shake of her head.

"It's fine," Aiden grits out. "Just let him be right now."

Derek catches Brent's eye, and they have some silent conversation, then they both look at Aiden. I really just want to yell, *What the fuck is going on?*

"Just lay off him, okay?" Aiden says.

Derek pats him on the arm and the conversation ends. Actually, all conversation kind of ends for a bit. No one talks while we wait for the waitress to return. I take a sip of my margarita, hoping I can ignore the whole thing if I'm drunk enough. What I really want to do is leave. I wish I could. But of course, I let them drive me here.

The table is quiet until Gloria comes over and takes our order. Brent ends up getting chicken enchiladas. For a second, I wonder if he's flipping back to his old ways. The girls are talking about the baby, and I pretend to listen, but I can't seem to focus on any of it. Brent is talking to Aiden and Derek about tour details. I tune those sounds out too.

"I'm gonna go use the bathroom," I excuse myself, then head into the bathroom.

I take three deep breaths, sitting there in the stall by myself. "Everything is going to be okay. You just need to calm down," I say out loud.

Three more deep breaths and I'm headed back to the table, where Audrey has rearranged some seats. I'm now seated in between Emma and Audrey. The guys are on the other side of the table, and Brent is the furthest away from me. Now he can comfortably ignore me, and I can enjoy some girl time.

Emma keeps on filling up my glass with more margarita. Strawberry is my favorite, and it goes down the easiest. I giggle and gossip with the girls. We talk about the absolutely gorgeous guy who walked in, and the girls tell me to go over and talk to him, but Derek shuts it down.

"But he might actually like to meet me," I say, giggling along with them.

"Nope, not happening. He's probably stopping in so he can pick up takeout for his girlfriend," Derek says, trying to burst our bubble. But it doesn't seem to matter; they just giggle at him and I giggle along with them.

"We should dance!" Audrey yells after we've eaten our meals. "We need to go to the dance floor and work off our dinner. Come on, Blair, let's see those hips work!"

"Yes! We need to!" I reply. I get up and follow her to the dance floor.

"I'm coming. Wait for me!" Emma says, coming after us. "Watch the bags, guys," she yells as she runs up beside me.

Salsa music is playing, but the three of us are just standing in a circle like we're at a middle school dance. We move our hips to the beat and laugh. Gloria even comes over to dance along with us. Her face is red, and she keeps glancing around to see who all is watching the scene.

"Gloria, how did we not know you could dance like this?" Emma says.

She just laughs along with us, then walks back to another table.

"Aiden!" Emma screams. The whole restaurant is looking at her, but she doesn't seem to care. "Come and dance with me."

"No, but I am going to bring you some water. You girls need water." Aiden and Derek get up and ask Gloria for fresh glasses of water.

"Here, drink this. No one likes a sloppy drunk," Derek reminds us, handing Audrey and I each a water.

"Let's go sit down now," Aiden says, leading Emma to the table.

"Or we could leave," Derek replies. "We ate and I've paid the bill. Let's get you all out of here so that we're allowed to come back."

The girls and I laugh as we're led off the dance floor. I drink down some of the water Derek gave me and follow them outside.

It's nice outside, and the cooler air is a little sobering. I didn't realize how hot I'd been inside. I guess it was the alcohol and the dancing. Either way, I look up at the sky and see the pretty stars and smile. Brent is watching me. I give him a nod, and a small smile crosses his face. Maybe all he needed was a little food.

CHAPTER TWELVE

The quasi-married couples ready themselves to head to their cars. I look around and wonder how I'm getting back to the studio, where my car is parked.

"What's the matter?" Brent asks me.

It's the first time tonight that he's really talked right to me on purpose. I pause, unsure how to respond to him. I stare at the ground, wishing Emma or Audrey would jump in and offer to take me home, but that doesn't look like it's going to happen. Audrey and Derek are whispering quietly to each other. The look in their eyes tells me I would be intruding. Emma is talking quietly to Aiden while he cuddles the baby. There must be something about seeing the man you love with your baby, because the look on Emma's face is telling me she wants to rip Aiden's shirt off.

"You're going to have to answer me. We cease to exist to them right now." Brent gestures toward his friends. His eyes travel up and down my body, and it causes me to shiver.

"Oh. That must suck for you most of the time," I say lamely. I really don't want to admit to him that I need his help, mostly because I'm sure he won't want to help me. He'll just feel obligated to do it.

"It's fine," he says with a shrug.

His brown eyes bore into mine, and it makes me nervous. I shift my footing, hoping he relents and walks away. But Brent won't. Even though I've wounded him and he's sure he'll always hate me, he's the good guy. The guy who takes the girl home, so she's not left stranded in a restaurant parking lot, instead of walking away and turning his back on her, the same way she has him.

"So, I repeat, what's the matter?" There's a ghost of a smile on those lips.

I sigh and give in. "I don't have a way home. I came with the girls, remember?" It's now just Brent and I standing there.

"I can take you to your car," he says and begins walking away.

"What?" I ask him, my brain still catching up with the words that have come out of his mouth.

"Are you coming or not?" He turns around and begins striding backward.

"Sure," I say and reluctantly follow him toward his car.

Brent stops in front of a motorcycle and extends a helmet out to me.

"I only have one, so here, this is for you." He extends the helmet out to me, and I stare at it like it might reach out and bit me. "Take it. Trust me, you'll want it."

"I've never driven one of those before," I stammer out. Drive isn't the right word, and I know it as soon as it leaves my mouth.

He snickers and rubs his bald head. "Yeah, well no one expects you to drive it. You just have to ride on the back of it."

I shake my head. "Yeah, sorry. I meant that I've never ridden on the back of one of those before."

"It'll be fine. Just put the helmet on and hold on tight." He makes it sound so simple, but the last part of his directions has me worried.

"I hold onto you?"

"Yes, it doesn't have handles," he says with sarcasm.

"I can't do that." My palms are sweating at the thought of

holding on so tightly to Brent. The idea both excites and scares me.

"And why is that?" His eyes dance with amusement. My discomfort is amusing him a little too much for my liking.

"Because you don't want me that close to you, holding onto you like that. And I'm not sure I want to either."

"Well, this is what I drive. So how do you propose you're getting home if you don't hold onto me?"

Yep, he's enjoying my discomfort, if his mile-wide smile is any indication.

"Do *you* want me holding onto you like that?" I ask him before biting my lower lip.

"Blair, I'll be fine with you riding on the back of my bike. I've done it with lots of girls before. There's nothing to it, trust me."

The words are like a gut punch. I'm not sure which bothers me more, that he's done this with lots of girls or that there's nothing to it.

"Right," I say, taking the helmet from him. I place it on my head and wait for him to mount the bike.

"Make sure you hold on tight," he says with a wink and proceeds to swing his leg over the bike. "Also, watch the pipes. They can get hot."

I nod as I do my best to get onto the Harley without getting too close to him, but it's inevitable. My arms come up and rest around him. He grabs my hands and pulls them tighter around me.

"I'm not going to let you fall off and kill yourself. Apparently, the band needs you now." There's a bit of bite to his tone. "You ready for this?"

"As ready as I'll ever be," I say, my voice shaking a bit.

"Relax, I'm an exceptional rider. You'll be just fine."

I don't miss the way his voice dips over the words "exceptional rider." If I wasn't already straddling his bike, I might have clenched my thighs tighter, but I fear he might feel it if I did.

The bike roars to life, and Brent drives slowly at first but then picks up speed the further along we get. I close my eyes. It's both thrilling and scary all the same time. When I finally gather the courage to open my eyes, the world is flying past me. The red hair that isn't covered by my helmet is whipping around wildly. My arms tighten around him because it makes me nervous when he turns. I wasn't prepared for all the leaning that the bike would do. His hand leaves the handlebars for a brief moment, and he brushes his fingers over my hands. It's a simple gesture, but it's sweet.

I rest my head on the back of his shoulder and let the world rush by. I relax into him, and it reminds me of all the times we used to lie together in the tree house. Except during that time, I was lying cradled into his chest while he promised me it would all be okay. I doubt there'll be any of those promises this evening.

We stop at a stoplight, and I pick my head up from his shoulder. His long legs reach the ground, and he looks over his shoulder.

"Thinking of making a pit stop first," he says over his shoulder. "Do you mind if I don't take you straight to your car?"

"That depends. Are you going to dispose of my body before you take me home?"

He chuckles. "No, babe, I won't be doing that."

"Then I guess it's okay," I say with a shrug.

I like that he called me babe. I like being on the back of his bike even more. Brent always was attractive. I knew that even when we were kids. The other girls used to look at him and fall all over themselves to talk to him, but he only spoke to me most of the time. He only took care of me. It had become a theme in my life; the only one who cared about me or made sure I felt safe was Brent.

I bury my nose into his back, breathing in his scent. It's a musky, spicy smell. I inhale a time or two, trying to pick out the exact spice, but I'm failing. We're nearing the ocean and the smell of salt from the beach takes over. A sign to right of us shows we're at Paradise Cove.

Brent goes rigid beneath me. There was already a bit of stiffness to his muscles in order to keep his form on the bike, but right now he's tense. I'm not sure if the feeling of me being this close to him is welcome.

Paradise Cove was the first beach I came to when I moved to LA. Being from Georgia, the nearest beach I could visit was four hours away, and my dad wouldn't dare take me there. Brent went on family trips, but that was about it. Of course, I wasn't included on those family trips, even though his mom took care of me from time to time like I was her own. I hate that I haven't seen her since I left.

The bike slows and Brent pulls up to a small parking area. He dismounts and begins heading out toward the pier, which looks like it could fall into the sea at any minute.

"Brent!" I call after him as I struggle to unhook the helmet. "Brent!"

He just keeps striding toward the pier. Is he going to stop, or will he just keep on walking right off it? There's a storm brewing between us, one that may come to a head here shortly.

Fuck. I guess I have to follow him.

rent is walking briskly to the pier, and a few fishermen stop and stare at him. He must look so intimidating from the front, black T-shirt, dark jeans, and tattoos on full display. His bald head is gleaming in the little bit of sun that hasn't set yet. He looks menacing. I wouldn't fuck with him.

But yet here I am, about to do just that. I hurry after him as fast as my long legs can take me. He stops short of the end of the pier, which is split in two. There's a decent amount for walking and fishing, and there's a gap about five feet wide that separates the pieces of the pier. I've heard a storm has caused the separation. I wonder if anyone has ever tried to jump to the other side. If they've dared one another or tried to show off to friends or girlfriends. I sure wouldn't. It looks like a long way down into the likely cold and dark water.

"Brent!" I call to him as I reach where he stands at the end of the pier. "What's wrong?"

He turns toward me, brown eyes blazing with fury. "Why did you leave me?"

I stuck in a breath. I knew it was only a matter of time before he asked me this question. I don't have a good answer for it, at least one that he'll accept. How could he? He's been angry over this for years.

"I had to," I say solemnly.

"Bullshit."

"It's not bullshit. I couldn't be there anymore. I had to get out of there, and it had to be that exact minute, or my circumstances would suffocate me. Leaving you wasn't easy, Brent, not by a long shot."

"But you still managed to do it," he points out.

Brents arms are crossed, and his eyes are smoldering with anger. Has this conversation been playing out in his head since he discovered I was gone?

"I did," I tell him, turning my head and looking out at the dark, cold water. It suddenly feels like a better option than being on this pier. Damn it, if I wasn't so broke, I could have taken an Uber. "I'm sorry I left you, Brent. I *really* am. But I never wanted to hurt you."

"No, you just wanted to vanish in the middle of the night and never speak to me again."

"Well, I wouldn't say never." I manage a weak smile and hope for one in return, but he remains stone-faced.

"Blair." His voice is laced with disappointment, and I shrink into myself.

"Nothing I say to you right now is going to be enough."

"Fucking try me," he grits out.

"He tried to touch me." I say the words in a whisper, hoping no one else on this pier heard me.

"What?" His voice is full of venom and malice. *He* heard me.

"Please don't make me say it again."

"Why didn't you tell me? I would have killed that mother-fucker." He takes a step toward me, but his hands don't move from his sides. "I wish I would have known."

"That look you have in your eye right now, that pity...that is why I didn't," I say, a sob breaking through. My shoulders begin to shake, and I turn and hold onto the railing for support.

He comes up behind me, but he doesn't touch me. It's the exact reason I stayed away from him for all these years. It's why I never told him. I knew he would treat me differently, look at me differently, and that we wouldn't be Brent and Blair anymore. So, I went away before any of that could take place.

"I wish I would have known this all along," he whispers. "I would have fucking killed him."

I turn and look at him, but he's staring out at the sea. His brown eyes look almost black with anger.

"That's one of the reasons I never told you," I admit. "Then you would never be what you are right now. You'd be stuck rotting in jail."

"You're assuming I would have gotten caught. Besides, if I would have told the police all the fucked-up shit that piece of shit did to you, add in the touching, no jury would have convicted me."

He sounds so sure of himself. I just shake my head, my gaze going back to the ocean.

"Well, either way, it seemed like the best approach was to leave him. But it wasn't easy leaving you. I thought of you every second of every day when I left. I saw your success in Crave a few years ago, and I knew I had done the right thing by leaving you. Look what you've become."

"Yeah, but I lost you." He comes over the railing and stands beside me. "When Derek called and took me to Cary with him to start this band with Aiden, I would have taken you with me. I never would have left you there in Georgia, especially with him and no one to take care of you."

"Brent, you have a certain sense of responsibility when it comes to me and part of me never really liked that because I felt like I was holding you back. And as freeing as it was for me to leave you there, I thought it would have been as equally freeing for you."

"It was hell. I attempted to find you at first, but it proved to be useless. I went to the sperm donor's home, and he said he had no idea where you were. He had some other colorful things to say, which I won't repeat to you, but he had no idea. Not that I expected he would. I just asked him what had happened the night before and he didn't mention it."

"Why would he?" I ask him, chuckling darkly. "He never did admit to what he did to me. He would see the bruises and have the audacity to ask me what had happened."

"Asshole," Brent says a bit too loudly.

A fisherman looks in our direction. I can't tell if he's listening to us or not. A few of them have left or moved further down, but not the two old men who are about ten feet away from us. They must have found a lucky spot for the day.

"It's fine. It's over now."

"Is it?" he asks, staring at me, daring me to say that it is.

"No. I mean, it ruined this." I gesture between the two of us. I always could read him so easily. Being with him was as easy as breathing but leaving him tore a hole in my heart the size of a glacier. It's something you never get over. Clearly, he hasn't, and every time I see him, my palms sweat and my heart races. But then I remember that the handsome rock star in front of me isn't mine to touch anymore.

"You did, but that's not what I was referring to." He pauses and glances around the pier, his tone growing low and deadly. "Do you ever see him?"

I shake my head. A lump of emotion forms in my throat, and a tear slides down my check. I wipe it away with the back of my hand. "No, I haven't seen him in a long time. My uncle Thomas reached out to me a while ago and asked me if I could help him at all. He needed a lawyer. Something about stealing a car, which, according to his brother, wasn't his fault."

Brent scoffs, shaking his head. "Yeah, right."

"I thought the same thing, so I Googled."

Brent smirks, and it actually makes me smile.

"It wasn't true," I tell him.

"Miserable bastard," Brent says, grabbing a hold of the railing so tightly the whites of his knuckles appear. If the pier were any weaker, he would break the railing. "I remember the one time I found you and you had that broken arm. I wanted to kill him. But my mom wouldn't let me anywhere near your house. She kept me so busy making dinners for you and some freaking gift basket of all of your favorite things."

"I was twelve when that happened. What would you have done?"

"I was big for my age. What wouldn't I have done for you?"

I look over at him and smile. I don't miss that he said *wouldn't*. We're talking about the past. It's not like I need protected from anyone anymore. Maybe just myself and the occasional debt collector.

"And then I had to go and leave you."

"Yeah, you did."

"I'm sorry," I say again.

"I know you are."

"But it doesn't change anything, does it?" I ask him. I turn and look at the sea, trying to see what he's staring so intently at. I see nothing but a black abyss. It's fitting really.

"I appreciate the apology, and I know you *are* sorry, but something like this doesn't go away overnight," he admits with a shrug.

We turn and face each other. "I understand. We're going to be seeing each other a lot more now with the press tour."

"Oh, I know," he says with a shake of his head. "If I didn't know any better, I'd say you did this on purpose." He holds his hand up to silence me because I'm moments away from interrupting him. "I know you didn't. You just really need this."

"I do, or I wouldn't be here."

"Then I guess you and I are going to find a way." He reaches out and brushes my cheek with the back of his hand.

I shudder at the touch. He misreads it, though.

"You must be getting cold. Let's get you home." He turns to head back down the pier.

I nod. "Yeah, let's."

I'm not cold; the shudder was caused by the heat of his body touching mine. That familiar jolt of electricity is still there after all these years. It makes me smile, my steps lighter as I follow him down the pier and back to the bike.

We hop on, wordless. This time when I grab ahold of him, it's tighter, just like he instructed me to do before. Now I'm doing it correctly, holding onto him on purpose. Me leaving without a trace or a backward glance had to hurt. It hurt me, so I can't imagine what it did to him, the not knowing. It must have killed him.

A tear trickles down my cheek, thinking of how enraged and lonely he must have been. He really only had me. Sure, there were friends he hung out with and a band he noodled around with. But none of them were really serious about music. Not the way Brent was. He wanted to make it a career and he has. I have no idea what happened to the other guys, but they had planned to attend college that fall. Not Brent, though. He was going to make something of himself in the music world, and boy did he ever.

CHAPTER FOURTEEN

The motorcycle slows to a stop in the parking lot of the studio. We're the only two left. It's late and I look around as the wind picks up, causing my red hair to whip into my face.

"It's still trying to kill you," he jokes as he pushes the thick strands out of my face.

"Yeah, still is." I flush, feeling happy that he remembers. "Are we okay?" I ask him, rocking on my heels. It seems like a weird question to ask him, but it's one I need the answer to.

"How do you mean?"

"I mean, do you still hate me?" I ask him. "Will you be nice to me when you see me now? Was there some form of a truce started tonight?"

He watches me for longer than I would like him to. I nod, knowing the answer.

"Blair," he says my name and sighs. "I can't get over what you did. I should, but I can't. It sounds shitty of me, but you have no idea what it was like to wake up and find the light of your life had been shut out. Sorry, I don't bounce back that easily. But I won't scratch your eyes out every time I see you, how's that?"

I chuckle and shake my head. "I guess that's going to have to do."

"For now, huh? That's what you aren't saying?"

"Who said for now? Who says I'm not just good with being your friend?"

"Because you and I have known each other far too long to just be playing pretend." He smirks and I beam back at him. It's my favorite expression of his. I used to fall asleep to that picture in my mind when he wasn't beside me. It helped relax me when I was stuck at home, and it gave me some peace from the war zone my house was.

"I would have to agree with that," I say. I sigh and head toward my car.

"You heading home?"

"Yeah. Why, wanna join me?" I tease.

He shakes his head, laughing. "No, where do you live? I'd like to see you home and make sure you get there safely."

"I'll be fine. I've gone home a million times by myself." I throw the last sentence in because I don't want him getting the wrong idea.

"I know you have, but that doesn't mean I'm going to let you do that now. Not on my watch. My mama raised me better than that." He winks at me. My whole-body flushes at the simple gesture.

I really need to be careful with this man. He could easily have me wishing we could fall back into old patterns again and have me falling back in love with him in no time. It would be a bad idea, not just because we are working together, but I never mix business with pleasure. Not that he would anyway; apology seemingly accepted or not, he wouldn't go there. I shake my head, wiping away those thoughts.

"What?" he asks.

"Nothing," I reply with a shrug. "If you want to follow me home, I can't stop you, but I'm not inviting you up." I saunter over to my car.

"I'll be right behind you." He mounts the bike, and it roars to life again.

I slide into my Jetta and pray that it starts. Thankfully, it turns over right away. I pat the wheel and silently tell her thank you. I wouldn't mind holding onto him again as he drove me home, but I can't handle another humiliation of him seeing that my car is a piece of junk.

I ease out of the space slowly and onto the streets of LA, then begin taking him toward my apartment. It's not in the nicest areas of the city, but still, it manages to feel safe, and it is home. Something about him following me makes my uneasy. It makes my palms sweat as I clench the wheel. He remains at a safe distance—he must not have forgotten I have a heavy foot and am a late breaker. I play with a string on my jeans that's hanging from the hole in my knee, rolling it between my fingers as I navigate home. The radio ironically plays a Crave song. It's not the one from the video, but it's another one of their popular ones from the last album, *Lost in You*. Aiden and Derek are both singing on this one, making me wonder which one of them wrote the words and who it's for—Audrey or Emma? I hum along as we make our way to my apartment.

I steal a glance in the rearview mirror and notice he's driving cautiously behind me, but he's looking around as we make our way to my home. What does he think of the area? Again, not the safest, but I've never had any trouble. My landlord is extra careful with the lighting in the lots, the porch lights, and also making sure we have strong locks. There are a lot of women who live in my building. A lot of actresses and dancers who came to LA in search of stardom.

Living here now isn't much different than when I first moved in. I could barely afford it then, and I can barely afford it now. The starving artist gig is starting to get a little old. Thankfully, the job with the band will help things. Dale is paying me for the press tour and dancing in the video. I think he's doing it because he feels bad for me, but I don't care. Growing up the way I did and being poor doesn't mean I'm ever in the position to be too choosey.

We pull into the complex, and I ease my way into my usual spot. By now, the sun has set completely, and the parking lot lights are on. The twenty-minute drive seemed to fly by. We hit every light just right, and traffic was even at a minimal, which never happens. Normally, I'm stuck sitting through several light cycles and endless lines of traffic trying to get home. I can't decide whether or not I'm happy about that. Because that meant Brent was no longer behind me, analyzing my every move, or that I couldn't be studying him in the rearview mirror any longer. It was a double-edged sword, and I wondered if he could tell that I was doing it.

I sigh and place my head on the steering wheel, bracing myself for getting out. I'm not sure if he parked or where he went. The guest parking spaces aren't near the tenants, so he cannot be seen from here. A tapping on my window jolts me from my thoughts.

"You okay?" he says through the glass.

I nod, moving to open my door. Brent backs up and waits for me to exit the car. "There, you saw me home. You can head out now."

"Nah, I'd like to think my mother raised me better than that. I'm supposed to walk you to the door."

I smile. "Thank you."

"Lead the way." He gestures for me to take him to my apartment.

His eyes are darting around, taking in the scenery. Thankfully, it's well lit, so I won't hear that lecture from him, which I'm sure I would have. Calling it a complex is probably a generous description. It looks more like the two-story hotels we used to stay in when his mother took us to the beach. The entrances to the dozen or so apartments are shielded by an awning that goes all the way around. We head up the stars since I was able to score a second-story unit. I'm more in the middle of the stretch of units. I'd rather have an end, but it's what was available.

"Fuck," I say.

"What's the matter?" He asks from behind me, close on my heels.

As we get closer, I can see there's a red notice attached to my door. I slow my pace and try to figure out how I'm going to explain this or if I can just get him to turn around now.

"Well, we're at my floor, so I'll see you later."

"But this isn't your door," he says, looking from me to the doors. He must have spotted it. "That's your door, isn't it?" He gestures toward the one with the notice on it.

"Yeah, that's me," I say, quickly striding over to it. It's what I expected it to be—an eviction notice. I have thirty days to leave.

"So, you're being evicted?" He looks over at me.

"Looks that way," I reply.

"When did your landlord put this up?"

"If you're asking if this was up when I left for the studio, no it wasn't." A slight edge has crept into my voice while hot tears brim my eyes. I hate this. I hate that he saw this, and I hate that my landlord is doing this to me. Well, he's not doing it to me so much as I've done this to myself.

"Sorry. What if we talked to your landlord? I could lend you the money to pay your rent and then you could stay."

"Brent, I can't take your money." A sob is working its way up and out. I don't want to cry in front of him. I want to rush into the apartment and slam the door closed so that I can deal with this by myself. But he won't go away easily, I can tell you that much. "Besides, he won't just take the money and let me stay." I walk toward the railing and look out over the parking lot.

"Why not?" he asks, coming up and standing beside me. "How many times has this happened before?"

I sigh and look down at the ground. For a millisecond, I consider jumping to avoid having to talk about this. It's so embarrassing. He's the last person I would ever want to know how hard it's been to make it on my own. But now he knows, all because the exact time he followed me home was when my landlord decided enough was enough. I mean, I knew it was coming, but I had hoped he wouldn't actually do it. I suppose I left him no choice.

"He's had enough. I can't be a tenant anymore because I'm not reliable," I say, letting my shame all out there for him to see. "He's given me more chances than I deserve, actually."

"What are you going to do now?" He bumps his shoulder into mine.

"I don't know. I've got thirty days to figure it out, and I have a consistently paying gig now, so maybe I can afford something else."

"Yeah, that's an option."

"Why do you say that like I've got any others?"

"What if you came to stay with me?" He turns me and hold his hand up to silence me. I'm ready to protest immediately. This isn't something I expected from him, but I instantly realize that I can't. "Just until you're back on your feet," he quickly adds.

"I can't do that." I shake my head vigorously. "You don't *actually* want me living with you, do you?"

He smirks. "Do you have any friends you can stay with?"

"I don't have a lot of friends." Every once in a while, the girls that live here and I will sit around and talk while drinking a can of soda. It's sad, but it's the only type of girls' night I've had in a long time. And sometimes, having friends costs money. They want to go out and do things, and I can't always do that. Also, when I worked in the restaurant, any extra time I had was spent there so I could pay rent and take classes.

"So not much has really changed, huh?"

"I suppose not," I say, wiping a tear away. "You don't have to offer me your place, Brent. I'll figure it out."

"How? Where will you go?"

"I don't know. Home, maybe? When you've been here as long as I have and you've made little to no progress, that may seem to be the only solution," I admit. I hate the idea of going back to Georgia. At least my father is locked up, but I still have uncles around who will encourage me to see my dad or try to control my life, just like he did.

"You're making progress. Look at the video. It could do huge things for you, Blair. And you're too talented to just waste your life in Georgia. That town doesn't have anything for you. This one does." He gives my shoulder a squeeze. "You should just stay with me until you get back on your feet. When we get back from New York, you can move in. What do you say?"

Brent looks at me with those big brown eyes he knows are hard for me to resist. He's playing hero again, a game he played all too well when we were kids. All the times he saved me from my father or from the boys at school, and now he's still doing it.

"I hate to put you in this position. It's not the most attractive offer, having me live with you. Do you really want to be around me that much?"

"It's a nice-sized place. We don't have to see each other if we don't want to."

"Let me think about it." I hate that the offer is so tempting.

"Yeah, because you have so many other options." Guilt is instantly written all over his face. His eyes widen just a bit like he can't believe the words actually left his mouth. "I'm sorry. That wasn't right."

"But it's true," I say, sniffling. "I have nowhere else to go."

"Well, then it's settled." Brent wraps me into a hug. "I'm glad I was here. I'm glad I saw this so that I could help you and stop you from heading back home."

"Yeah." I'm not sure if I'm agreeing with him or just putting words out so that he knows I'm listening to him. "I appreciate it. I won't overstay my welcome, and you can just do you and I'll take care of me. I won't be another mess you have to mop up." The shame of what he sees is written all over my face, and I'm exhausted at this point. I want to go lie in my bed and cry myself to sleep.

"How much shit are we moving?" He gestures toward the door.

I let out a bitter laugh. "There's not much in there that's mine. These beauties come fully furnished. So, it's just clothing and a couple of personal items."

"Okay, well after NYC, let's get you moved out, yeah?"

"Yeah. Thanks, Brent. Like, I'm sure I'm the last person you want to offer refuge to, but I really do appreciate it."

He nods. "It'll be fine." The words come out so uncertain that I'm not sure if he's trying to convince himself or me. But I don't read too much into it.

"Good night, Brent."

"Good night, Blair."

With that, he turns and heads back down the stairs. I go into the apartment that will only be mine for another week. I didn't bother to point out to Brent that I had thirty days to find somewhere else to go, that living together doesn't have to start that soon, but I decided against it. I didn't want to press my luck and end up homeless, or worse yet, heading back to Georgia.

CHAPTER FIFTEEN

Brent: I'll pick you up at 8 to take you to the airport.

I wake up to that message and a pounding headache. After Brent left last night, I broke down pretty hard. It was rough to see the eviction notice on the door and to know that the last-ditch effort I have been given to make it work here has failed. And of course, Brent had to see it. It's the type of failure you didn't want anyone to see. It wouldn't have been better if Dale had seen it or any of the band members' significant others who I enjoy talking to.

I take two Advil to attempt to cure the pain in my head and work to make myself look presentable. I'm not sure what it will be like to travel with Brent and the band. Crave has found success. Did that mean we're traveling by a private plane or maybe first class in commercial? Dale hadn't mentioned what our travel arrangements would be, just that he would send over the final itineraries once they were finalized. I haven't seen anything yet.

Blair: Thanks. Do you know when we take off?
I haven't seen the flight details yet.

I sigh and roll my neck. Time to quickly pack and make myself look presentable for the flight. When the press tour started, Dale had a stylist send over some clothes for me to wear. He has no idea how much I appreciate that. Sure, I have some things I could wear, but I don't want to look foolish in front of the guys or embarrass the band. I certainly can't afford to go out and buy the things I would need; let alone the nice things he had sent over.

My phone dinged again, and I looked at it. Brent had replied.

> Brent: I'll show you when I pick you up. We take off at 11.

Great. I guess Dale hadn't bothered to send it to me after all. I try not to think too much about that as I throw some leather pants and a dress into my suitcase. I steal a glance at the clock. It's almost eight, so he'll be here soon. I move around my apartment for what could be the final time before he moves me into his place. I'm still a little shocked that he offered so quickly. Force of habit, I think. Maybe he's just so used to playing hero when it comes to me that he decided he would do it again.

I will miss this place. It's the first place where I've felt safe on my own. You could throw a stick from one side of it to the other. There's a small kitchen that leads into the living room, my bedroom is right off the kitchen, and the only bath is attached to my bedroom. It's not much but it's been home. It was just what I needed once I could afford a place of my own. I'll be sad to leave it. And I'm even more nervous about living with Brent. I guess this quick trip to New York will be our little test. See how we do together when it's just us.

I head down the stairs to meet him. I didn't want him to pick me up at my door, so I decided to wait for him by the Jetta. Thankfully, my car is paid off and no one can take it from me. I look over at it. The rust has gathered in some areas around the rear fenders. The paint is fading and chipped in some places, but she's mine. And she was almost where I had to live in or what I had use to trudge back to Georgia in.

A black SUV pulls up, and I immediately straighten up. That's the thing about being a dancer—it's taught me great form and grace, especially under pressure. It makes situations like this, when I want to craw inside the Jetta and hide, seem much easier.

Brent steps out of the car in dark jeans and a plain white T-shirt. God, he looks hot. I immediately scold myself for thinking it. I can't help it; I've always appreciated the way he looks, even when he wasn't mine to appreciate. And even when he's hated me, I've loved the way he looks. So much like the boy I used to know, but now a man.

He rubs the back of his head, a nervous habit that hasn't changed since we were kids. "How come you're waiting out here? Were you kicked out early?" He wiggles his eyebrows at me.

"Very funny," I say, sticking my tongue out at him.

"Real mature there, Blair. So glad you're coming on this press tour with me. Do you think you can manage to keep yourself from sticking your tongue out at reporters if they ask you stupid questions?"

He tone is teasing, but part of me wonders if he's concerned about how I'll do on the tour. Truth be told, I'm concerned about how I'll do. Other than the previous interviews, I haven't had to talk to the press before. Dale did prep us with the types of questions they would ask, and someone from his firm is going to be there to ensure we're well taken care of or to step in if the questions become too personal in nature.

"Well, for the press tour, I figured I would stick up my middle finger instead of sticking out my tongue." I flash him an innocent smile and he smirks at me.

"I knew you were going to be a handful on this trip."

I giggle and stick my tongue out at him again. It earns me a laugh—a real laugh. He reaches for my bag and takes it to the back of the SUV.

"I'm impressed," he calls over his shoulder.

"With?" I ask him, confused.

"You didn't overpack. Or at least it appears that way." He comes around to the side and opens the back seat. "Come on, get it. We've got a plane to catch."

I climb in, my arm brushing against him. I'm pretty sure a bit of my hair brushes his face. He inhales, judging from the noises I hear behind me. I smile, wondering if he still likes the smell of my shampoo. He always used to tell me he did.

We ride in silence to the airport, which isn't too far of a drive. I'm still worried that we haven't left enough time to get through security and onto the plane. Brent sits beside me. His leg is bouncing and it's making the whole back seat shake. I want to reach over and place my hand on his leg to still it, but I don't. I think it's being in such a confined space with me. He can have me riding on the back of his bike, no problem. But being in a car with me where he has no escape seems to make him nervous.

We're both playing this game of wanting to keep the walls up that we've built but also wanting to rip them down because we used to be so comfortable with each other. He seems like the same person he was back then. The fame and the millions of women screaming his name hasn't changed anything. The hurt I caused him, though, seems like it might have.

He's still so giving, but at the same time, he keeps me at arm's length. He hates me but he doesn't want to. Or maybe hate isn't the right word. His emotions are playing jump rope with a myriad of feelings. I can see it written all over his face. I hate that I caused it, and I understand it at the same time. I want to run back into his arms and give him some big romantic movie speech in hopes it fixes everything. But life isn't like a movie. And damn, if it were, this could be fixed so much easier. Maybe being around, him might not feel like walking on eggshells.

"We're here," he announces, jumping out of the vehicle. He says a few quiet words to the driver and pats him on the back.

We're at LAX but not at the front entrance. Airport staff are waiting for us with a side door held open.

"Stay close" is all he says to me.

I nod vigorously, unsure of what's going on.

Brent leads us through the airport as if he's done this a million times. I'm thankful on more than one occasion that I wore sneakers. I never would have kept up otherwise. He moves quickly, his long legs guiding him, and I pull my carry on closer to me, hoping I don't lose it.

"You doing okay?" he asks me once in a while, but that's about it. That's the only communication we have until we're through security and seated in first class. We're in the back, away from the other passengers. We boarded before them too, I guess to keep Brent from being noticed. The tall bald rocker sure stands out in a crowd.

"You good?" he asks when we're finally situated.

I nod. "Yeah, I'm fine."

"Not a nervous flier?" He smiles playfully at me.

It makes my stomach flip, seeing him like this. "Nope," I say, popping the 'p.'

"Okay, good."

"And if I was? If I made you take care of me the whole plane ride there, would that be so terrible?" I ask him.

He chuckles. "I've been taking care of you my whole life. Until you decided you didn't need me anymore."

"Oh, Brent," I say, reaching out and taking hold of the hand that's resting on his knee. "It's not that I didn't need you anymore. It's just that the evil that was living in that house was worse than leaving you."

"Yeah, well, it didn't make it any easier on me."

"It wasn't an easy decision to make."

"Was taking me ever a consideration?" he asks, brown eyes boring into mine.

"I didn't think you'd want to leave your mom. When did you finally leave Georgia?"

"Shortly after she died. Once I hooked back up with Derek, I went to North Carolina, met Aiden, and we formed Crave."

"Wait, we knew Derek from Georgia?"

Brent shook his head. "You wouldn't have. I knew him from the scene down there. He was a younger kid who was stuck with a mother who didn't take care of him, so he was able to sneak out easier. You wouldn't have met him. I didn't take you down there."

"Oh, so you're older than the rest of the band?" I ask him.

"Yeah, by two years. We're a little later in our twenties than they are."

I nod. "And now you take care of them the way you used to take care of me."

He scoffs. "Well, they let me easier than you ever did."

"A lot of good you've been doing. Aiden got a girl pregnant, and Derek hooked up with your bandmate's sister," I tease him, bumping his shoulder.

He shakes his head. "Woman, I've kept them from doing way dumber things than that."

The flight attendant begins doing her preflight speech, and our attention shifts to her. There are no more words spoken for a while. Brent and I both nap on and off on the flight to New York City.

The next day will be full of lots of press, so there's no going out when we get there. Brent says that will happen later. Instead, we each retire to separate hotel rooms and eat room service. He might have dealt with me enough today. Brent's always been the quiet one, introverted and needing time to himself, so maybe I'm reading too much into this, and maybe it's just his way of recharging. Which I get.

I eat alone and watch TV, but eventually, I become restless and find the courage to go to Brent's hotel room.

I reassure myself that it'll be fine. He'll either want to hang out or he won't. No big deal. Breathing in and out, I knock on the door and wait.

But he never answers.

I place my ear against the door, hoping to hear a TV coming

from inside, but there's nothing. I head back to my room and fall onto the bed. Part of me wants to cry, thinking that he's out meeting a girl or something. But it's not really my place. Sure, it can hurt me, but he's not doing it on purpose. He's living his life and doing what he would normally do when he's out of town.

A security guard met us here in New York, and he's in the room on the other side of Brent. I fight the urge to go over to him and ask if he knows where Brent is. He said we had to check in with him before we went anywhere. But my pride won't let me. Instead, I lie in my bed, watch TV, and scroll through social media before falling asleep early.

CHAPTER SIXTEEN

The outfits the stylist picked out are so cute. They were waiting for me in the hotel room when I came in. I hadn't bothered to look at them too closely until the morning. There are two choices: a black maxi dress with pink flowers or a black strappy jumpsuit. I go with the jumpsuit and gold wedges. I took my height into account—they aren't too high that I would tower over Brent. Although, I'm sure we're both sitting for press tours.

I finish off the outfit with my gold hoops and the gold 'B' that has hung around my neck for years. Brent's mother gave it to me when I turned sixteen. I let my wild red hair down and head out the door.

Brent texted last night, late, that he would meet me in the lobby at ten. I go down a bit early to grab some breakfast that the hotel offers, and that's where Brent finds me when it's time to go.

"You didn't order room service?" he asks in way of greeting.

I look up at him, confused. "Well, the hotel offers this for free," I explain.

He smirks. "We would have paid for your breakfast, and it would have been more private."

"I'm not like you. No one knows who I am. I can still go places without being noticed."

"Not true," he says, bopping me on the head with a newspaper like I'm a puppy. "You forget I'm the drummer. I'm not as easily recognizable as Aiden and Derek are."

"Ah, but I hear you've left your share of broken hearts on the floor after the shows."

He just chuckles and shrugs. "Well, the girls are hungry, and the guys have their own things happening, so why not?"

I nod and feel my heart squeeze. I'm curious to know what he was doing last night. I don't dare ask, though, because I'm pretty sure I don't want to know.

"What?" He narrows his eyes as he looks at me. "What's on your mind?"

"Nothing. Nothing at all. Should we get going? We wouldn't want to be late." I rise from the table and get ready to bus my dishes, but he beats me to it. He picks them up and discards them quickly in the bins and comes back over.

"Let's roll," he says, his voice dropping to a few sultry octaves as he does it.

I nod and follow him out of the hotel. As he walks in front of me, I take the opportunity to look him over, and the results are so delicious. The black button-up he's wearing fits him well, as do the dark jeans and boots. The boots remind me of what he wears when he rides. Brent sure does clean up well. Not that I never doubted he would. I've seen the pictures of him at the award shows and on the red carpets. A stylist may help out with the outfits, but he does a nice job of filling them out.

He opens the door to a waiting SUV and gestures for me to move past him and into the SUV. "You look beautiful, Blair."

The words are spoken so faintly that I barely hear them. I look over my shoulder and catch him winking at me. I'm more than a little thankful that the air-conditioning is cranked on in the car. I shiver as the warmth of my body hits the cool of the leather seats.

"You okay?" Brent asks, his dark orbs traveling up and down my body.

"Just fine," I murmur and turn my attention to the window so that I can watch the city fly by.

Brent just chuckles beside me. Every now and then I feel his eyes on my body, but I don't move and don't react.

We pull up at the offices for *Rolling Stone* magazine. They're doing a piece on Crave and the recent awards they've won, the new album, and the music video that accompanies it. That's why I'm here. So that the reporters can ask me questions about what it was like to dance in a Crave music video.

"It's going to be just fine. Don't be nervous," Brent whispers as we make our way through the building. "I'm pretty sure someone from Dale's office, Stephane, is going to be sitting in with us. That's the nice thing about Dale. He'll never leave us exposed."

"Yeah, that's what I've heard."

"You clean up good," he remarks as he regards me while we wait for the elevator.

"Thanks," I stammer out.

A security guard is with us, the same one that picked us up at the airport. I'm not sure what his name is, because he has yet to say two words to me. All he does is talk quietly with Brent. I get the impression they know each other, because they do talk and laugh with each other. Either that or he's just a really friendly guy. Brent looks around, seeing that it's just us waiting for the elevator. He steps closer to me so that he's invaded my space. I could lean forward ever so slightly and touch his body if I wanted to. Something about seeing him like this and being out here with him really makes me want to. But I don't.

It's Brent, though, that decides to make the move. He runs a hand down the cleavage of my jumpsuit, staring straight into my brown eyes. I swear they turn molten at his inspection. I'm burning for him, and I didn't even realize it.

"There's something about this fiery red hair that I've always loved." He removes his hand from my top and runs it through a strand of my hair. "It still looks the same. I'm so glad that this is one thing about you that hasn't changed."

I step into him so that our bodies are pressed together. "You are exactly the same," I say quietly to him. "Well, not completely. You grew up so fine, Brent Allen."

"Oh, Miss Masters," he starts to say, but the clearing of a throat stops him. It breaks the spell between us, and we step apart.

"The elevator, man." Security gestures toward the open door.

"Right, we should get going," Brent says, walking into the open elevator.

"Absolutely. Wouldn't want to leave them waiting," I say lamely as I pretend to adjust and remove nonexistent wrinkles from my jumpsuit.

"Oh no, we wouldn't." He chuckles and the security guy clears his throat awkwardly as the elevator climbs the floors of the skyscraper.

When the elevator doors open, a woman is standing there in a gray business suit. "Good morning, Brent and Blair. Let's get the two of you into the interview room," she says, not even bothering to introduce herself or wait to see if we're following her before taking off.

Brent and I hurry down the long hallway. I can normally walk very well in heels, but for some reason the wedges are making it tough for me to keep up with her. Brent reaches down and grabs my hand, then pulls me along with him. I squeeze his hand in thanks, and he returns it. I look over to see him smirking at me, and I return the look with one of my own. Something passes through his eyes, and it's not pained this time. There's an excitement there, and maybe even a hint of desire as he holds onto me, making sure I can keep up. Neither one of us is looking at all of the photographs on the walls of rock n' roll legends, pop singers, and rappers. Some pretty famous faces are smiling at us, but we pay no attention to them. It takes all the energy I have to make it down the hall with his hand in mind. There's no way I could focus on them right now. Right now, the only thing on my mind is how his hand feels in mine and how every few steps he rubs a finger over my knuckles.

———

We're settled in the conference room waiting for Jamie to come in and interview us. I've never met her before, but Brent apparently has. When the woman who led us here tells us that Jamie will be right with us, he replies with, "It'll be great to see her again."

"Friend of yours?" I ask when we're alone.

"Something like that," he replies, shooting me a wink.

It makes a flame of jealousy shoot up my spine, but I don't have a moment to react to it because the door flies open and there's Jamie, a petite blonde woman with curly hair. She's wearing dark jeans with holes in the knees and a Crave T-shirt—the one that I've been eyeing, with the red lips on it. I hate that she has that T-shirt, and I don't. I immediately school my face, remembering that Dale said that reporters are generally very perceptive people and would be able to read any emotion on my face. Well, at least the good ones can, and she's a good one.

"Brent, long time no see," Jamie says as she makes her way toward Brent to hug him.

He stands and embraces her. "Hey, Jamie, it's so good to see you again. What's it been, since the Grammy's? How have you been doing?"

"I'm doing great. That was a great night," she says.

I swear her smile just grew wider, and I have a feeling I don't want to know what she means by a "great night."

"This is Blair, the incredible dancer Crave was lucky enough to find for the video of 'Love Drunk,'" Brent says.

I look over at him and smile before turning my attention to Jamie. "Hi, Jamie, it's so nice to meet you."

"You too," she says, shaking my hand.

"I've seen the video," she finally says when we're all sitting down. "And it's incredible, just really incredible. I heard the song before I saw the video, and I knew it was something special."

"Thank you," Brent says. "Derek really did some incredible songwriting on that one."

"You write the music, right?" Jamie asks Brent.

"Yeah, I laid out the arrangement. You are right, this one is something special. I knew it, too, when I was putting the arrangement together." He is beaming.

I love watching the way he lights up when he's talking about Crave's music. He's so proud of the band and their work. It makes my heart swell with pride.

"Is that why you guys chose it for your next single?"

"It really is. Music videos aren't done all the time anymore and that's a shame. It's something I always enjoyed, watching videos growing up," Brent says. "The music industry has evolved, and we have to evolve with it. And we all have. Videos are still made, just not as regularly as they used to be. The guys and I heard this song, and we knew that it would be our first single. And with that, it was getting a video. The beat that plays is perfect for it. And let's face it, there aren't many Crave songs that are perfect for dancing." We all chuckle, and Brent continues. "So, we worked with Dale and got him to set up a video for us, and that is where this beautiful girl comes in."

Jamie's smile widens like she thinks she has some kind of scoop on her hands. She turns to me. "A music video was definitely something new for you. I've looked over your resume and didn't see one. What made you do it?"

Dale and I went over this answer a million times. There's no way I could say, "Well, I was broke, and it was a great opportunity." Instead, we needed something more in line with what Brent said. Except that it isn't that far-fetched. Brent and I grew up together, but we're not allowed to say that.

"Well, like Brent, I watched those same videos too, and I do miss that aspect of the music industry. So, when a music video is going to be made, it has to be made well. Crave did that with 'Love Drunk.' I heard the music and also saw the concept for the video and knew I had to be a part of it."

"You do some pretty impressive belly dancing in this video," Jamie compliments me.

"Thank you. I must say, I was surprised there was belly dancing in a rock song, but this worked so well. Brent lays down an incredible beat, and Aiden and Derek are insane on these vocals. It's just really a beautiful song and something I'm so proud to be a part of."

"I'm sure they're glad that you agreed to do it as well," Jamie says. Her attention is turned back to Brent. "Are you holding any type of premier for this video?"

"We're actually not. We had a performance in LA where we debuted it. It was low-key and intimate for our fans. It's out there now, and I know you got to see an advanced copy of it," he says, winking at her. "But we just felt that the best way to get it out there was to make sure it was introduced to the fans first."

"Crave is certainly all about the fans," Jamie says.

"We sure are. They have been so good to us and so great at embracing the decisions we are making as musicians and in our personal lives."

Jamie chuckles. I want to dislike her. I'm not sure if it's because she may or may not have slept with Brent or if I've been conditioned to dislike other women who might be a threat. Jamie is warm and friendly; it's really hard to not like her. She's just one of those people that you meet, and you know she'd be fun to hang out with. And that she's just a cool, good person.

"Oh, are you referring to Aiden and Derek? Two of the seemingly most eligible bachelor's in music pairing off recently?"

Brent laughs along with her. "Yeah, and the whole mess that was created with Serena. We really just wanted to make sure the fans knew it wasn't something done maliciously. It was just two friends falling in love. Serena is great and she will always remain a really close friend of the band."

The answer I've heard Dale recite to Brent over and over again rolls off his tongue with such ease. Without thinking, I reach under the table and squeeze his hand. He squeezes back and keeps talking to Jamie.

It becomes more about the band, the song, and the process. I'm enraptured by all the things he's saying. The passion that he has for the music they make and the guys he makes it with. It's great to hear.

"Now, Blair, if I can come back to you a bit," Jamie says.

"Sure," I say, smiling warmly at her.

"What's it like to be working with the boys of Crave?"

I laugh and shake my head. "It's great. They are so warm and welcoming. I really enjoy the time I spend with them. And it's great that I've been invited to be on this press tour with Brent. Really, I'm having so much fun hanging out with them."

"Well, they are great guys," Jamie gushes. "Let's get a picture." She stands up, and the three of us pose in front of a wall under the *Rolling Stone* logo. Jamie is in the middle of Brent and me. Our height really dwarfs her. She only comes up to my shoulder, and Brent towers even higher over her.

"Well, it was really great to spend some time with you, Brent. And Blair, it was so nice to meet you."

"Nice to meet you as well." I shake her outstretched hand.

"Do you have any free time while you're here?" she asks Brent.

He stutters over his words for a bit but manages to say, "Nah, I'm sorry. We're headed out first thing in the a.m."

"Well, maybe another time," she says, flashing him a wink and a wave.

"Definitely," Brent says to her retreating form.

When she's gone, I turn to Brent. "Maybe that's one of those questions Dale should have reviewed with you before we left. Had some trouble there, did you?"

He shakes his head. "Jealous?"

"Nope, but if you wanna change your mind and have dinner with her, you can. I hear I can eat alone in my suite if I want to. You know, instead of around people."

"No, we're going to dinner," he says, rolling his eyes. "I gotta say, I like that you're jealous."

"Am not," I grumble, crossing my arms as we walk toward the elevator. It's just the three of us this time, and we're moving a lot slower than we did on the way down.

"I need a nap before dinner." Brent rubs a hand down his face and yawns for effect. "So, if you don't mind, I'm gonna hit the hay for a bit."

"Long night last night?" I ask him.

"You know how it is. Being in a hotel, it's hard to sleep," he says, boarding the elevator.

"Right. I'm sure that's it."

The elevator descends, and just like that, we're headed back to the SUV so that we can head back to the hotel—where Brent will nap, and I'll try to relax and not get myself too keyed up at the idea of having dinner with him later tonight.

CHAPTER SEVENTEEN

Once we've both napped and freshened up, we're walking to a little pasta place he found on Yelp. My heels are making a clacking sound on the pavement.

"I told you we would be walking and not to wear heels," Brent says, glancing over at me from the corner of his eye. He has a sly grin on his face.

"The heels work better with my skirt." I carefully step around the cracks on the sidewalk.

"I can see that," he replies.

I almost don't hear the words because they are so quiet. The noise from the street almost swallowed them up. "Where are we eating?"

"It's just right down the block. Not a far walk." He touches the small of my back as we navigate around a man and woman who are making out in the street. "See, they enjoy a walk," he teases.

I shoot him a wide grin and say, "They aren't exactly walking, and maybe that was a kiss goodnight."

He throws his head back laughing. "It's barely eight. That is not a kiss goodnight."

"Whatever," I say.

He laughs again and we walk in silence. Brent seems really playful tonight. I like him like this. He doesn't necessarily seem unguarded with me, but some of the anger from our earlier exchanges has slipped away. The awkwardness has faded a bit too. I would love to say we've gone back to old patterns, but I don't think we have. There's no way I could tell him everything the way I did back when we were young. Although I've enjoyed the way his eyes have traveled up and down my legs more than once during our walk.

"I'm guessing you like the heels?" I ask him, but my eyes stay on the pavement in front of me. Partly so I don't fall and, and because I don't have the courage to look over.

"I do like the heels. I'm just worried you're going to fall on your ass, and then Dale will blame me."

"He will not," I say.

"Oh, but he will. I've gotten several text messages from him about you."

My head snaps in his direction so quickly that I falter.

He reaches out and grabs hold of my arm, steadying me. "Please be careful."

He doesn't release me immediately, and I have the urge to melt into his side. I want him to pull me close even though I know he won't.

"He's texted me a couple of times saying you're important to the band and that I'm supposed to be nice."

I chuckle. "Well, you should be nice to me."

"Yeah, well, I have been," he says as he pulls open the door to the restaurant.

Gesturing for me to go first with his arm, I walk into the restaurant. It's a quaint place, dimly lit with candles on the tables. The aroma of the dishes that are coming from the open kitchen window smell heavenly.

"Looks like you picked a good one," I say, taking in the room.

"I think so too." He struts over to the hostess and gives her a name.

I don't hear it, though, if it's his name or an alias. I make note to ask him.

"Come on, our table is ready." He motions for me to follow the hostess.

"Right this way," the hostess says, leading the way to the table.

She sits us in the back corner of the restaurant, where we're nice and hidden away. I immediately decide that I like it back here; it's lit mostly by the candles.

The hostess places the menus on the table and turns to Brent.

"Your server will be right with you. Enjoy your meal."

"Thank you," Brent says, smiling at her.

Brent gestures for me to take the seat that allows me to have the view of the restaurant. "You still hate having your back to open doors?"

"Yeah, I do." I reply, taking my seat. "You remember that?"

He nods. "I do."

"Thanks." I get myself settled into the booth and begin to pick up my menu when I catch him staring at me. "What?"

He gets ready to say something, but the waiter comes over and introduces himself. "Hi, I'm Shawn. I'll be taking care of you tonight."

We both nod and smile at him.

"Thanks, Shawn," Brent replies. "We'll take a bottle of the Justin Cabernet, and we still need a few more minutes with the menu."

"Thank you," he replies and hurries to check on another table.

"Do the people here know that you're *the* Brent from Crave?"

He shakes his head. "Really? *The* Brent."

"Do they know?"

"No, they don't know. I gave the hostess a fake name. But I can't help it if sometimes people figure it out. Looks like she hasn't yet."

I nod. "What's your fake name?"

"Don't worry about it."

"Tell me," I say a bit more sternly.

He sighs and shakes his head. "No, you don't need to know it."

"Okay, you don't have to tell me if you don't want to. But I'm dying to know what you would like to call yourself if you weren't Brent."

"It's not that I get mobbed that much. I just like to fly under the radar is all," he admits with a slight shrug.

"That much hasn't changed, huh? You never were much for attention, even when you were playing with the band back in school." The grin I'm rewarded with is enough to make my smile just as wide.

The moment is interrupted when Shawn returns with our wine. He hands it to Brent, who gives it a taste. I watch as he twirls the liquid around in his glass, breathes in, and takes a sip.

"Perfect."

With that, Shawn fills up our glasses before leaving us again. I decide that I like him as our server; he doesn't seem like someone who hovers.

"The food looks good," I say, trying to break the silence that has stretched between us. I look up and he's just staring at me. "What?"

"Nothing, just watching you for a moment."

"Why?"

"Why not?" he answers with a grin.

"Real mature." I pick up my wine and taste it. "You picked a good one."

"Thank you."

By the time our waiter returns, we've both decided on our food. As I was looking at the menu, I thought he might go with the Bolognese, and he did. I went with a risotto, knowing that I won't be eating the whole thing. A comfortable silence falls over us while he enjoys the bread and I fiddle with my napkin.

"Where did you go last night?" I finally gather the courage to ask him. I'm working on my second glass of wine, so I figure the liquid courage has kicked in enough to ask.

"What do you mean?"

I sigh and decide to put my cards on the table. "I went over to your room last night, but no one answered. You were gone."

He nods and watches me for a minute. "What did you want?"

"It doesn't matter."

"Were you looking for a quick, dirty fuck? Dinner? What is it that you wanted?" He leans forward and places his elbows onto the table.

I blush at his mention of a quick, dirty fuck. What does this that mean to him? "How do you do that?"

"Do what?"

"Go from hating me to acting like you would actually fuck me?" I don't miss the way his eyes darken when I say the word fuck.

"It's who I am."

His answer knocks the wind out of me. *It's who I am* plays in my head again and again.

"Stop," he says forcefully. "Stop and get out of your head. I was only kidding." He considers his words again. "Well, partially, but come on, Blair. It's you and it's me. I'm torn between wanting to scream at you until I'm horse and wanting to fall back into old patterns with you. It's a very confusing little dance."

I go to say something, but the words don't come out. I know what he means, though, and I want to say as much, but I don't get the chance. Our food is placed in front of us, and Shawn does his best to scurry away. Brent just laughs and shakes his head. He must enjoy the affect he's having on him.

The risotto touches my lips, and I let out a low moan. I can taste the butter, and it's so unbelievably creamy. I love the cheesy flavor and the scallops. I haven't eaten this good in a long time. I knew the band was paying, so I ordered whatever I wanted. I look up and see that Brent is staring at me, his fork midair; the sausage on it hasn't yet touched his lips.

"What?"

He clears his throat. "Nothing."

"Oh, that wasn't nothing. You liked the sound I made." I giggle when he just groans. "Are you trying to remember if I sound like I did back when we were young?"

He shifts nervously in his seat. "We were kids back then."

I nod. I know what he means. This Brent is a man now. He was always the taller one who looked older than he actually was, but this Brent has filled out more, and his voice is deeper. I wish I would have been around to watch the transformation, but I just have to take what I can get at this point.

"We were," I finally say, when it's clear he's not going to speak again.

"Imagining what it might be like if we did it now?" He waggles his eyebrows at me.

"Shut up and eat your dinner," I say with a laugh.

He does as I ask him to, and we eat in a comfortable silence.

"So, you came to see me last night, and what, couldn't find me, so you figured I went and hooked up with some girl?"

I shrug. "I honestly wasn't sure where you went. I mean, I'm not an idiot, Brent. You're the only one in the band who can still give the bus bunnies some attention."

Shaking his head, Brent laughs at me. "Are you Googling me?"

"Yeah, I've kept up with you throughout the years."

"I wish I could say the same, but I haven't," Brent admits. "I didn't want to know."

"Why not?"

"I didn't want to know that you were happy with someone else. I thought if I Googled you, I would find you with a husband and a couple of kids."

"Is that because that's what everyone from our high school has done?" I try to make light of the situation.

"No, because you were always so amazing." The words fall from his lips, and the pain shows in his eyes.

"Well, then it's a good thing I'm not anymore. I'm just the bitch who broke your heart."

"Yeah, there's always that," he says, but the words don't come off as funny as he means them to. "I wasn't out there hooking up with anyone. I just went downstairs to the hotel bar to grab some food and a drink."

"Oh," I say. I want to ask why he didn't invite me.

"I thought you might want some space," he adds. "Maybe you'd had enough time with me for one day."

"I didn't. It's kinda why I went looking for you."

"Well, since you haven't had enough of me, would you like to go grab a drink?"

"What do you call the wine we're drinking?"

"I call it a start," he says with a grin.

I watch him for a moment. The carefree side of Brent is back, and I love it.

"Yeah, that would be fun."

"Awesome. There's this bar not far from here that I wanna go to. It's a bit of a biker scene, but it could be fun. That's assuming I don't kill someone for looking at you the wrong way in that skirt."

I snicker. "Yeah, let's go see if we can get you beat up."

To my surprise, Brent just laughs. There's no witty comeback or telling me to fuck off. He finishes his meal, while I only push mine around. We leave the restaurant with his arm hooked into mine. Both of us are a bit buzzed on the wine and in search of some more mischief to get into.

CHAPTER EIGHTEEN

We walk into a dive bar. It's poorly lit and the walls are concrete block. The floor is wooden but has definitely seen better days with its scuff marks and faded stain. The music plays low, and it's old country, but I can't be sure. The clientele looks like they have been here since the place opened; there are burly men all around. It reminds me of a place we would have seen at home or somewhere my father would have frequented.

"Well, this place looks great," I say with a chuckle.

"What, are you too good for this place?"

"Not at all."

We make our way over to the bar and get ready to order some drinks. He seems so comfortable and at ease here. This isn't the type of place I thought he would frequent in NYC. I assumed it would be somewhere a little nicer than this, without being too trendy.

"Two beers," he says to the barkeep, who looks me over a little too long for my liking.

Brent must notice it, too, because he moves closer to me and places an arm on the small of my back.

"Worried about something?" I tease him.

"He doesn't need to look at you like that," he replies.

"Like what?"

"Like you're something to eat," he grumbles just loud enough for me to hear.

I snicker. "Well, I do look absolutely amazing tonight."

His eyes travel up and down my body. He looks like a man who's starving and has just found his first taste of forbidden fruit. "You certainly do," he says quietly.

"Thank you. I thought you might have complimented me sooner."

"Is this a date?" he asks me, a teasing mischief in his eyes.

"Well, no," I reply, shooting him a playful smile. "It's not."

"Then why would I compliment you, darlin'?"

I can hear a bit of that Georgia twang in his voice. I haven't heard that in quite a long time. In all the interviews he's done and the times he's spoken around me lately, it's been missing. I wonder for a moment if he's like me, where it only comes out with a good buzz.

"I don't know." I let the words hang out there in the air.

Our beers arrive and they stop whatever conversation was starting as we both take a sip. Brent's eyes are wandering around the bar, like he's checking his surroundings to make sure no one knows who he is or that there's no threat to us.

"I thought you'd want something more upscale than this," I say, breaking the silence.

He considers my words for a moment before speaking. "When I go out, I like to go to places like this. It's better than heading somewhere I might get recognized. Sometimes there's a live band playing, so I have a chance to scope out some new talent. This was how Derek found our last opening act, by frequenting little dive bars. Plus, it's a Thursday night. Better chance of it not being overcrowded in a place like this."

"Something tells me this place doesn't have live music." The small space and concrete walls wouldn't make the best acoustics for live music. Hell, the music coming out of the speakers barely sounds good bouncing off the block walls.

He snickers. "Not everywhere I pick is a home run."

"Shocking, even for you."

"What is that supposed to me?"

"Well, back in high school you were always so sure of your-self. Always had that know-it-all swagger about you. Has that fallen off with the success of being a rock star?"

"I wasn't that cocky in high school."

"Oh, you were. You had this don't-fuck-with-me-because-I'm-the-shit aura," I remind him.

"And yet I hung around you and you only." He shoots me a wink as he delivers the burn.

I shake my head. "Well, yeah. Someone had to."

"Are you still as closed off as you used to be?" He takes a long sip of his beer.

I shrug. "I guess so. Old habits die hard." I grab a pretzel from the dish in front of us. I have no intention of eating it. I just keep playing with the salted disk in my hands. "Besides, it's a pretty cutthroat business. I'm never sure if they're being nice to me because they like me or if they're gunning for the jobs I'm booking."

He nods. "This isn't an easy business to be in."

"You've found success."

"We did."

I like that he adds the *we* to it. The band is so close. I love that little family they've built. I'm not sure that the dance community would have the same type of one. Or maybe I just haven't met the right dancers.

"You guys are so close."

Brent nods slowly. "Just like we were."

I openly grimace. "You're never going to let that go, are you?"

"I don't know, it's kinda fun to hit you with that every once in a while." He winks at me, and I swear my stomach does a backflip. "See, that flush tells me you like it when I tease you."

"I'm sorry I screwed things up between us," I reply, and I mean it. But he's grinning at me like an idiot, and it's making it hard for me to take him seriously right now. "Stop it, I'm being serious."

"I know you are, but it's not like it's something that can be fixed overnight. You're going to have to give me a minute with it." He takes a drink of his beer and adds, "A long minute."

"Great," I say with a roll of my eyes.

He drains his beer and motions for the bartender to serve us another round.

"Better finish that, darlin'." He gestures toward my beer, which is resting at about half.

"Are you trying to get me drunk?"

"What makes you loosen up just a bit?" He wiggles his eyebrows in my direction.

My face heats. "Why are you trying to loosen me up?"

"Because I want things to stop being so heavy between us. We have a night off, and I just want to have some fun."

"Okay." Disappointment seeps into my tone. I thought he would tell me there was a totally different reason. A more intimate one. I hoped he was looking to move on from our uncomfortable past.

"Why do you look so disappointed?" he asks me before thanking the bartender as he accepts our drinks.

"I don't mean to."

"Uh-huh. Were you hoping I was trying to get you drunk because I wanted to take you back to the hotel and ravish you?" He leans in when he says the words, his brown eyes having darkened into a molten color. "Because I don't think that's such a good idea."

I lean in just a bit so that if he moved another inch, our lips would be touching. "Why is that?"

"Because the only sex I could have with you right now is angry sex." With that, he leans back with a chuckle while I let out a deflated sigh. "You doing okay over there?"

"Just fine," I murmur.

We each finish our second beer, and the conversation has

started to flow a little easier. It stays surface, though; nothing too deep and nothing about the past.

"I can't believe you've become the levelheaded one of the band. It's hard to imagine," I admit after he's done telling me all of the trouble Aiden and Derek got into for the ways they've found love.

"What can I say? Taking care of people just seems to come naturally."

My face falls at his words. It feels like it only took fifteen minutes for us to get into uncomfortable territory. I'm not sure we can even have a conversation that doesn't.

"Sorry," he says. "That wasn't exactly keeping it light, now was it?"

"You and I aren't that simple, are we?"

He shrugs. "We might not be now, but one day I think we will be."

"Will you always hate me?" I ask. The beer is starting to affect me. I'm warm all over and my thoughts are swimming with all the ways we could be irresponsible and cause Dale some real heartache with the press.

"Nah, I don't think so. You're a hard person to hate. Why else do you think I'm still hanging around you willingly?" he teases me before sticking his tongue out in my direction.

I flush. I want him to use that tongue on me. Yep, it's definitely the beer making me feel warm all over. Sober Blair would not want him to do that, right?

When I don't say anything, he laughs and shakes his head. "Get out of your head, Blair. As infuriating as you are, you're a hard person to hate."

I study my beer. "Okay," I finally say.

"You think too much."

"Do you not remember the way you came at me for being there and being in the video?" I remind him, shaking my head. "I thought you were actually going to physically throw me out."

"I was surprised to see you. And I'll admit to not wanting you in my world."

"What changed your mind?" I ask him when he's clearly not going to say any more on the topic.

"Dale told me I had to."

I stare at him for a moment. "That's it? Dale told you to be nice to me and suddenly you're all nice to me? I'm sorry, but I don't buy it."

He takes a drink of his beer and then looks around the bar. I get the feeling I'm not going to get an answer, but then he says, "Well, I might have had a long talk with Derek and Aiden about it."

"And they helped you see that I wasn't such a bad thing to have around?"

He chuckles. "Something like that."

A burly man walks up to our table and leans close to me. "How are you doing tonight, darlin'?" His breath smells of cheap beer, and I instantly want him to get away from me.

"I'm doing fine, but I need you to get away from me, please," I retort with the take-no-shit attitude I've adapted to having when men approach me.

"Are you sure, sweetheart?" He leans in closer to me, taking his hand and running a fingertip up and down the plunging neckline of my shirt. "I bet you and I could have so much fun."

Brent immediately stands. "The lady asked you to get away from her." His voice sounds low and deadly, and the extra effect of Brent standing up straight shows him just how tall he is.

"Look, buddy, it's obvious you aren't hitting it. Now let me see I if I can take a run at it." He keeps leering at me.

"No," I say a little loudly, causing a few other bar patrons to stare at us.

"The lady said no." Brent walks over to where he is standing. "You can leave now."

"Is she sure about that?" the man grumbles, his eyes still trained on my breasts.

"Back the fuck off, asshole," Brent growls out. Clearly, he's had enough.

I rise from my seat and make my way over to stand beside him, but the man reaches out and grabs my arm before I can make it to Brent. Then it all happens so quickly.

Brent's fist connects with the man's face. He grumbles, having been pushed back a step or two, but he keeps on coming at Brent. A lot of commotion fills the bar, and I'm pushed around as men come over to stop the fight.

"Brent!" I scream out as the man attempts to punch him in the face. But Brent's quicker and lands a punch to his face again.

"Stop! Stop it right now!" I scream, but no one pays me any mind.

It's not until the barkeep comes around and bangs a bat on our table that the fight comes to a stop. "Knock it the fuck off, or you both can leave, and you will never be allowed back here again! Do I make myself clear?" Luckily, that seems to do the trick.

I rush over to Brent to see the man managed to land a punch. Brent's lip is bleeding. "Are you okay?" I ask him.

He nods. "Yeah, I'm fine." But he doesn't look at me. He's too busy staring at the man, making sure that the fight is in fact over. "I need a minute to clean up."

Brent says something I can't hear to the barkeep, and he hands him some bills. Then it's off to the bathroom in the back of the bar. The attention is turned to me for a brief moment. I shift uncomfortably and decide to follow Brent. I'll feel safer when I'm closer to him. And right now, closer to him means being inside the bathroom. I steal a glance around the bar and notice that the attention on me has waned. I decide to enter the bathroom so that I'm near him again.

CHAPTER NINETEEN

I enter the bathroom and find him standing in front of the mirror, his hands braced on either side of the sink, head hung low. I can see the whites of his knuckles; he's gripping the sink like he could rip it off the wall if he chose to. The bathroom matches the rest of the place—faded paint on concrete walls and poor lighting. It looks like they could literally take a hose to this place at the end of the night and call it clean. In fact, that might be how they clean it—it looks that fifthly.

"Brent..." I want to thank him for standing up for me.

"Don't." His voice comes out cold and hollow. His eyes meet mine in the mirror, full of rage.

I step closer to him and place a hand on his shoulder. He tenses at my touch.

"Don't, Blair. I'm angry and I need a minute."

"Take it out on me," I tell him.

"What?" he asks, confused. He turns around so quickly that it causes me to take a step back. "What are you talking about? It's not you I want to hurt."

"Take it out on me," I repeat, finding my courage and stepping forward.

Seeing Brent like that, all fierce and in protective mode of me after all these years, has stirred something in me. We haven't been together in years, and right now it's the only thing I want. It's what I *need*.

"Please." I plead with my eyes for him to see what I'm talking about.

He shakes his head slightly. There's confusion written all over his face—a furrowed brow and grim expression like he's trying to figure out what it is I need from him.

"Wipe away his touches, Brent. Wipe them all away and take me."

"I'm not going to do that, not when I'm in this state of mind."

"I want you to. I need you to. Punish me. Take it all out on me."

"Blair, I don't want to hurt you." He's starting to understand what I need from him. What I want from him.

"You won't. You could never. Besides, we both might enjoy it. We both need this," I goad him, hoping it works.

He shakes his head, but his resolve is fading. I make my way closer to him and place my hands on his chest. His eyes dart around the room like he wants to run from me, but there's nowhere to go. I have him boxed in.

"Blair." He says my name again, but this time it comes out like he's begging me to make the next move.

I step into his space and let my lips meet his tentatively. Brent stays frozen, and it's going to take a bit more to get him to react to me. I press my lips roughly into this and jut my hips forward. He groans but stays still. I don't budge, though. My lips continue to work his. I nibble on his lip and hear him groan. It's then that I take his bottom lip in between mine, sucking a bit at first and then biting down. His hips rock forward. He's coming undone, unraveling, and I'm going to get him to give in. He needs this as much as I do; it's just a matter of getting him there.

I pull back slightly. "Brent," I moan before placing my arms around his neck and moving my body flush with his, hips bucking against his, begging him to take action. Begging him to take me in this bathroom.

Brent takes control of the kiss. His tongue roughly enters my mouth, and his kisses become more urgent and punishing. There's a bite as he nibbles at my bottom lip, the same way I did his. His mouth presses roughly against mine, and his tongue darts in and out of my mouth. I needs this. I want this. I can hear myself moaning. It's then that his hips slam into mine, but I don't back down. I meet that thrust, pushing mine farther into him. Trying to show him that this is right. That this punishment is something that's going to make us both feel better.

That's the movement that makes him come undone. I've never been so happy to be wearing a short leather skirt in my life. Brent yanks us apart roughly. Switching our positions, he places me in front of the sink and jerks my body around so that I'm facing it.

"Put your hands on the sink and stick your ass out," he commands.

I can feel myself growing wetter with anticipation. This is exactly what I was hoping for. I do as he orders me and ready myself by spreading my legs wide and sticking my ass out. I'm looking at him in the mirror and see that he's studying my body, looking up and down my legs and checking out the view of my ass, ready and waiting for him to invade my body. I feel like prey that's been caught by a predator. Little does he know; I've wanted this predator to catch me all my life. I've wanted him to be rough with me since the day Brent showed me what sex could be like when we were teenagers.

And now it's finally time.

"This might hurt a bit," he says.

I hear the clanging of his belt and the zipper of his jeans going down. "Bring it," I reply.

He chuckles, reaching around and grabbing at my thong. "This feels like it might be pretty. But I'm sorry, darlin', this is going to be ruined."

"I don't care," I grit out. I'm so ready for him to touch me or enter me. My body is humming with anticipation. Our eyes meet, and the same hunger in my eyes is mirrored in his.

"Good girl," he replies with a wink.

He gives my thong a hard tug, and the cheap fabric snaps on one side. Reaching around, he completes the same action on the other side. He pulls off my red thong and tosses it onto the dirty bathroom floor. "You won't be needing that."

His hand remains under my skirt as he caresses my wetness. He's touching me, rubbing just the outside of my folds. But what I really want him to do his dive those fingers deep inside me. I let out a whimper, trying to ask him through sounds for what I want.

"We'll get there," he replies.

I push my ass farther back, hoping he realizes that I can't wait anymore. My senses are on overload, and I need release. I swear the smell of my sex is filling the small space, which should make me embarrassed since he's barely touched me. But I don't give a damn. I want Brent. I've always wanted him this way, possessive and without any resolve, and I finally have him here. Who knew that it would just take some toothless man palming my ass to make it happen.

Without saying so much as a word, he's ripping open a condom. I look over my shoulder and see he's sliding it over his length. I smile at the sight. He's huge and I'm anticipating that this may hurt in the most delicious way possible.

His hands grip my hips roughly, and he pulls me back slightly before slamming into me. I let out a yelp, but it's quickly replaced with a moan as he continues to slam into me again and again, punishing me with his thrusts. It feels so fucking good. I sound like a slut continuously moaning at everything he does to me, even though there's a hint of pain to it.

"Fuck, you feel so good. Who knew this would feel like this?" Brent grunts out as he continues to assault my pussy.

I don't complain or ask him to stop; it feels too good, the lines of pleasure and pain blurring.

"Fuck, you feel so good," he keeps repeating as he takes what he needs from me. I couldn't move right now if I wanted to; his thrusts are too violent.

"I love this," I manage. "I need this so fucking bad."

"Me too," he replies, leaning down and placing a kiss at the base of my neck before working his way around, lightly sucking on my neck.

The sensations he's creating are making my knees weak. I want to fall slack, but I don't want him to stop, so I do my best to steady myself as my legs begin to shake. He must notice, though, because he pauses for a moment and picks me up. My feet are just dangling down as he holds me tightly around my waist. He's doing his best to drive in and out of me.

"Fuck, this isn't working. Can you stand for me, darlin'?"

"Y-yes," I stammer out.

He puts me back down, and I grip the sink as he continues the thrusts that are nearly sending me over the edge.

"Oh fuck, Brent I'm so fucking close. This is so fucking good, so fucking good."

He just grunts in return as my orgasm takes over. I can't move or think. I swear I see stars as the waves of pleasure overcome me. I hear him curse, but I'm not even able to comprehend the words that are coming out of his mouth.

A pounding at the door makes us both still for a moment.

"Come on, unlock the fucking door," a voice calls.

"You locked the door?" he asks into my neck.

"Well, yeah," I reply.

He chuckles. "You are so fucking unexpected" is all he says before he continues to pound into me. The knocking continues and he grumbles something about finishing if it's the last thing he does, before yelling, "In a fucking minute."

Turning his attention back to me, he says, "Darlin', you're going to have to help me here a bit." With that, he removes him hand from my hip, which I'm sure is bruised by now, and places it on my clit. He rubs quickly and with some pressure. My head slumps forward, and I moan loudly in the bathroom.

"Fuck, fuck, fuck," Brent calls out. The pounding on the door intensifies, as do his thrusts.

My body releases and relaxes as the waves of pleasure and pain overtake me. Brent is coming too; he stills, gripping onto me. To block out all his moans, he leans down and bites my neck, and I moan as a second orgasm overtakes me.

"Holy shit," I say as I breath in and out, trying to keep my body upright. I want to cave and fall to the floor, but it's dirty and I can't.

"You can say that again," Brent says.

I feel his eyes on me, so I meet his in the mirror.

"It was never like that," he tells me.

I nod in agreement. "You would never be that rough with me before."

"I was a lot younger then," he admits, reminding me that this is the first time we've had sex in years. And back then, we were kids who were just figuring out what we liked.

Yes, sex with Brett in a bathroom may have been a bit dirty, but it was just what we needed, and it's something I would never change.

"We gotta do that again," I say, smirking at him.

He chuckles. "Let's focus on getting out of here without getting our asses kicked for taking up this bathroom."

"I have a feeling with the type of establishment this is, they won't mind so much."

We both chuckle as we right our clothes and prepare to exit and face our audience.

CHAPTER TWENTY

The walk back to the hotel is quiet. I'm not sure what to say or what came over either of us. Maybe it was the alcohol, but I don't think that was entirely all of it. It had been a while for me, so God, did I need that.

When we get back to the hotel, he stops at my hotel room door and leans in for a hug. I misread it and kiss him on the cheek.

"Ooh, sorry," I say awkwardly.

"It's fine," he says with a chuckle, leaving me at my door. "Get some rest. We have an early day tomorrow." And that's where he leaves me, standing outside my door, not sure what to think of it all.

I have a hard time falling asleep, so when my alarm goes off at seven the next morning, I'm in a world of hurt. My head is pounding from the beers and wine that we had. My sex is a bit sore from the pounding it took last night, but man, did I love it. I've thought about it over and over again, about the courage I had to go into the bathroom and beg for it. After seeing him defend me like that and the wild look in his eyes, I knew I needed him.

Now, however, I'm second-guessing myself.

I rise from the bed so that I can shower and ready myself for the day. It's going to be a morning interview and a travel day. This means the black lacy shirt with jeans will be the perfect outfit. This interview is for a radio station, so we don't have to be as dressed up. I was told I could be more casual. I decide that I'll wear my black Converse so that I'm comfy for the interview and the travel back to LA.

I keep my hair simple and wild, the red waves cascading down my back in loose waves. With one last look in the mirror, I gather all of my belongings and head out the door. Once outside my hotel room, I'm met with the security man who has been assigned to us.

"Good morning, Miss Masters. Brent went downstairs for breakfast. I'm here to collect your bags. If you wish to join him, he's in a corner of the dining area." He says matter-of-factly, like he's practiced that exact sentence.

"Good morning and thank you." I leave him with my suitcase and head toward the elevator. He follows me, taking my bag along with him. I figure he must have already taken Brent's down to the SUV, because mine is the only one he's towing.

I enjoy the comfortable silence all the way down. Once the elevator doors open, I walk slowly to the breakfast buffet. I'm not sure what to say to him this morning, or if we just act like this never happened. It was probably a one-time thing. A symptom of the alcohol and the overly charged situation that we found ourselves in. I'm not sure how Brent feels about it or if he'll want it to happen again. If given the chance, I would welcome it.

I spot him over in a corner, his back to me. Wardrobe has kept him dark again. He has on a black T-shirt and dark jeans. I can't see his feet, but I don't doubt that he's wearing his boots again. I decide to grab my breakfast first before I sit down with him. It'll give me something to focus on instead of those choco-late-brown eyes.

I make my way over, already knowing that I'll have yogurt

with granola and fruit and some coffee. I will definitely be needing the coffee today. I can feel his eyes on me. They follow me as I pick up my breakfast items and head over to the table he's occupying.

"Good morning," I say as I lower myself into the seat, hoping to get the awkwardness out of the way. One simple word won't actually make that happen. One can hope, though…

"Morning," he says. His voice is low and husky. He sounds incredibly sexy this morning.

My thighs clench together as I remember the way he grunted as he pounded into me from behind last night. I take a minute to glance at his shirt—it's a Crave T-shirt. Luscious red lips cover the shirt. It makes me smile. It's the logo I've seen around a lot lately.

"How did you sleep?" he asks me.

"G-good," I stammer out. I'm not sure what to say to him, so I begin to eat my yogurt.

He lets me go for a bit, pushing around the eggs on his plate and drinking his coffee. "Is this going to be awkward now? Because I've been thinking that there's no reason for it to be. We've had sex before, and this was just blowing off a little steam in the heat of the moment."

"Sure," I say, not looking up at him. I don't know why hearing me say it makes me sad. It's probably how we should play it, especially since we're going to be spending a lot of time together and he did invite me to live with him since I have nowhere else to go.

"You okay? You look a little sad."

I just nod and don't bother to look up and meet his eyes.

He reaches over the table and lifts my chin so that I'm looking at him. "Hey, what's going on? Talk to me."

I sigh and shake my head, refusing to allow my eyes to meet his. "I just…I don't know. I'm not sorry it happened, Brent."

He smirks. "It was pretty good, wasn't it?"

I return his smirk with one of my own. "It sure was."

"Definitely wasn't like that when we were kids," Brent says, watching me closely.

"No, it wasn't. I guess the reputation they say you have has done you some good," I tease.

I don't miss the way his face falls when I bring that up, but he recovers quickly.

"I guess it did" is all he says.

The silence stretches back between us. Is it too early to drink something? We seem to do better when there's alcohol involved. Something about it makes it easier for us to talk. I want that now, so badly. I just don't know what to say to him sober. Buzzed Blair may have some ideas. Although they might not always be the starters ones, like "When can we do that again?"

"What's going on inside that head of yours, pretty girl?"

His words throw me off-kilter, and maybe that was the whole point. Maybe that was his game. I flush and shift in my seat. "A million little things" I smirk.

"A penny for your thoughts," he says, flipping a penny over at me.

It makes me giggle a lot more than it should. He used to do that when we were kids. Flipping quarters into cups or over little ramps he would set up, just to make me smile. It makes me smile even bigger to see that he can still do it.

I pick up the penny. "You can still do that."

"Well, yeah, it's not something you forget."

I lean back in my seat so that I can study him for a minute. "I guess not."

He winks at me. "We're going to be heading out soon. Is what happened between us going to be an issue?"

His tone has switched back to business. I shake my head. "No, it won't be a problem for me. But can I ask you a question?"

He looks at me for a moment before responding. I can see the questions written all over his face, in his furrowed brow and his eyes searching for mine, like the answer is written in there somewhere, and maybe it is. "What?"

"Is it ever going to happen again?"

Brent breaks out into a wide smirk. "Is it something you want to happen again?"

I shrug and a flush covers my face. My sex clenches—she definitely wants it to happen again. I happen to agree with her. "I don't know. I kinda do."

"But?" he asks me, obviously hearing the unspoken doubt in my voice.

"I'm not sure it's such a good idea considering we'll be living together."

"Yeah, it would suck if it happened again and jeopardized that. Or even if Dale got a hold of this. He wouldn't be happy with me."

"Something tells me you don't care about either of those things."

He's got this devilish grin on his face that I haven't seen in ages. There are so many things that have changed about Brent, but so many have also stayed the same. I can still read his smiles and smirks. He's up to no good right now.

"I might. I might not. I'm not real great with rules. And who knows, pretty soon you might wish for it. If that happens, well, I might have to give in." He winks at me and stands. "We gotta get going. It's time for some more press on that video. So, let's go explain to them how much you like to shake it while I play the beat."

Then he's gone, discarding his dishes in the bins. I get up and follow him, shaking my head. Oh my, Brent is so many more things than he used to be, and I just might like every one of them. Even the protective side that he still seems to have for me, even when I've broken him in two more than once.

We pile into the waiting SUV. Being this close to him seems to be setting off a fire in me. Sure, there's a seat between us, but Brent is taking up so much space, and I feel like if I move an inch our bodies will touch. Part of me wants that to happen. I want to feel him on me and against me one more time. But it's not a good idea. There are so many things that could go wrong if we gave in again. I decide that the incident in the bar had to be driven by the alcohol and that it won't happen again, as long as I stay sober around him. Right?

"Why are you so quiet? You have this serious expression like you're trying to solve some equation or some shit like that." He laughs at his own joke.

"I'm fine."

"Is this fine, fine or is this girl fine?" he asks me with a wink.

"This is fine, fine. I don't do that passive-aggressive shit, Brent."

He chuckles. "I'll remember that."

The interview goes off without a hitch. There's more talk of the upcoming video awards and how Crave is a strong contender for it. We travel back easily to LA, with Brent depositing me at my doorstep.

"I'm coming by this Saturday to get you, so make sure you have your shit together," he says before getting ready to climb back into the waiting SUV.

"But I have some time yet. The notice was just put up the other day." I look back at my apartment, not so sure that I'm ready to give it up yet. It's only Thursday evening. I would have one day to get it taken care of.

"Well, why prolong it? You're already past due. Let's get you out of here before he decides you have to go sooner."

I shake my head. "He wouldn't do that to me."

"Yeah, because everyone always keeps their word." He turns and climbs into the SUV.

His words are hinting at what I did to him. Will he always bring it up? Throw it back at me? I sigh and head to my apartment. He's right, though. My landlord could just up and decide that a paying customer is more important than me and kick me out. Nothing's making him keep me here other than that he's a decent person.

Living with Brent might have been one of the dumber decisions I've made. What's the plan for when he brings a girl home, if he does? There's no concern about me bringing anyone home. I don't want that right now. And while I'm sure that I'd rather have Brent than any other guy, so much has changed since we were last together. There's no going back. There's no reset button where I didn't hurt him. Besides, how much hurt can one man take before he decides that the knife that keeps cutting him shouldn't remain around anymore?

CHAPTER TWENTY-ONE

I would have loved to be a fly on the wall when Brent told the band I was moving in. I wasn't there, but they're all around when I take my Jetta and all of my possessions over to Brent's.

"I thought we would need a truck or something," Brent says. He's searching behind me to see what's in my car. There's not much there. I have a few trash bags full of clothes and one small suitcase that I took when we went to New York. I only have a few small boxes of personal and kitchen items I've bought over the few years I've been in LA. Not much to move, and certainly not enough to call for a truck.

"I thought we were here to do some heavy lifting," Aiden says. "Where's the heavy stuff we have to lift?"

Emma stands to his right, a baby carrier across her front as she comforts Jade.

"I don't have anything heavy to bring in. Just a few boxes and some clothing." I look down at the driveway, suddenly feeling a bit ashamed that I'm in my mid-twenties and don't have anything to my name other than clothes, some kitchen stuff, and knickknacks.

"Your apartment was a furnished find, huh?" Brent asks me, coming over to stand beside me.

I don't miss that he puts a protective arm around me. I don't think the rest of the group does either. Aiden's mouth is hanging open. Derek is grinning, and so is Emma and Audrey, like they knew something would happen between us.

"Yeah," I reply lamely, unsure of what else to say.

"We can help unload the car," Derek says, heading toward the Jetta.

"Oh, you don't have to do that. I can get all of this stuff in, no problem."

"Well, he called us over here"—Derek gestures toward Brent — "so what can we do to help you?"

"Nothing," I murmur. I suddenly feel very self-conscious around them. Do they know the reason I have to stay here? They must. I mean, there's no conceivable reason I would need to move in with him, other than the fact that I'm a loser who couldn't pay her rent. And for a awhile, too; it's not like they just throw you out for only missing one month of rent.

"Hey, we can help you get your closet set up," Emma says, hurrying toward me. "That would be so much fun!"

"Yes! I love to help organize." Audrey grins at me.

I smile back at them, because how could I not? They're both such happy and bubbly girls. They're trying to make me feel included in this little family they've created. While I would like that, I'm not sure Brent would.

"Sure, thanks," I say, not wanting to say no to them. I don't have a lot of clothes, so there won't be much to organize.

"Does she need the grand tour?" Audrey asks.

"Yeah, she hasn't been inside yet," Brent explains. "I thought *I* would show her around the house, though. You know, seeing that it is my house."

Audrey just laughs. "Yeah, I'm sure you thought that, but really, it's better if the girls have some time together."

He just shakes his head and laughs. "You are so lucky that I love you, Aud."

She grabs me by the hand. "Let's head on in there and give you the grand tour."

I smile and hurry after her. Emma trails behind us, reminding Audrey that she has a baby attached to her and not to run.

Brent's house is what I expected and not at the same time. It's sleek and modern, much bigger than I had pictured. I thought it would just be a condo like Derek and Aiden have, but he has a full-on house. The floor plan is open and spacious. There are large navy-blue couches in the living room and a TV mounted to the wall. The kitchen is directly behind it, with stainless steel appliances and clean gray lines. The dining room is off to the side, but I don't bother to walk in there. I just see the long black table with wooden chairs. In a small cove off the living room are large bay windows and a drum set sitting in the middle. The word Pearl is written on the base drum. The other drums are a glittery dark red, almost like the color of the Crave logo he wore the other day.

"His bedroom is back that hallway," Audrey is saying, motioning toward a hallway. "I think your room will be down this hallway."

I'm glad to hear that his bedroom is in a separate hallway from mine. At least this way there won't be any of these uncomfortable moments of hearing him bring home another girl and the noises they might make. I may be a strong woman, but my heart couldn't take hearing that.

Audrey leads me down a short hallway where there are two closed doors. "These are his guest rooms," she tells me. She opens the door on the left and closes it. "That one doesn't have a bed made up. Let's try this one." She opens the other door on the right, and sure enough, there's a bed made up.

It's beautiful. The blinds are open, and there's a pale purple comforter on the bed. The closet doors are open, showing that it's empty, though full of hangers for all my things. I step in to find a full bath in my room as well.

"Wow," I say, not meaning to say it out loud.

"Yeah, he has a nice house," Emma says from behind me.

Tears fill my eyes. This is even nicer than the little apartment I rented. It wasn't much, but it was all I could afford. I can't imagine having enough to own a house just like this.

"He has a pool too," Audrey says, leading me out of the room and back through the living room to the side door where I can see a nice in-ground pool and BBQ area. "Brent made sure to pull out all the stops for this house. It was one of the first things he bought when the boys started making some money."

"How long has he lived here?" I ask.

"Not long. Not even a year yet," Emma replies. "It was when the song hit big with Serena that he was able to afford it."

"Wow, good for him." Looking around in awe, I can't believe he's able to have a house like this. My chest swells with pride for him achieving his dreams. A fence swings open and there the guys stand.

"Did you give her the grand tour?" Brent is asking the girls.

"We did," Emma says as she puts her around Aiden when he joins her. "She was impressed with it. And you bought her bedding. That was so sweet."

"Aw, you went shopping?" Derek teases him.

Brent swings at his shoulder and playfully punches it. "Yeah, dickhead, she was going to need something to sleep on."

I don't miss the way Derek and Audrey exchange glances. Either he told them something or they suspect something.

"Is purple okay?" Brent asks me, shifting uncomfortably from foot to foot. "I wasn't sure if you still liked that."

"It's perfect. Thank you."

"We brought all of your stuff inside for you. It's sitting in your room for you to put away whenever you want. Or if the girls are going to help organize things, y'all can get to that whenever you're ready." A little bit of that drawl has seeped into his voice. I'm betting it's because he's nervous.

I smile a bit, thinking that I made him nervous. But I have

no room to talk because, honestly, the man makes me nervous too. Cohabitation is sure going to be interesting.

I hear a door close and see that everyone went inside. In a flash, it's just him and me on the lawn. "We're alone out here now," I remark.

"Looks like it," Brent replies, rocking on his heels.

The silence begins to stretch on, so I just gush about the house. "Really, this is all so great. You have a really nice house here. It's what you always wanted. One like we talked about when we were kids."

"One like I thought you and I might share together," he says quietly.

"Well, we're sharing it now."

His chuckle is low. "Yeah, but this isn't how I thought it would be."

"Life never is," I reply with a shrug.

We both know that. He just kicks at the ground like there's an imaginary rock on his perfectly trimmed lawn.

"I really appreciate you letting me stay here. I can pay you some rent if you would like. And once I get back on my feet more, I'll be looking for another place. The money from doing the video and the press will certainly help. I just need to pay some things first, like the back rent I owe on my old place."

"Blair." He comes over and places a finger on the tip of my lips. "Don't worry about it. I'm not worried about how long you're here or you paying me. You can stay here as long as you'd like."

"Well, come tomorrow, I'm going to start looking for a part-time job or something," I mumble.

"It's fine." He's watching the inside of his house. "I guess we should get in and see what the commotion is in there." He gestures with his chin toward the sliding glass door.

I look over and see a lot of hugging. "Yeah, you can go ahead. I'm just gonna stay out here and let you all have your moment together."

"Blair, what I don't think you really understand is that those girls in there won't let you stay out here. You're one of us now. You're like family to them now, and you'll just have to suck it up and come in there with me."

"They barely know me. How could they consider me family?"

"Oh, darlin', they most certainly do consider you family already. So just suck it up and get in there."

I chuckle and start following him inside. I have a little found family I wasn't expecting. I want to think it's weird and back away from it, but being on my own for so long hasn't always been easy. Sometimes it's been downright lonely. I relish in the fact that I get to partake in this little family. I'm not sure how someone who hurt one of their own gets into this family, but apparently, I do. And I love them for it. Because maybe it means that Brent has forgiven me, and things just might be a little less awkward for us. I would like that.

I'm just not sure how much he likes the idea of it and how much he'll include me in his life. And if, when he does, it will start to feel like old times.

CHAPTER TWENTY-TWO

B rent pulls the door open and gestures for me to follow him into the house, and I immediately hear a lot of fast talking and what looks like celebrating.

"What is going on in here?" Brent asks.

"We're engaged!" Audrey screams. Derek is standing right beside her and leans in and kisses her temple.

"Congratulations," Brent replies, going over and wrapping Audrey into a hug. He fist-bumps Derek before hugging him as well. "And you're okay with this, man?" He throws a grin in Aiden's direction.

"Yeah, it's about time he makes an honest woman out of my sister and stops just shacking up with her," he teases.

Derek pretends to look wounded and explains, "He wasn't always so cool with this whole arrangement. At first, he didn't like me being with her. No one could date the little sister of Aiden Zaks—from little on up he had that rule. Kept my poor *fiancée*," he says, grinning at Audrey as he tries out the word, "from dating a lot of guys. Some of whom were jackasses, but still, he wasn't always so nice to her about it."

Aiden just shrugs. "But I came around."

"What made you come around?" I ask.

"Seeing how happy she was," Aiden replies.

"Look like it's working out really well." I move over to Audrey and hug her. "Congratulations."

"Thank you," she says, hugging me back.

"Congrats," I say in Derek's direction.

He extracts me from Audrey and wraps me in a hug of his own. "Thank you."

"This calls for a bit of a celebration!" Brent exclaims. "And since I'm the only one of you who was a big boy and bought a big boy house, how about we have it here? I can grill up some grub, and we can all hang out by the pool. What do you say?"

"Sounds like a plan," Derek says. "Thanks, man. It's cool of you to host us."

"Well, what good is this place if I can't host my friends and let random girls stay here." Brent shoots me a wink.

"I am not random!" I exclaim.

Brent chuckles and shakes his head. "You are something, though. You guys all have swimsuits here, so go get changed. Blair, you got a suit?"

"Uh, yeah," I stammer.

"They're here enough using my pool, so they might as well keep suits here." Brent moves over to a closet and grabs what looks like a pack 'n play. "And of course I have to have something for the little princess." He begins setting it up. My heart melts at the fact that he has something like that for baby Jade.

"Thanks, man," Aiden says, walking over to make sure every-thing is secure.

I wander back to my room, where all my boxes and bags are there against the wall. It's nice that they kept the bed open for me. I'll have to sort all of this out later, and I'll have to do it faster than I did when I was in my old apartment. My heart squeezes as I think of it. I will miss that little oasis I called home when I first got to LA, but it'll be nice to be here in this house with Brent. Even though we're not the same as we were back then, it's still a comfort being here in this house with him. And it's a nice one, at that.

I look through the trash bags and find my electric-blue bikini and a white mesh cover-up. My hair goes up in a high ponytail as I give myself a pep talk about handling being around him like this. Seeing him in his suit and his bare chest and knowing what it feels like to have his body pressed against mine is something I can handle. It'll be okay. He won't be thinking of the same things when he sees me in my suit.

Taking a deep breath, I exit my room. Everyone is already dressed and out by the pool.

"There she is," Aiden yells.

"We thought you chickened out on us and didn't want to hang," Derek teases.

"Nah, it just took me a minute to find my suit," I say lamely. A stack of towels waits on a cart for everyone. I take one and head over to an empty chair.

Emma and Audrey are sitting on the side of the pool with their feet in the water. Both of them are just in their bikinis, so I decide to disregard my cover-up as well.

"Cute suit," Audrey says, adjusting the strap of her yellow one.

"The groceries are here," Brent says with a clap of his hands, and the guys follow him inside.

"How long was I changing?" I ask with a laugh. "How can he already have groceries on the way?"

"Expedited pick up," Emma says, glancing over in the direction of the pack 'n play, which is set up under an umbrella. Jade must be sleeping, because there isn't a sound coming from it.

"So, how was New York?" Audrey asks, her eyes glittering with mischief.

I smirk. "Why are you asking me that question?"

"What do you mean?" she asks, feigning innocence.

"I see he told you guys." I thought he might keep it quiet,

but I guess not. Makes sense though, I guess. It must have come out when he said I was staying here.

Emma laughs. "He didn't tell us a damn thing, but you sure did. So, my dear, spill the beans. What happened?"

I shake my head, realizing that I have to be on my toes when I'm around these girls. "Ugh, I can't believe I fell for that."

"Sorry," Emma says, reaching over and squeezing my leg. "You don't have to tell us if you don't want to."

I sigh. "No, it's fine." For some reason, I trust these girls. I'm not sure if it's because Brent considers them family or if it's because they're just the kind of warm, inviting women who seem to have your best interest at heart. They don't appear to be like the catty ones I've met through dance. I like them, and that's why I spill the beans. I explain all about the fight and the sex in the bathroom.

"Holy shit, girl," Audrey says with a knowing smirk on her face. "I knew Brent had it in him to be dirty. Hell, Derek does too."

"So does Aiden," Emma chimes.

"Ew, that's my brother," Audrey squeals.

"You asked," Emma replies.

"Actually, I don't think I did. But anyway, back to the matter at hand. What did he say once it was all over and done? Did you guys talk about it, or did he pretend it never happened?"

I stare at the water for a second, remembering the quiet walk back to hotel and the slightly awkward breakfast, where it seemed to be a bit more charged than normal.

"We just kinda talked about how it could suck if it happened again. The only thing we really agreed on was that it wouldn't be a good idea because I'm living here. And also, Dale wouldn't really like it if we started hooking up." I pause, then decide to say the thing that's been on the tip of my tongue since it happened. "I'm not sure if he regrets it or if it wiped the slate clean for us in some weird way."

"What makes you think he regrets it?" Emma asks me.

"My own insecurities, I think." I pinch my eyes closed.

"I'm gonna go out on a limb here and guess that wasn't the first time you two slept together?" Audrey asks.

I nod. "Yeah, that wasn't the first time."

"So, while you practically lived together when you were in high school, you two were screwing?" Audrey asks.

"Wow, Derek is really rubbing off on you," Emma teases. "You used to be a little more proper when we talked about sex."

Audrey sticks her tongue out at her. "That must have been interesting, having your boyfriend at your beck and call like that in high school. I'm surprised his mom was cool with that."

"She wasn't, but she also kinda let us do our thing in some ways. She just realized that Brent and I were a little more mature about things because of the situation I was dealing with at home." I don't say any more about that; instead, I switch gears. "I don't know, though. It was never like that—the way it was in the bathroom. I'm chalking it up to a buzz."

"Do you want it to happen again?" Audrey asks me.

I flush. I'm not real sure what else to say. Thankfully, I don't have to say anything else because the back door opens, and the guys are bringing out some beers.

"Hey, look. It's alcohol back to see if we can recreate some situations," Emma teases.

I shake my head, laughing right along with them. I get up to go and get one, and Brent's eyes glide up and down my body as he licks his lips.

"I need one of those," I say when I reach the beers.

He hands me one and our fingers brush. "Here you go," he says, his voice faltering a bit.

I smile. "Thanks," I croon out. I know what I'm doing. I'm playing a dangerous game here to see if I can get him to crack again. And maybe rail me in the bathroom again. I turn to walk away but then decide to go back and get beers for the girls. "Emma and Audrey need one."

"Yeah, sure," he says, handing them to me.

"Thanks," I reply again, making my voice sound a little husky. I also make a point to walk slowly back to the girls. I can feel his eyes on me the whole time.

"Brent, you okay, buddy?" I hear Derek call out. "You need a minute, or maybe a drool rag?"

There's some laughter, and as I turn, Brent shoots him the finger.

"Well, that was worth the show," Audrey says, accepting her beer from me.

The rest of the afternoon is spent with Brent's eyes avoiding my body and me eating good food and making friends with his friends. I knew I liked them. I did the second we all went to dinner together. Sure, they're fiercely protective of one another, but even after what I did to him, they still decided they liked me enough to invite me into the fold.

Once everyone is cleared out, Brent is in the kitchen washing dishes.

"Do you need some help?" I ask him, coming out from my room. I'm wearing a T-shirt and shorts. I just spent some time in my new shower and loved every minute of it. His bathrooms are heaven.

"Nah, I'm good. Are you finding everything okay in there?"

"Yeah, I am. Thanks. I wish I could help or do something for you, as a thank-you for today. It was fun joining in on the celebration of Audrey and Derek's engagement."

"It was a good day," he says in return. He carefully studies the plate he served the chicken on.

"I can dry if you need me to." I come up right beside him. If I moved a fraction of an inch, we'd be touching.

"I'm good," he replies again, a little more curtly this time. "Did you know your room has a TV? I put one in there. You can go watch it if you want."

"Sounds like you're dismissing me." I catch his shrug from the corner of my eye. I don't dare look in his direction.

"I just thought after the long day in the sun and pool, you might wanna lie down."

"And give you some space?" I ask him, reading between the lines of what he isn't saying. "I take it it's not as easy as you thought it'd be, having me here."

"Bingo," he says. "It's just gonna take some time getting used to having you here like this, with me every day, like you used to be."

"Understood." I turn and start heading back the way I came. "But Brent, thanks for having me here, for bringing me into the fold of your friends. I know it's a lot of me invading your safe space, and I don't want to hurt you."

"It's fine," he says.

"Night," I say in return.

He simply nods and I disappear around the corner. When I'm in my room, I spend a lot of time thinking about this having something to do with me teasing him during the BBQ about how much he watched me. Or the way his eyes wandered all over my body. I'm sure the girls will go home and tell Aiden and Derek all about how we fucked. It'll be another reason he puts up a wall of safety around himself. Sighing, I wish that I wasn't such a mess and didn't need him to rescue me again. It might make it easier for him to let me in, knowing that I don't need saving again. Knowing that I'm on firmer ground and someone he can lean on instead of being that person who always needs to lean on him.

I put my pjs on and switch on the TV. I didn't get a lot of channels in my old apartment, but he probably does. Brent doesn't want for much. The stress of moving and being in the sun tuckered me out. I'm asleep in the extremely comfortable bed before I know it.

CHAPTER TWENTY-THREE

I'm standing in the kitchen staring at the open fridge. It's full of food, but none of it has been opened. I get the feeling he stocked the fridge just for me. There's an array of fruits and veggies. I don't know if I want to be the first one to cut into them. I feel like a mooch, and I don't want to be the one who eats all his food or eats something that he might have wanted. Although the selection of his food looks out of place for him.

In the little bit of time that I've been back in his life, I've seen him devour burgers, wings, and pizza, but never a salad. Which makes me think he bought it just for me. I sigh. The guilt I've been feeling about taking up residence in his apartment is only growing.

"You've got no choice," he's reminded me on more than one occasion.

I hate that he's right. I had no choice. The only other option was to head back home. Not that there was anything there for me. Just my mama, whom I could have worked beside in the diner while the hometown boys attempted to nail me at the local honky-tonk. Not the life I've dreamed for myself.

I decide I just want a simple yogurt, but he didn't buy any of that. I'm sure if I would have asked, he'd have done it, which makes the guilt sting even more. It doesn't matter how much of a bitch I've been to him, he keeps on doing things for me, making my life easier, while I continue to blow in like a hurricane and destroy his.

"There's a light in the kitchen. You don't need to use my fridge to brighten it up." His voice comes out soft like he's trying not to startle me, but I jump anyway. I wasn't expecting him to come in here, even though it's his house. I thought I might have the late night to myself.

"Sorry," I say, snapping the fridge closed. Without the light of the fridge, the kitchen is dimly lit, with only a small light on over the sink. It makes it hard to see him. Maybe that's a good thing.

He's studying me, the intensity of his gaze traveling up and down my legs. I can't see what his eyes look like. Are they wide with desire, or is he pissed off when he gets to the shirt I'm wearing? Instinctively, I wrap my arms around myself. I block the logo of our old high school, but it's useless. He's already seen it. I still like to sleep in the old football T-shirt that used to be his. It's ratty and well worn. Over the years men have told me that I look so good in it. The thought makes me shudder. Since this is Brent's shirt, only he should enjoy the view. Oddly enough, now I'm hiding it from him.

"I already saw it." The words come out flat. He's either angry or he's just stating facts.

"Yeah, I guess it's silly to cover it up." I don't remove my arms from around my body. I continue to hide the shirt, but it's not just the shirt I'm hiding. I keep my arms wrapped around my midsection, trying to hold myself together.

"Why?" he asks.

"Why, what?"

He sighs. It's the only sound in the room except for the hum of the fridge. "You know what." He sounds annoyed and he's shifting his weight from one foot to the next.

I shrug again. I'm not sure if my answer will suffice or if it even matters. He can probably guess what I'll say.

He leans against the counter, eyes still boring into mine. We're at an impasse. Over a shirt. Awesome.

"It reminds me of a simpler time."

He scoffs. "Try again."

I smile. He can't see it, but I do anyway. "Fine, it reminds me of you."

"Thank you."

"For?" I ask him, confused.

"For being honest with me."

We're both quiet for a beat. I feel so exposed standing there in his kitchen wearing nothing but his old shirt and my sleep shorts, which barely peek out of the shirt thanks to my small frame.

"I'm surprised you have it. I thought you would have chucked every memory you had of me out the window the day you left town."

His words hit me like a ton of bricks.

"I didn't." I state the obvious and roll my eyes at myself in my head. This is not going well. I want to say more, the words are right there on the tip of my tongue, but I don't say any of them. Hell, I've had sex with this man recently—I should be able to use my words. My conscience is telling me that if I can't talk to him, then I definitely shouldn't be having sex with him.

"I tried to wipe away every memory I ever had of you." His admission feels like a gut punch, but not nearly as bad as his next words. "Didn't work, though."

"Oh," I say. My mouth feels so dry, like he's sucked all the air out of the room. I wish I had gotten water when I first came into the kitchen, instead of looking for food.

"Yeah, oh." The slight shake of his head is just barely visible in the darkness.

"I can go if this is too much." I have nowhere else to go, but I offer it up anyway. What else can I do? "I don't want to torture you by being here."

"Darlin', you don't know what torture is. Torture is knowing you're out there somewhere and me having no idea where. Not knowing if you're safe or if you're dead. I had no idea what had happened to you. You just vanished without a trace. I went mad trying to find you. Did you know that?"

"Why?"

"Because how could I not? I protected you for all those years. I wasn't prepared to wake up one day and have you gone. I was worried he was looking for you too, so I knew I had to find you before he did."

"He never found me," I admit.

"Neither did I." His voice is thick with emotion. I can't place it, but it sounds like he's in pain.

"I..." The words fall dead on my lips.

"You don't need to say anything. Lord knows you don't owe me anything. Just tell me one thing: did he ever try to contact you?"

I shake my head. "His lawyer reached out a few years back. Something about wanting me as a character witness at his trial. I never returned the phone calls." I no longer feel guilty for that. I did a long time ago, but the hell that man put me through makes me glad I never took the stand and painted some false picture of the man who beat and raised me.

"Some things never change."

"No, they don't." Can he tell that I mean him and not my father? Because here he is again after all of these years, still protecting me and cleaning up the mess I made.

"What would you have done if I hadn't offered you my place? Would you really have gone back home?"

"Yeah. I mean, what other choice did I have? I wasn't going to live homeless here on the streets of LA."

"Being a dancer doesn't pay the bills, huh?"

"Well, not the kind of dancer I like to be," I quip.

He chuckles. "What are we paying you to dance in the video?"

"A fair wage."

"That doesn't answer my question." He sounds annoyed.

"I'm not giving you that information, and Dale won't either. You don't need to fix this. It's not your job to fix my finances."

"Blair," he pleads with me.

"I'm going to get another waitressing job. That's what I was doing before I got fired."

"What happened when you got fired?"

"The owner liked to grope me, and when it got to be too much, I quit."

"You're fucking kidding, right?" he seethes.

"No," I reply with a flat tone.

"Why the fuck would he do that? Was it some sleazy joint?"

"No, it wasn't. It was a decent bar and grill, but that's this town. That's the way the world works. I'm a pretty girl," I admit with a shrug, "and he knew I'd been working my ass off to be a dancer. He knew I needed every cent I got for rent and my classes. So, he took advantage of that fact. Thought he could get me to do some things for money because, well, I needed it."

"Asshole. Where did you used to work?"

I let out a hollow laugh. "No, Brent you will not go over there and beat the shit out of him. That's not happening."

"Well, someone should."

"You can't fix the world for me, Brent. I love that after all these years and what I did to you, you feel like you still need to, but you don't. I'm fine on my own."

"Clearly," he says sarcastically.

"Like you've never struggled," I throw back at him.

"Not quite like this."

"Well, everyone pays their dues, and that's what I'm doing. Things will come and it'll be fine."

"I'm going to ask Dale to pay you more."

His tone suggests there will be no more discussion on this. It's stern and demanding, very much the way I remember it when we were younger, when he was trying to convince me to stay with him and not go back to my house, where my dad was.

Little did he know, I never wanted to go back. I wanted to stay with him forever. But I was always afraid my dad would come for Brent, and I wasn't sure if teenage Brent could survive. The man he's become easily could have. He's just as tall as he was, but his body has filled out into hard lines and firm muscle.

"I don't want special treatment," I tell him.

He shakes his head. "I feel bad that I am able to live in this" —he gestures around his house— "and you're still working on making it."

"Tougher business, I guess," I reply with a shrug.

"Bullshit," he says with enough force that it makes me jump. "It shouldn't be that way."

He's playing all of these hot-and-cold games tonight. I'm not sure what to think or do. He was softer earlier, when his friends were here, but now he's more stern and harder. I'm not sure if it's because I woke him up or if the reality of my situation has come crashing down around him.

"I heard the girls ask you to go shopping with them tomorrow. Are you going?"

I ponder this a moment before answering him. "I like spending time with them. They're really nice."

He nods, seeming to hear what I'm not saying. "Are you worried they'll try to buy you things? Or that you'll be some sort of charity case?"

I sigh, leaning against the cool fridge. The bite of the cold against my skin feels good. He advances so that he's caging me against it.

"No one thinks you're a charity case." He pushes back the hair that's escaped my bun. "I just want you to know that."

I nod, and I almost let out a whimper. He's so close to me; if I moved just slightly, his body would be pressed against mine, and oh, how I want that. It was hard watching him today, hanging out in the pool without a shirt on. Then when he went and held Jade, crooned in her ear, I swear my uterus skipped a beat at the sexiness that was Brent holding a baby.

"You okay?" he asks, his voice quiet and almost curt in this small space.

"Yeah, I'm fine."

"Did you get all the snacking you needed?"

"Uh-huh." I barely get the noise out of my mouth. Words aren't even possible with this man pressed almost right against me.

"Good," he croons.

His lips come down on mine. It's soft and tentative. "I want you to know that I'm not trying to use you. Trying to get something out of you because you need a place to stay," he replies before pulling back. "So just know that you if you want something to happen again, you're going to have to come to me. Because I won't be that guy."

Fuck, I shouldn't have told him that. I certainly don't want him thinking he's anything like my old manager, but I can see where he put the pieces together.

With that, he turns and heads back down the hallway that leads to his bedroom. I sigh and let you the whimper I'd been holding in.

CHAPTER TWENTY-FOUR

"You okay?" Brent asks as he comes up beside me. He doesn't sit down on the couch beside me; he just lingers behind it.

I make the mistake of taking a deep breath in order to smell him further. I sneak a peek over my shoulder and catch him grinning at me. "What?" I ask him, but I know what.

"Do you want a bottle of my cologne, or do you just want to take deep breaths every time I'm around?"

I shake my head, and my face reddens. "Sorry."

"It's okay. It's kinda nice to see that I have this effect on you after all these years."

"I don't think you had this type of effect on me when we were kids."

He smirks. "I have to head down to the shop and get some things for the drums, new heads and such. The fam is gonna hang out while I'm gone. You're welcome to stay here if you want, or you can hide out in your room, whatever is easier for you. They can be a lot, but trust me, their hearts are in the right place." His brow furrows as he examines what I'm doing. "You okay?" he repeats, gesturing toward where I'm rubbing at the arch of my foot.

"Those girls can shop," I admit with a shrug. "I wasn't prepared for all the trips up and down the mall and all the stores we went into."

"I guess I should have warned you. They mean business when they shop. Not like when we were kids, and we quickly ran into the mall for the things we needed."

I laugh along with him. "I don't think they're necessarily worrying about shopping for things they *need*. It's like a sport to them."

He nods in agreement. "Are your feet going to make it, or would you like me to give them a rubbing when I get back?"

My cheeks heat and my body tingles at the offer. Brent's foot rubs were amazing when we were kids. I bet they'd even better now.

"You think about that and let me know." He leans down and places a kiss against my temple.

I turn my head in his direction, in shock that he did it. But he's already gone, and over comes Derek to sit down beside me.

"Hey, did you have a good day with the girls?" he asks me.

"I did," I reply, hoping my expression doesn't give away the way my stomach flipped at the contact with Brent.

He hands me a bottle of beer. "Here, I feel like you might need this. I didn't learn how much energy they take until we were home from the tour. Those two women over there could run a whole country and barely break a sweat."

I giggle. "They are some amazing women."

"That they are."

"And you're going to marry one of them."

"That I am," he says, smirking at me. Derek leans back against the couch and props his arms on either side of the cushions.

"I don't remember you from Georgia." I didn't mean to say it, but it just came out of my mouth. It's been needling at me more than I had originally thought.

"I had heard of you, but no, we never met when I lived there."

I nod, hoping he's going to say more. Aiden and the girls make their way to the couch and sit down too.

"He kept you from me when I lived in Georgia," Derek continues. "I didn't live there for very long, if it makes you feel any better. My mom only saw fit to stay there for about five months."

I swallow, trying to figure out how someone who cared so much for me kept someone like Derek from me.

"Oh," I finally manage to say when it's clear he's not going to talk until I acknowledge his words.

Audrey places her hand on Derek's thigh as he says the next part of his story.

"I wasn't living in a great part of town. I saw Brent when I was pretty young. He stopped me from getting beat up when we were only like, twelve. Brent would have been—"

"Fourteen," I finish for him.

Derek nods. "I don't think he kept me from you on purpose. We just stayed at my place or sometimes went to that old, abandoned warehouse and jammed. He really had a gift, even back then. I kept in touch with him after I left. He would send riffs and beats he was working on. Sometimes I even used the songs he wrote in our band." He gestured toward Aiden. "I always liked Brent. He's a good guy."

"He is," I reply, suddenly feeling stupid. "I just couldn't imagine how he had such a strong connection with you, and I had never heard of you or even met you. It must sound stupid after all that I did to him."

He rubs the back of his neck. "If it helps, he did tell me all about you."

I smile. "Of course he did."

"He just didn't tell you about me because he was trying to protect you or something. I had a lot going on back then. My mom wasn't always the most stable parent for me, and Brent was a big help with that."

"Sounds like my Brent," I say. I haven't called him my Brent in a long time. Finally, I say the thing that has been whirling around in my head. "He was always the one saving everyone and doing what he could to protect them. Everyone but himself. He let himself open up to me and I just scattered it. I didn't mean to, though. That's what everyone says, but I really didn't."

"You don't have to explain anything to us." Derek runs a hand through his hair and shifts nervously on his feet. "I know you didn't. *We* know you didn't. I could tell the second you stepped on set that his presence had just as much of an effect on you as yours did on him."

"How did all of this get started?" I ask him, trying to pivot the subject to something that might be a little less emotional for us.

Aiden nods. A wide knowing smile covers his face. "Well, once Derek and I decided that college wasn't for us, which by the way did not make my parents happy, we knew we were starting a band. We were so excited, and we went to our old drummer, Neal, thinking he would be just as excited. But guess what? He wasn't. He actually wanted to go to college and do what his parents wanted him to do."

"Oh, come on," Audrey breaks in, smacking Aiden on the shoulder. "How did that work out for Neal? I think pretty damn well considering he's a lawyer now. Neal always enjoyed being in your band, but it was never what he really wanted to do."

"Yeah, yeah." Aiden waves her off. "Derek and I were brainstorming who we could ask, and this guy immediately knew he wanted to ask Brent. That he would be the perfect fit for our band. But there was one wrinkle we weren't sure about. You," Aiden says, punctuating his statement by pointing at me.

"I was sure he wouldn't leave you," Derek says. "But by the time we called him, it turned out you had already left. So, he packed up all his shit and kissed his mama goodbye and came out to Cary with us. And this band has been together and tight ever since." He reaches back and smacks Aiden on the shoulder. "I can't imagine it any other way."

"That's how you should tell it," Emma says, a wicked grin on her face. "When you're on *Behind the Music*, that is exactly how you should explain it."

Aiden turns around and shakes his head, while Derek flips her off.

"I can do that because she's not my wife," Derek says, patting Aiden on the back. Meanwhile, Emma and Audrey are busy cracking up.

I just laugh and shake my head. "Well, I'm glad I wasn't around when you called."

"Why is that?" Derek asks.

"Because then he wouldn't have found this. You're right about one thing, he wouldn't have left if I was still there, and I'm not sure if I would have gone with him. So, it's good that he got to come out here with you and start this."

"Yeah, it did work out pretty well, and it looks like you coming back into his life has had some positive impact here too." Aiden winks at me.

I try to hide my smile. "That might be a bit of a reach. But it is great to get to be around him again."

"But you knew who he was before you agreed to do the video, right?" Aiden asks.

I nod. "Yeah, I knew. But I needed the money," I say lamely. I hate this conversation suddenly. I hate that I have to explain to them that I'm poor. "I really had no choice in the matter."

"Hey, what's going on over here?" Brent asks as he comes in the door. He's holding a large brown flat box and some takeout bags.

"Whatcha got there, Mr. Man?" Emma asks, getting up to check on the baby, who is sleeping in her car seat.

"I thought maybe we could all use some dinner," he says, studying me. He then looks over at Derek and Aiden. They must be having some kind of silent conversation, because they all keep staring at one another intently. Brent eventually shakes his head slightly.

"You good, Blair?" Brent asks.

"Why wouldn't she be?" Audrey asks.

"Because I left her home with the three of you."

"There are four of us here," she corrects him.

"Yeah, well, there are only three of you that worry me." He shoots her a wicked grin.

"Glad you can trust me, man," Derek says at the same time Aiden says, "I know it's not me."

"I'm not answering which one of you I meant," he says with a chuckle.

We all gather around his dining room table and have dinner. It's a nice end to a long day. I push my food around my plate, only taking in a little bit of it. Brent brought home Chinese food, and the grease and salt aren't the best for my stomach or diet.

"There's fruit in the kitchen if you want some," Brent says, leaning in from where he's seated beside me at the table.

"Thanks. It's fine."

"You don't have to hide it from me, Blair. I can tell when you don't want to eat or when you're placating me. Just go get yourself some fruit. I might not have the best diet, but that doesn't mean you don't have to."

I smile and make my way into the kitchen, where I grab a bowl of the melon salad I cut up this morning. He had so much fruit in there, I had to do something with it. I pause at the entrance of the dining room because I can hear that the conversation has turned to me.

"Guys, just let it be. She'll be back any minute," Brent is saying.

"I really like her," Audrey says. "She's so sweet."

"Yeah, she's a blast," Brent says with a bit of edge to his voice.

"Man, we talked a bit about us back in Georgia," Derek explains.

"Oh really?"

"Yeah, I only told her pieces."

I'm frozen in the doorway, trying to figure out what the other pieces of that story are. I might not have the right to be mad because of how I left him, but I wonder what he's hiding from me. I slowly make my way into the dining area, then take my seat. The conversation is flowing easily, but I barely hear any of it. Instead, I push the fruit around on my plate until we all can get up and leave.

Once dinner wraps, I make an excuse about stretching and head into my bedroom so that I can hide away for a bit. It's nice to have some solitude. That is the one thing I miss about having my own place.

CHAPTER TWENTY-FIVE

A sharp blow hits the side of my head, and I'm knocked to the floor. "I can't believe I've raised such an ungrateful daughter. How can you act this way? Leaving me alone for all hours of the day. Not taking care of your old man like you should be! You ungrateful bitch!" he screams as he lobs another blow to my head.

I fall to the ground and lie there, protecting myself. It's one of the things I've learned from all the beatings I've taken from my father—protect your head.

Crying makes it worse, too. It's like he thrives on my pain or the fact that he's hurting me. I've learned to just lie there and try not to react. It helps it be over faster if he doesn't think he's getting a rise out of me.

"How could you not come home and make me dinner?" he says, landing a blow to my stomach.

I grunt because the punch he lands is enough to knock the wind out of me. He chuckles darkly, again enjoying the pain he's inflicting. I get a whole other host of insults hurled at me. I'm called a bitch, a slut, and ungrateful. Although, I have no idea how I could be seen as ungrateful, because it's not like he's taken care of me in quite some time...

Mentally, I'm back in Brent's arms at his house, while physically, I'm on the ground, my dad beating the shit out of someone he's supposed to *love. Blow after blow reminds me that I'm not worthy of that kind of love.*

I break my rule of not screaming and let out an awful howl when his boot connects with my ribs. I'm sure he broke more than one with that blow, which is why I scream bloody murder, hoping and praying that someone will come save me.

In the fog, someone shakes me. I whip around, trying to find the source, my dad's face fading fast.

"Blair, Blair," a voice is saying. "Wake up darlin'. Wake up."

"Huh?" I thrash awake, my arms swinging around.

"Whoa, whoa. Careful there, you're going to hit me. Are you okay?"

I open my eyes as I slowly sit up and look around the room. I don't recognize it immediately. There's no shabby comforter from my old apartment. The couch isn't to the left of the bed, with the TV opposite of it. No, instead there are clean lines and purple. A spacious room with no furniture. Once my eyes focus, I see him.

He's here.

I sigh, my hand going over my heart as it beats rapidly. He wasn't here in my dream. I had called for him, though he hadn't showed up. But he's here now.

"How are you here? I was looking for you." The words come out in a hushed tone as I struggle to put everything together.

"Oh, Blair, it was a dream. And from the sounds of it, it was a bad dream." He reaches over and switches on the bedside table light. A soft glow fills the room. "Do you recognize your surroundings now? You're safe, darlin'. So, so safe."

I just sit there for a moment, trying to process everything. "It all felt so real," I manage to say. This is so weird to me, having someone here to comfort me. I never used to get nightmares when I stayed with him before. I was living my nightmare. But ever since I fled from home, I've had dreams about it. And it usually takes me a minute to realize that I am not back there. That I'm safe, and he can't hurt me anymore.

"Do you wanna talk about it?" Brent speaks again, his wide chocolate eyes searching mine. His brow is furrowed and he's biting his lip.

"Can I get some water?" I ask him.

He springs up from the bed, happy that he's being asked to do something. That he has a task. He's out and back into the bedroom in a flash. In fact, the water sloshes up over his hand before he hands it to me. "Sorry about that."

"It's fine, thank you." I take the glass from him. Small sips and deep breaths are what I practice. That's what has helped in the past, at least. He's staring at me, and I wonder if it would make him feel better if he knew what the nightmare was about. I want to tell him, but I hate that it'll anger him.

"I'll talk in a minute. Just let me get my bearings a little bit," I tell him.

I look over and he nods. A comforting hand comes out and rests on my knee. He rubs a small circle on my knee, offering me what comfort he can. I remember when he used to do this. It always helped me and calmed me down.

My father wasn't always like this. He wasn't always the drunk who beat his daughter. My mom left him, running off with her high school sweetheart. She said they were destined to be together, and she didn't love him anymore. He took that really hard, and at first, he was a decent father to me. But then he found the bottle and all of that changed.

He lost job after job and did his best to keep it all together, but it was hard for him. I tried to rationalize it at first because I knew my dad was brokenhearted. I thought about finding him someone else to date, thinking that if he wasn't sad, he wouldn't hit me anymore. But there was no way anyone in my town would go for my dad. He was a drunk and had a temper. He'd been in bar fight after bar fight, even stole things and got busted a time or two.

The police always came and got me and took me to my aunt's. It was better there, but she didn't want a child, so she barely bothered to pay attention to me. And then I found Brent and his family. They took care of me, and sometimes when my dad got busted and was in jail, that was where I went. And now, even in my dreams, Brent's still saving me.

"How often do these happen?" he asks me quietly.

"Not as much as they used to, but from time to time, I get them."

"Okay. And they're about...?" Brent always has been a nervous Nelly. What he doesn't know scares him.

"Yeah, they're about being back in that house with my dad and the things he used to do to me," I reply, sipping my water again. My eyes find the carpet, and I just stare at it, not daring to look him in the eyes.

"I'm so sorry, Blair. I wish I could take all of the dreams and nightmares of those times away from you."

"Thanks." There's a question on the tip of his tongue, so I say, "Just ask me what you want to ask me."

"Have they gotten worse since you started coming around me more? Do I cause them?"

I'm shaking my head before he can even finish the thought. "No, Brent, this is not because of you. I've had them before, when I lived in my apartment by myself."

"I hate to think of you going through this alone. Waking up and screaming like that and having no one there."

"I wake up screaming?" I knew I was screaming in my dream, but I had no idea that it was how I actually wake up.

"Yeah, you do." He sits beside me and pulls me into a hug. "Tell me about your dream, Blair. Let me help you."

I sigh and repeat the events of the dream to him. The hand that was resting on my thigh is now balled up and is lying on the bed. He's careful to keep it away from me. His anger is boiling up. He always hated when I would tell him about the abuse. I had to restrain him a couple of times so that he didn't drive over to my house and beat the living shit out of my dad.

"It's okay, Brent. It isn't happening to me anymore. Look at me." I grab his face and force him to look me in the eyes. There's fire there. "Everything is okay."

"It doesn't feel like it," he murmurs.

"Well, it's as okay as it's going to be at this point. You and I are here, and we're together like we used to be. Miles away from Georgia. Miles away from where he rots away in prison. It's okay. It's okay," I repeat. I'm not sure if I'm saying this more for my benefit or his own.

Brent pulls me into him. I'm nuzzled against his chest and breathe in that familiar scent from earlier. I fist his T-shirt and hold on as he rocks me gently—like he used to. And that's it. That's when I lose it. I let out a sob into his chest, and strong arms wrap around me tighter as I cry. It feels good to be held like this for a change. I've missed the feel of his arms around me. I haven't had this feeling in a long time.

My sobs have quieted down, and we're still sitting like this, him holding on to me and my fist wrapped in his shirt. I sigh and go to sit back up.

"Oh sorry," he says, releasing me.

My body registers the loss of him immediately. I wipe at my eyes, and he's back to staring at me.

"Have you ever talked to anyone about your nightmares?" he asks.

I shake my head. "Um, no, I really haven't."

"Maybe you should," he suggests. He's looking at me like he used to when we were kids. His expression is tentative, like he knows he could potentially get yelled at for the things he's about to say to me, knowing that I might blow my lid if I don't like the answer, like I used to do. But I won't, not with this.

"Yeah, I probably should. And I will someday. I just need to get some things taken care of first. Plus, it does help having someone here," I reply, hoping that helps. I can still see the doubt in his eyes. "They aren't that often, but I get your point. I should be talking to someone about it."

He nods and looks a little satisfied with my response. "Do you want me to stay with you tonight? Will it help?"

I'd really like him to stay, but instead, I say, "Nah, I'm okay. But thanks. I'm sure you'd rather be in your bed and not mine."

"I wouldn't have offered if I didn't actually want to stay with you, Blair. But I get it if it makes you uncomfortable."

"I would actually like that." The smile that I am greeted with is enough to make me wish I would have just given in sooner.

I scoot over so that he can lie on his back. Once he's situated, I lie down beside him, placing my head on his shoulder, but there is some space between his body and mine.

"Scoot in a little closer," he says, and I look up at him. "Come on, darlin'. Just get in here and let me hold you."

It feels awkward and intimate lying with him like this. It's like we get so close and then we back off. I'm not sure which is happening now. We're getting closer, but come morning, then what? I'm so busy in my own head that I let out a yelp when he drags me to him.

"Stop worrying and thinking it over so much. Just lie here with me, okay?" Brent chuckles and I feel his head shake against mine.

"Yes, sir," I tease.

"Get some sleep. Didn't you say you had some dance class or something tomorrow?"

"Yeah, I do. A full day of classes."

"Alright, well, staying up all night isn't going to help things. Let's get some sleep."

I want to ask him what he has going on tomorrow. I'm curious if he'll be up or at home when I return. My alarm is going to wake us both, but I try not to think too much more about it as I drift off to sleep in his arms, breathing in and out and taking in that the scent of Brent that I've really come to enjoy. My last thought is about him, which makes my dreams more pleasant.

CHAPTER TWENTY-SIX

It's been two days since Brent has slept in my bed. Thankfully, the nightmares have stayed at bay. We're in this weird space where we're just a little flirty, but he keeps his distance from me. Meaning, there's been no sex or touches, but there's been glances and words spoken. No promises, but the air around us is definitely charged at times. Does he feel it too? There are times when I think he just might, based on the way he looks at me, but I can't be sure. He's so much better at holding his cards close than I am. I have no poker face, and it's proving to make me easier prey for him.

Today, we're headed for more press on the video. It's local, but not all of the band members are coming. Aiden had something with the baby, so he decided to not come out. It'll just be Brent, Derek, and me.

The black SUVs take us everywhere we need to go. I'm sitting in there brushing my sweaty palms on my jeans.

"Are you guys always driven around everywhere?" I ask. I've seen the garage that has not only his motorcycle but also a black sports car of some sort in the garage and a black BMW SUV. He has cars, but whenever it's band business, it seems like we're driven places.

"Dale likes to make sure we're on time. There was one time when Aiden and Brent showed up twenty minutes late. The producers were not happy with us. So now, whenever possible, he'll arrange a car service for us. It also helps with security."

"Yeah, and sometimes it's just nice not to have to navigate this traffic," Derek says from the other side of me.

He's right, the LA traffic can be brutal, and right now, we're sitting in a line of traffic while we're on our way to some magazine that wants to interview us.

"I never knew there was so much press surrounding the release of a music video. Like, since when?" I ask the guys as we creep along.

Derek chuckles. "Well, Dale is trying to get some good buzz surrounding the video. And besides, he never does anything half-assed. We're aways doing things up big—lots of press, red carpet walks, and other fancy things to get the band attention."

"He's a smart man," Brent chimes in. "He's helped us so many times and has gotten us pretty far."

It almost sounds like he's defending him. "Well, I guess it's good that he's managing you guys then. He seems like he's a big help."

"That he is," Derek adds in. "Hell, he even managed to bring you back into Brent's life."

Brent's lips quirk up into a smile. "You can't give him credit for that. He had no idea who she was."

"No, I suppose not," Derek says with a chuckle.

It's a creep and crawl all the way, but we eventually end up at the interview. I find out when we get there that it's for a magazine called *Billboard Hits*. I've never heard of it before, but the boys seem pretty excited about it, so it must be good.

Brent and Derek position us so that I am in the middle of them again.

"Are you sure you don't want me off to the side?" I ask them for what feels like the millionth time.

"Is she always so squirrely at interviews?" Derek asks.

"She warms up when they start talking to us," Brent replies, laughing along with him.

"You guys know I'm sitting right here, and I can hear you, right?" I say with a roll of my eyes.

"Oh, lighten up, darlin'. You're going to do just fine." Brent reaches beneath the table and gives my thigh a squeeze. It causes my insides to light up. I love the feeling of his hands on me. I want more of it, but it's a long, slow, and complicated dance to make it happen.

"Sorry." I swallow and rub my hands on my jeans again.

"You sleeping okay?" Brent asks, angling his body to me so that Derek can't hear us as easily. "I haven't heard you having any more nightmares. Or are you quieter lately?"

His eyes are filled with genuine concern. "No, no more nightmares."

"Trouble sleeping?" he asks, a mischievous smirk covering his face.

"Yeah, a little," I admit.

"Need help with that?" He shoots me a wink.

Before I can open my mouth to reply to him, the door opens, and in walks the woman who will be interviewing us. She's the tiniest woman I've ever seen. When Derek and Brent go to hug her, they dwarf her; she doesn't even reach their shoulders. Her hair is short, black, and cut into a blunt bob. On her small frame, she wears dark skinny jeans and a black long-sleeve T-shirt. It has the band's logo on it. On her feet are motorcycle boots.

"How are you, half-pint?" Brent asks her when they separate.

She smiles widely at him and giggles. It's a flirty giggle, and I can see her smokey eyes are shining brightly at him. She knows him well, that much is evident.

"I'm doing just fine. We've missed you at the last couple of rides. Where have you been hiding, Brent?" She playfully pushes on his shoulder.

"Oh, you know. I've been hanging out in the studio, on this press tour, and just trying to do my thing."

"Well, if you need any help with doing your thing, just let me know, okay?" Her voice drops to a sultry low.

They both laugh and my stomach flips. The only thing in my mind right now is if he fucked her. I can't ask the question. I can't even act like I'm affected by all of this. That reaction would make the band look bad, not just me. I'm sure Brent wouldn't think twice about telling Dale that I acted inappropriately.

I do my best to breathe in and out, trying to act like this isn't shaking up my whole world. I feel eyes on me. It's Derek, but I don't dare look at him. I don't want to see either the sympathy in his eyes or him glancing at me like he's figured out the keys to the kingdom. Instead, I turn my gaze to the floor and try to remain calm and not fall apart. Especially since I have no claim on this man. I'm only the girl who's living with him because she's been evicted and needs him more than he needs her.

"Gia, this is Blair, the dancer from our video," Brent says, suddenly remembering that I'm here.

I look up and meet her eyes. "Hi, Gia. It's so nice to meet you."

I pull off my best fake smile and voice. She shouldn't be able to tell; she's never met me before. She can't tell if I'm being genuine. Brent might be able to, but at this point, I can't worry about that.

"You did an amazing job in that video," she gushes.

"Thank you," I reply lamely, unsure what else to say to her.

"So, what I thought we would do is sit down here and talk for a bit," she goes on, "and then get a picture of all of you for the website and the article that we're working on. Does that sound like a plan for all of you?" She may say "all of you," but her eyes are glued on Brent.

This time I do look over at Derek. I don't mean to, but his eyes are boring a hole into me. I can't help but look at him with the intensity of his stare. The grin that explodes on his face tells me he can see the jealousy written all over mine. I bite my lip in an attempt to get my emotions in check.

"Yeah, sounds good. Let's do it," Brent says, taking his seat.

Derek gestures for me to sit back between the two of them. Gia is on the adjacent side of the table. She angles her body so that she's facing us, but I could swear she's only interested in just looking at him. She places a tape recorder on the table, then hits the record button and prepares herself to get started.

"Tell me about this drum solo. How did that come to be? It's amazing. I haven't heard a solo like yours in a long time, Brent."

He blushes at her praise. I love the humility in Brent. He's so humble. But she is right, the solo is amazing.

"Thank you, Gia. You are too kind. I really loved the chance to write it in there, as selfish as that is to say. It was something I thought would work out perfectly for the song. The heavy beat that 'Love Drunk' has calls for it. Thankfully, the guys were on board."

"Well, we had to be," Derek chimes in. "He writes some pretty dope beats, and it's hard not to listen to him. This man here is too humble, though. He really doesn't give himself the credit he deserves. He's big on giving each one of us something special to play on guitar or base, and he rarely does it for himself. So, we were thrilled that he took a moment in time for himself. And to have it blow up like this, and to have an outstanding video like this with an incredible dancer, is just awesome." Derek stretches his arms out and pats both Brent and me.

"It is really blowing up the charts," Gia remarks. "In fact, you dropped it just in time for the VMAs. I hear it's going to be a tight race but Crave looks like they are in good position for awards season. You must be pretty happy about that." She's beaming with pride for the boys, as am I.

"Well, thank you," Derek replies. "We're pretty stoked. It's all kind of working out pretty perfectly for us. We're hoping to be heading back on tour here pretty soon." His perfect answer almost sounds rehearsed, but she doesn't seem to notice. Her big grin is focusing in full force on Brent.

"Will you take Blair on tour?" she asks him.

I look over at Brent for the answer to this. They've never talked about me and the tour. However, I have heard the mentions of one between the guys and Dale.

"We'd like to," Brent replies, looking in my direction. "But those details have to be worked out with Blair. She's an in-demand dancer, after all. We need to work around her busy schedule."

I'm caught off guard, and I flush a bit. I know what he's doing, making me sound like I work more than I do. I appreciate that instead of saying that I'm out of work and barely getting by.

"What do you think, Blair? Is there a tour in your future?" Gia asks me.

"We'll have to look at those dates and see what we can do. I'd love to be on tour with the guys." My answer must be well delivered, because I turn to see Derek's big grin and Brent puts his hand on my thigh. I look over at him and smile brightly, covering his hand with my own.

And Gia being Gia doesn't miss the look that passes between us. "Am I sensing a little romance here? The boys of Crave are certainly very lucky in love."

I can feel my face heat. I'm not sure how to answer that question. No one has ever suspected us of dating before. "Um, well—" I start to say, but Brent takes over.

"No, of course not. Come on, Gia, you know me," he says with a laugh. "I like my freedom."

She giggles. "That is true." Her green eyes bat in his direction, which he returns with a megawatt smile of his own.

I inwardly cringe and do my best to school my face. Derek chuckles lightly beside me, but thankfully, neither Brent nor Gia notices. They're lost in another conversation.

By the time the interview is wrapping up, most of the talking has been done by Brent.

"Should we get a picture?" Gia asks, standing up from her chair.

"Yeah, we totally should." Brent rises along with her.

"Yeah, let's get one so we can document that I was actually here," Derek murmurs. "I don't think they actually needed us, Blair." He says it softly enough that I don't think that either of them heard.

I giggle. "She's just lovely," I say.

"Admit it, you hate her," Derek says as we watch the two of them talking as if we're not even there.

"Oh no, not all," I reply. "Besides, we're not anything, so what does it matter who he talks to?"

"Except that the two of you are certainly not nothing. I can see that, Aiden can see that, and the girls have been telling me so all along. So yeah, you're jealous."

I go to say something, but he puts his finger on my lips.

"Let's get this picture taken and get out of here."

CHAPTER TWENTY-SEVEN

The ride back to Brent's house is fairly quiet. Derek and Brent do most of the talking, while I stare out the window. I don't hear much of what they say, but I imagine it doesn't involve me, because no one tries to pull me into the conversation.

We pull into Brent's driveway, and I instantly turn toward Derek. "Thank you," I say to him. I repeat the same thanks to the driver and hop out.

I hear my name, but I don't bother to see who called it out. I'm on a mission, walking to the front door. I reach for the keypad, when Brent's hand covers mine. His body becomes flush with mine as he pulls me toward him.

"What's the matter?" His voice is quiet in my ear, and it sends chills down my spine. "Why are you acting like this?"

I freeze, unable to say anything. I attempt to push him off, but he only backs off slightly and releases the hold he has on me.

"Talk to me," he says.

I sigh. "Just let me go into the house. I wanna change."

"Why?"

"I just do. I want to do something away from you, okay?"

"No, that's not okay, because I don't get why you're running," he hisses in my ear. "Just talk to me."

"Back up," I say sternly. "Back up if you want me to talk to you."

He sighs and my body registers the loss of him immediately. He did exactly what I asked him to, yet I hate it. I wanted him to stay close to me.

"Now talk to me darlin'."

I spin around and there he stands, watching me with his hands on his hips. I shake my head. Yes, I'm upset about him and Gia—their closeness and how they probably don't have a jaded past. It's that and jealousy. He seemed to be easy and relaxed with her. He's probably that way with every girl he meets, but damn, to have to watch it... I hated it.

"I don't know where to start," I say. For someone ready to tear him a new one, I'm now at a loss for words.

"Okay, well, I'm thinking this has something to do with Gia. Wanna explain it? Or at least explain to me why you're jealous?" He looks way so happy with himself. Sure, he may have hit the nail on the head, but I'm not sure I like that he was able to put it together so quickly.

"Not really," I say bitterly.

"Okay, so yeah, I am right. Want to talk about it?"

I groan and he laughs at me.

"Come on, let's go for a ride," he says, walking in the direction of his garage.

I hear the door going up, and I walk over to see him getting his bike together.

"You and I could use a change of scenery," he tells me. "Let's go for a ride while you gather your thoughts."

I watch him carefully. I have on heeled booties, so I can't say that my shoes are a reason to say no, but I don't feel like being this close to him right now. "I'd rather not" is all I say.

"Why, because you don't like it that Gia may or may not have been this close to me on the bike? Is that what worries you?" He takes a predatory step toward me. "Or are you worried that our bodies were pressed up against each other in a more intimate manner, and you can't stand the thought of that either?"

I can't take the words that are coming out of his mouth, because once again, he's spot on. "Stop!" I yell at him.

"Blair." He comes close to me, his hands up in surrender like he's approaching a caged animal. "Can you help me a bit here? I want to talk this out with you."

I shake my head, hot tears burning in my eyes. "Did you fuck her?" I ask him. I clamp a hand over my mouth, closing my eyes and hoping he doesn't get angry at me, or even answer me.

"Blair, we should just go for a ride. You'll feel a little better if we take a ride and clear both of our heads, and then I'll answer any questions you have."

"Why won't you answer me now?" I spit at him.

"Because if we talk all of this out right now, it's not going to go well. We're not going to talk; we're going to shout. And darlin', I don't want to shout at you right now. Go for a ride with me." He punctuates each of his words by pushing the helmet back and forth in front of me.

I sigh again and look up at the blue sky. "You are so irritating."

"I'll be less irritating on the road," he promises.

"Fucking fine," I say, taking the helmet off his hands. "I'll go for a ride with you, but on one condition."

"What's that?" he asks me, his grin growing by the second.

"We talk and you tell me everything once we get to our destination."

"Deal," he replies. He's won, but right now, going with Brent on a ride actually does sound like a good idea. The bike roars to life as I'm finishing strapping the helmet to my head. "Come on, pretty lady, get on."

I do as he asks and wrap my arms around his waist. It's nice to be this close to him even though a few moments ago I wanted to kill him. As I settle onto the bike, he revs it loudly one time, then peels out of his driveway and drives through the gated community where he lives. When we get to the gate, I look over his shoulder and watch as he punches in some digits and the gate opens. Out we go into the open road. Brent drives faster and faster as I hold on to him. I love being on the back of his bike. I still wonder if Gia ever was, though.

I roll my eyes at my own thoughts as we drive. I'm being bratty. Brent must think so too.

I run my hands along his middle, noticing that he's really, really ripped. Sure, I saw him with his shirt off at the pool, but I've done my best to keep my distance from him. I kept my eyes from really appreciating his body. But being pressed up against him like this, it makes me appreciate his strong body even more. You could grate cheese on his abs. I'd actually like to run my tongue over them. When we were together last time, he was behind me, and there was no appreciating his body. My mind is racing with thoughts of what it would be like to get to openly puruse his body.

His hand comes off the wheel and brushes across my finger-tips, then he gives me a gentle squeeze. I smile and give his middle a bit of a squeeze back. My head falls down and rests between his shoulder blades. I hate that I acted bratty earlier. I wish I could apologize to him right now for flipping out. I place a kiss on the back of his neck.

As he rounds a corner, he calls over his shoulder, "It's alright, sweetheart. I thought you could use a ride to get a little bit of perspective before we both said things we didn't mean."

"What could you have possibly said?" I ask him.

"That I'm not perfect."

We ride in silence to the beach and then park and get off. I take in a deep breath of the ocean air as he move over to a spot on the sand, though we stay away from the water.

"Not getting any closer to the water, huh?" I ask him.

"Well, neither one of us is really dressed for it, so…"

It's quiet for bit. I watch the waves crashing and families out there playing. It's a nice sight to see. "I always wanted a family to take me to the beach and play." I'm not sure where the words come from or why. We're supposed to be here talking about Gia.

"Yeah, you never really had that, I guess. We would have taken you," he says with a shrug.

"You would have. But it would have been nice if my parents could have taken me."

"You don't think they did before she left?"

I sigh. "I'm not sure. I don't remember. And it's not like my father kept any of the photo albums around for me to see if they did. I only have the one picture I hid away of her."

"Bastard," Brent growls out.

"Yeah, maybe. But he was brokenhearted. I'd like to think that's why he did what he did." I shrug. It seems silly that I'm defending him. It's not like it makes it any easier.

"Nah, I think he was always a bastard."

I nod in agreement. There's no reason to defend my dad. He has no defense for the things he's done. I finally get up the courage to ask my question. "Did you fuck Gia?"

Brent chuckles. "I did." He says it so simply, like he's telling the waitress that he does in fact want more bread or something.

"I thought so. Is that why she agreed to interview the band?"

Brent throws his head back laughing. "No, that's not why. Everyone is connected in this town. I met Gia a while ago, when I was riding around LA. I used to hang out at a biker bar and made some good friends there. Gia hung out with the group too, and we would go on rides up and down the coast."

"You mean like *Sons of Anarchy*?" I blurt out.

"No, not like that. We just hung out and rode together. A lot of the guys I ride with are in the industry. You have a couple of singers or band members. There are some studio executives and Gia, who is with the press. And that's how I know her. But I like that you were jealous of her." He shoots me a wink and looks back at the ocean.

"So, was it just the one time, or did you guys have a relationship?"

"You really want all the sordid details, huh?" He shakes his head. "We didn't really have a relationship. We just met once or twice and had sex. You know, blew off some steam after a long ride or some shit like that."

"Oh," I say, dumbfounded and slightly hurt by his reply.

"I haven't had the past of a saint, Blair. I'm not sorry about it. It's who I was back then, and maybe who I am still, I don't know. It just helps me get through the trips on the road. I like women, and being in a band like this, they tend throw themselves at you."

I watch him while he watches the surf. "Are you ever going to settle down?"

"Are you talking about sometime in the future, or did you have a certain scenario in mind?"

"I guess I'm just wondering if you would ever come back to me." The words are out of my mouth, and I wish I could reel them back in. I shake my head and play with the sand in front of me.

"Do you want me to come back to you?" He scoots closer to me so that our knees are touching on the sand.

"I-I'm not sure. I don't think I really meant *me*. Maybe I just meant that it would be nice to know if you would ever go the distance with someone. Anyone," I stammer, trying to find the right words.

Brent nods. "I would go the distance. Who knows, it might even be with you." He bops my nose with his fingertip and winks at me.

"I made it weird, huh?" I ask him.

He laughs. "I liked how jealous you were of her today. Kind of made my dad. The interview was pretty awesome, and it went well. Add on top of that the way you were seething because I was talking and joking with another girl. It was a hell of an ego stroke."

I shake my head. "You're an ass."

"True, but I never pretended to be anything different."

"Yeah, you did. I remember when we were together in Georgia. You weren't like this."

"Time does a lot to people."

"Maybe to some people, but it left you pretty much the same," I say, tapping his leg.

"I've spent so much time being mad at you. I hate that, considering how close we used to be. Maybe it's time all of that stopped." He's staring at me intently.

"Are you sure it's been long enough?" I ask, trying to lighten the mood.

"Not really," he teases. "But I like it better when we're playful and not angry at each other."

I smile. "Me too. So, are we done with all of that?"

He chuckles. "I'm not sure about being done with it. I mean, I still like to give you shit. But you're off the hook."

"For leaving you?" I ask him, and he nods. "You're a good person, Brent. But don't do it because you feel like you have to. Because you have a sense of duty or honor to uphold when it comes to me. I hurt you and I get that. Let go of it if *you* are ready to, not because you feel like you have to."

"Thank you for saying that, but I realized that while you are in front of me, it's better if I don't hate you. I like it this way. The way that allows me to be here with you like this and not roaring and yelling all of the time."

"Oh, but I like you roaring and yelling," I tease.

"I could roar and yell in different ways." He wiggles his eyebrows at me.

It makes me laugh, so much so that I throw my head back. "Oh, Brent, thank you for that. I needed a good laugh tonight."

He throws some sand at me. "Well, now you know how I felt when you were jealous."

I stick my tongue out at him.

"She's nothing compared to you," he says, leaning over and

placing a tender kiss on my lips. It doesn't last long, though; he pulls back and winks at me. "Yeah, nothing compared to you."

Brent pulls me to him, and we lie there, my back against him, watching the people on the beach laugh and play. It's a slower ride home. When we get home, he makes us dinner and we cuddle on the couch together. There's no touching or kissing, but I like the time we have together. There are no promises made or words spoken about what we may or may not be, but it feels like a step in the right direction.

CHAPTER TWENTY-EIGHT

I'm in the kitchen eating a yogurt, scrolling on my phone. I just got in from dance class, so I'm not sure where Brent is. Both of his cars and his bike were here when I pulled in, so I imagine he's here somewhere.

It's kind of awkward to be here by myself. It doesn't quite feel like home. And it's not because of anything Brent says or does; I know he wants me to feel at home here. It's just my own awkwardness that makes it difficult. I don't want him to feel like I'm taking advantage of him or his generosity. That's why I'm trying to find a part-time job. He doesn't want me to, but I want to. He feels that the video is really going to help things take off, especially if it's nominated for a VMA, and even more so if we win. I hope so too, but I have bills to pay and debts to pay off, so I want to make sure that I'm continuing to make money.

Being a broke and struggling artist is definitely getting old. I've dealt with it for a while. A few times, I've almost found a cheaper city to live in and abandoned my dreams of making it as a dancer. But I just want to be able to dance in videos, and maybe even get a chance to dance in a musical or Broadway play. Something, anything, to add to my resume and my experience. Hell, being a backup dancer and dancing during a concert for stars like Beyonce or Taylor Swift would be a dream, but I have no idea how to get my foot in the door for those. They haven't been flaunting those auditions lately. They seem to have their teams in place.

Brent walks into the room with a big smile on his face.

"Where were you?" I ask.

"Miss me, huh?" He wiggles his eyebrows at me while sweat drips from his brow. His clothes are drenched too.

"Were you working out?" I ask him.

"Well, yeah." He laughs, seeming to enjoy the way I keep staring at him. "Are you enjoying the view?" He pulls up his shirt and wipes the sweat from his brow. "I had a rough one today. Sorry for all the sweat."

"Y-yeah. Looks like it," I stammer, struggling to get the words out.

"Maybe it's okay, though. You seem to be enjoying it," he teases.

I just look at the counter as I finish my yogurt. Out of the corner of my eye, I see his shirt come off, and my eyes snap over on their own accord. My brain must have known I wanted a look at his body.

And damn does he look good.

He catches me watching him but doesn't say a word, just sips on his water, watching me study his body.

"Sorry," I finally say, forcing my eyes to look away.

"It's okay. I kinda like that I have this effect on you. Feel free to stare at my body as much as you want. I work hard for it." His tone has dropped to a sexy, low tone.

And God, does he ever work hard for it. I can see the sweat glistening off him. His muscular arms look like they would have no problem throwing me up on this island. He has abs that are rock hard. And damn, the *V* that trails down into his shorts is enough to make a girl stupid. Which is why I'm having trouble getting words out around this man. I want him to put his shirt on, but at the same time, I want him to find a job where he never has to wear a shirt again. Or maybe he could just serve me yogurt and strawberries shirtless for the rest of our lives. Which may not be very long for me. My heart is beating fast, and my breaths are coming out fast and short.

"You'll be alright, kiddo. I'm going to put a shirt on after my shower. Or I could go jump in the pool and show you what I look like all wet."

"Enjoying yourself?" I ask him, forcing myself to look at his eyes and not at his chest.

"Not as much as you are," he quips. "Would you wanna go grab something to eat tonight? Or maybe go see a movie?" He looks anxious suddenly.

I smile at him. "Do I make you nervous, Brent?"

He chuckles. "Only worried that you'll say no. I've never actually had to ask you out on a date before. You just willingly went everywhere with me. We were kids back then too, so..."

I nod, understanding what he's saying. "I would love to, Brent. Thank you."

"I'm gonna go grab a shower. Just let me know what you wanna do and what time you wanna leave. Especially if it's a movie, okay?"

"Sure, will do."

He leaves and heads for the shower, while I'm leaning up against the island trying to decide what type of date I would like to go on with him.

It might be lame, but I chose to go to a movie. I haven't been in years. There's a theater here in LA that shows old movies, so I ask him if he'll take me to see *The Way We Were*. It's one of my favorite older movies. My grandmother watched it with me once. I was probably too young to watch it, but she had no idea I was still awake. She thought I had passed out on her couch, but I watched the whole thing.

"So, you really love this movie, huh?" he asks when we're walking into the theater.

"I do."

"I had no idea," he admits, shrugging nervously.

"It's fine. I knew you wouldn't want to watch it when kids were, so I never brought it up."

"Yeah, but I made you watch all those horror movies," he reminds me.

"You didn't exactly make me. I like watching those movies."

"But you jumped, screamed, and held on to me the whole time."

I stop and turn to face him. "Yeah, I certainly did. I held on to you nice and tight."

"Oh," he says, flushing a bit.

It makes me smile that much bigger to know that I caused him to blush. "Come on, baldy. Let's get you in here to watch this movie. You're going to love it."

"Oh, I'm sure I will. But keep in mind, little one, if I get scared, I'm holding on to you." His voice deepens, and I swear his eyes darken a bit more.

"Oh" is all I can manage to say as he leads me over to the ticket counter. We get our tickets and snacks quickly, then head into the theater room showing our movie. "Seats in the back or front?" I ask him.

"Back," he says.

"Don't want to be seen at this movie?" I tease.

"Don't want to be seen period. I don't want anyone interrupting our date."

So that must be why we're here thirty minutes before the movie actually begins. The theater is empty, and Brent loaded us up with candy, popcorn, soda for him, and water for me so that we wouldn't have to leave the theater again.

"Oh, I'm sorry. I didn't think about that aspect of it."

"I don't expect you to. I'll worry about all that. Had we

chosen dinner, I would have taken you to some little out-of-the-way place."

"To minimize the pictures?" I ask him.

"Yeah, I'm not ready to share you with the press yet." He winks at me before explaining, "Believe me, once that happens, you won't be able to go anywhere without having your picture taken."

"So, after the VMAs?" I ask him as we settle into our seats.

"Probably" is all he says on the matter, and he reaches out and wraps his arm around my shoulder.

"Making your move early?" I tease him.

"Oh, I have all the moves. Don't you worry, little one."

My body heats at the mention of the moves he has. I kinda want to experience some of those moves in this dark theater. We watch the people file into the theater, though not many come in, and most of them are older people.

"We might be the only young people in this theater," he comments before snickering at me.

"Shut up. This is a great movie."

"I don't doubt that. Here, have some snacks." He gestures toward the popcorn bowl and the carrier of candy he's balancing. "Come on, have some peanuts."

"What?" I exclaim. "What did you say?" I hiss, noticing that I've caused a few people to turn around.

"I said peanuts, but clearly, you heard something else, dirty-minded girl." He laughs and then adds, "Be cool, nerd, you're going to blow our cover."

"Sorry," I mumble as I eat a few pieces of popcorn. He pushes the bucket toward me and motions for me to take more, but I don't. If he's ever noticed how careful I am with indulging in such things, he's never said anything. It's almost not fair, though, because he eats all kinds of junk food, and he's still as slim as can be.

We watch the screen and answer the movie trivia as the questions come up on the screen. He knows so much movie trivia, but I'm not surprised. He always was good at remembering little obscure little facts about things.

The movie finally begins. I do a little clap because I'm so excited. I haven't seen it in a long time—probably a year or more. I never owned it, and it's been a while since the theater has played this particular movie. He only fidgets a few times, but I catch him watching me more than once. I bounce up and down in my seat a bit, and even though it's a chick flick—according to Brent—he does seem to actually enjoy the movie. The line comes on when she says about how lovely his girl is, and that breaks me. I wipe at my eyes, and he pulls me to him. The song comes up and the credits start to roll, which makes me cry a little harder.

He pulls me closer and kisses the top of my head, "Now, little one, it's a just a movie," he says with a laugh.

"I know," I sniffle out. "It's just so sad."

"Sure is." He sits there watching the credits roll across the screen, and we wait until everyone has left the theater to make our exit.

On the way home, I tell him, "I always thought that would be us, you know? Seeing you one day on the street with a new girl. I just kinda figured I had that kind of karma."

His knuckles flex on the wheel. "Well, that wouldn't happen. I wasn't really that kind. Until recently," he throws in for good measure.

I laugh and shake my head. "I hadn't known about your new attitude toward things. I just figured any girl would be lucky to have you."

"Thankfully, you're the only one that gets to." He reaches over and squeezes my thigh.

Once at home, I enter the house and notice he's walking in slowly behind me.

"What are you doing?" I ask him.

"Just watching you. If I forgot to tell you, you look beautiful."

I smile. "Thank you. I'm just in jeans and T-shirt."

"Darlin', you don't need to be in a fancy dress and heels to look beautiful. I like you like this."

"Well, thank you. I like you in a T-shirt and jeans too."

He walks over and places a gentle kiss on my lips. "I have wanted to do that all night long." The timber of his voice is low and sexy.

I put my arms up around his neck and pull him closer. "Come here. I need you a little closer right now."

"How much closer?"

I just grin and pull him toward the couch, then gently push him down on it. I straddle his hips and attack his lips with mine.

"Have you been waiting for this, my love?" he asks between kisses.

I grin at him, grinding my hips against his as he begins to moan.

"Should we go to the bed?" His voice comes out all husky and alluring.

"No, right here," I breathe out. "Unless you need it to be in the bedroom."

Brent answers by flipping me over and laying me out on the couch. My jeans are unbuttoned and dragged down my legs. He wastes no time taking my thong with it and diving his face into my slick folds. My hips buck off the couch, and I cry out for more, rubbing the top of his head and pulling him closer to me. When he inserts a finger, and then two, I lose it, screaming and moaning out obscenities and his name.

Brent looks up at me, grinning. "Was it good for you?"

I swat at him, and he chuckles. Then he lays his body out over mine and kisses my neck, his hands roaming underneath my shirt.

"Are you ready for me?" he teases me, bucking his hips against mine.

I nod vigorously. I love him like this, in control and domineering. He's not expecting me to touch him. He's the one giving me pleasure and I love it.

Within moments, my shirt and bra are discarded. He takes his time sucking on each of my nipples and kneading them with his hands. I buck off the couch, a ball of want and need by the time he undoes his pants and slides them off his legs.

"Brent, get here faster," I grit out.

He chuckles. "Easy there, needy girl. You're going to get me."

I love how husky his voice is when he's like this. Covering my body with his, he kisses me—gently at first, but then harder as his hips circle with mine. He lifts my leg and slowly enters me, and I moan at the sensation of him filling me.

"Oh God, Brent. You are fucking amazing." I moan as he keeps on driving me into the couch. It's tentative at first, but then he picks up the pace. When he sees that I'm getting close, he'll switch to a teasingly slow pace that I'm not sure I can handle.

"You doing alright there, darlin'?" He knows exactly what he's doing, and he's enjoying it, by the look on his handsome face.

"Please," I moan.

"Please, what?"

"Please let me come," I beg him. The pressure is building, and I'm getting close, but just when I'm there, he changes his pace to deliciously slow again. "Brent," I growl.

After a few more times of refusing to let me come, I flip him over and begin to ride him, hard and fast, then moving slower again. I'm making the same sounds come out of him that were coming from me minutes ago, the moaning, panting, and begging, and I love it.

Finally, when I truly can't take it anymore, I ride him harder and harder, chasing my orgasm. I start falling over the edge so much that I can barely move. He grabs onto my hips and rocks me harder until he's coming, screaming out curse words.

"Holy shit, woman," he says when he comes down from his high.

I'm lying there on his chest, listening to his heartbeat slow to a normal rate. "That was amazing. Best date night ever."

He chuckles. "Best date I've ever been on."

"Have you been on many?" I ask him. He pinches my ass, and I chuckle. "Come on, you can tell me."

"It's been a while; in case you were wondering. What about you? Was your first date a long time ago?"

I draw circles around his toned stomach. "Yeah, it has. I only went on one date here in LA before I decided I couldn't. I couldn't date anyone who wasn't you. It just wouldn't work."

"You're beautiful," he says in reply, and I forget about asking questions about his last dating experience. We lie there for a while and then head back into his bedroom so that we can shower, where he takes me again and then again. It's the best night of my life. I'm not sure anything could ever top it.

CHAPTER TWENTY-NINE

There have been a lot of headlines lately about Brent and me. It seems like the more press we do, the more they suspect something is going on with us. Dale says it's our chemistry. I'm not sure if he knows that we're doing this dating thing, but he definitely knows we're living together. I had to tell him so that he had a forwarding address for the firm, a fact that I think he either enjoyed a little too much or took a little too much credit for. Either way, it pissed me off. Brent not so much.

The headlines lately, though, are all about what a manwhore Brent used to be. They've even gone as far as to find some girls to interview who claim to have banged him at shows and describe what their night was like. Some of it is such bullshit. They make it sound like a porno movie—too unbelievable to be true. But there's that one percent that makes you wonder.

"The Bad Boy of Crave," the latest magazine headline reads. I'm lying out by the pool with Emma and Audrey, having a girls' day while the guys are rehearsing. Jade is here too; Brent set up an umbrella over her pack n' play so that she's protected from the sun. I love the little things that he does, not just for his friends but for the baby. That baby has him by the balls sometimes. I wonder what he'll be like if he ever had kids of his own.

I'm sure he'll be great at it. He seems like a natural with Jade—a side of him I never saw growing up. But I'm glad I'm seeing it now.

"That's what they call all of them," Audrey says with a giggle. "At one point or another, they've all been the bad boy of Crave."

I shake my head, looking down at the picture on my phone. It's the one from the press shoot we did in LA, where I'm positioned on Brent's lap. We're staring intently into each other's eyes. The photographer caught something between us. The picture was published with the article; however, a tabloid site has taken it and is selling it as Brent, and I are dating.

Honestly, in these last few weeks, I'm not really sure what we are. I'd like to say that we're dating or that he's my boyfriend, but he's got such a long torrid past in the short time I've been apart from him, bedding girl after girl in each new city they went to. He said it was just something to do to pass the time.

"Don't stress over it." Emma reaches over and gives my knee a squeeze. "Fuck, they even called Aiden that when I was pregnant with his child. You'll make it through this bit of press. We all did."

"I don't even think it's about the picture," I admit lamely. "It's more about the article. All the things they write about him in it. How they try to paint him as some womanizer who's just moving on with his latest kill. I hate that."

"We all did," Emma says.

She clearly deals with it better than Audrey did. I notice she's chewing on her fingernail, not saying a word.

"Tell her, Aud." Emma bumps her knee.

"I get why you're worried. I was too, and half the world hated me because I broke up America's Golden Couple of Rock," Audrey says, shaking her head. "But all of this does get easier. You get used to being called names and having their names and faces being splashed all over the tabloids. You just gotta special order yourself a thicker skin, and everything will be okay."

I nod. "I honestly didn't think this would bother me as much as it does."

"I knew it would bother me. Hell, it still does when he's pictured with a woman, and they try to make it out like he's cheating on me. I could claw their eyes out or scream at them to print the fucking truth for once. Emma deals with it better than I do."

"Well, yeah, I used to work in the industry. I know what their tricks are." Emma takes a sip of her wine before saying, "If you ever want to know if a picture is real, come to me. If you ever need help tracking down a girl they say he fucked, come to me."

"That doesn't make me feel any better," I say.

Audrey gets up and wraps her arms around me. "It'll get easier. It really will. And you do love him. You can say that it's all new and you're still figuring it out, but you love him. All of the rest of this bullshit will work itself out. You just have to give it time. And talk to Brent. He's the one who will help keep you sane."

"Did Derek keep you sane?" I ask her.

"Well, sane and distracted." We all burst into giggles when she wiggles her eyebrows. "Brent's a good guy. He may have had his share of fun and left some pretty broken hearts, but honestly, he's a good man. You know that."

"I do. I just hate this side of it."

"They'll get bored and find something new to focus on. You'll see," Emma says in way of reassurance.

I look out over the pool and sigh. Tossing the magazine aside, because it won't hold the answers I'm looking for, I decide to focus on the day with the girls. I've only known them a short time, and they're easily working their way onto my list of favorite people.

"There's shit that doesn't matter and there's shit that does. This falls into the pile of shit that's not worth getting worked up over," Emma tells me, topping off my wineglass. She looks at my face and seems to know I'm not buying it. "Look, it's not easy and I talk a big game. It's just my way of dealing with it. But the two of you are the only ones who can understand what's happening in your relationship, and you are the only two who matter. It'll get better and you'll have ways to communicate with each other about it. It won't always be easy, but one thing I can tell you from watching Audrey and Derek and then being with Aiden is that these boys are worth it. One hundred percent worth it."

"Thanks, Emma." I smile sincerely at her.

She winks and adds, "Plus, they are pretty good lays too."

Audrey yells, "Ew! Please don't tell me such things about my brother."

Emma and I are laughing, while Audrey pretends to pout.

"You love that I take care of your brother," she replies before sticking her tongue at Audrey.

"I love this niece you gave me," she says, walking over and picking up a sleeping Jade.

"Wake her up and you're dealing with her," Emma teases.

But of course, Jade doesn't even stir. Audrey cradles her close to her chest and sways her hips back and forth, taking in the sweet scent of the baby as she presses her nose to the top of her niece's head.

It's that moment that the boys come barreling into the back yard.

"Oh, please don't wake the baby." Emma gets up and hurries in the direction of Aiden, her finger wagging back and forth in his direction. Her attention then turns to Derek and Brent.

Aiden laughs and picks her up, then makes a run for the pool. He immediately jumps in. When they surface, she looks like she's trying to scowl but can't, too busy laughing as he holds her in his arms. I look away when the moment becomes too intimate. Aiden's lips are buried in her neck, and he's talking softly to her.

Derek has his arms wrapped around Audrey while she cradles

the baby, and Brent makes his way over and drops down beside me.

"Are you still looking at that magazine?" he asks, nodding in its direction.

"Yes." There's no point in denying it. The evidence is right in front of me.

"Are you feeling any better about it?"

I nod. "I am. The girls really helped me with some perspective about it all."

"Good. How about a different perspective?" Brent wiggles his eyebrows and stands, then he picks me up and runs for the pool.

"No, no! Brent, put me down," I yell, but there's no use.

Brent leaps into the pool, and we're both quickly submerged. Underneath the water, he presses his lips to mine. We come up kissing and hooting and hollering. Being quiet for the baby has clearly been forgotten.

When we pull apart, he's laughing. "I've always wanted to do that."

"What, throw me into the pool?"

"Darlin', if I wanted to throw you into the pool, I would have done just that. I wouldn't have gone in with you." He leans in and kisses my temple. "I meant the underwater kissing. What did you think?"

I just giggle. I love it when he calls me darlin'. He used to do it as a kid; even at the age of twelve, he was a charmer. It's nice to see nothing has changed and that I have the nickname I used to. "You're something else. And I wouldn't call it kissing. I would call you assaulting my lips while I tried to figure out what the fuck was happening."

"Call it what you want," he says, carrying me bridal style to the shallow end of the pool.

I look up into his brown eyes and just smile at him.

"What?" he asks.

"You are just so unexpected."

"Surely there aren't many things I could do anymore that

would surprise you. We've known each other long enough. I feel like it's all just expected."

"No, Brent, it's not. There's nothing expected about you. Besides, every time I have you figured out, there's another layer."

He smiles at me. "Wanna go peel some more back?"

"You have company," I remind him.

"They've left me alone before to go fuck their girls, what would be the difference?"

I laugh. "No, not happening. Not with me."

"Fine, but one of these times, I'm going to say it and you're going to want me so bad that you're going to jump at the chance to go and fuck me, guests be damned."

His eyes turn a molten-chocolate color, and I don't doubt that he's right for one second.

CHAPTER THIRTY

It's a lazy rainy day in LA, and my butt has been parked on the couch all morning long. I have no intention of moving until Brent texts me when he'll be home. I want to cook him dinner; he doesn't know that part yet because I want it to be a surprise. He's out with the band. They're working on some new material and going to meet with Dale to discuss the details of the tour. I'm not sure if it'll involve me, but he says he wants it to. I want to go along too. I love watching them play live. Plus, Emma, and Audrey are going, so it would be fun to hang out with them.

The only part I'm not keen on is the fact that we will all basically be sharing a bedroom in bunks. That could be weird, but Audrey told me you get used to it. I'm startled from my thoughts when the door opens up and some woman comes walking through it carrying grocery bags.

"Can I help you?" I say, walking over to the woman.

She's kind of small and looks like she could be about our mother's age, with her short gray hair and small frame.

"Hello, dear, I'm Lesly. I'm just here to clean up a bit and restock Mr. Brent's fridge," she explains in her English accent.

"Oh, hi. I don't believe we've—"

"You're Blair. Brent told me you would be here and that I should make you tea. Or even a snack."

I smile and shake my head. "Yes, I'm Blair, but I'm sorry I wasn't aware you were coming over today. Or that you ever come here," I say with a laugh.

"Oh, he hasn't told you about this, huh? Well, apologies. I take care of him on a weekly basis. It's the least I can do since he's so busy and can't go to the store without someone seeing him."

I shake my head, a smile on my face. "He does it because he hates shopping and hopes someone will always do it for him."

"That might be, but I like taking care of him. He's such a sweet boy."

I want to laugh because sweet isn't necessarily the word that my tatted, bald rock star is often called. "He sure is," I say lamely.

She's busying herself by putting away the groceries while I watch the small woman who I never knew existed move around the kitchen much better than I do.

"Well, I'm going to get started in the bathrooms and bedrooms," she says, moving back in the direction of Brent's hallway. "You enjoy yourself out there, dear. I won't be in your way."

"Okay," I say to no one. She's already left me alone to start her tasks. I shake my head. Of course he has a cleaning lady. I think back to last week at this time and remember that I wasn't here to see this because I picked up a dance class, so I must have missed her.

> Blair: Thanks for letting me know you have a cleaning lady.

I add a smiley face and hit send.

His reply comes almost instantly.

Brent: Yeah, I saw on the Ring she arrived.
Sorry. Guess I should have mentioned that.
She'll be in and out. Don't worry, she won't
bother you.

Blair: I'm sure it's fine I just wish I would have
known she was coming.

Brent: Hey, she's showing up to clean. Be nice.

I roll my eyes at his reply.

Blair: I'm always nice.

Brent: Sure you are. No scaring Lesly.

Blair: Sir, yes sir.

I send him the saluting face, and he replies with the kissing face. I grab my Kindle and begin reading the book I've been enjoying.

Lesly eventually crosses over and cleans my room and bathroom. I notice that she's also changing sheets too.

"Wow, you do a lot for him," I tell her when she's dusting the living room.

"He pays me to, dear," she says with a wink.

I decide that as weird as it is to have her here, I like her instantly. Brent didn't need to ask me to be nice to her. She's very likable and kind of reminds me of the grandmother I always wish I had growing up.

"Have you ever seen any other woman here when you're cleaning?" I finally get up the courage to ask her when I head into the kitchen, where she's currently cleaning.

She looks at me and smiles. "Are you trying to figure out how important you are to him?"

She nails it on the head. I mean, I know, but I'm just curious.

He never really answered me when I said something about the number of woman he's dated, so a girl can't help but be curious.

"I guess so," I finally admit.

"I don't think you have anything to worry about. He never has any other woman here. You are the first one I've seen."

My face lights up when she admits this.

"When I was cleaning for him in the early days," she continues, "he would stay here sometimes and talk to me. Follow me around while I cleaned for him, asking me about my family and my children. What my husband was like when he was alive."

I smile. That sounds like Brent. He looks tough as nails, but he's the nicest guy around.

"Anyway, he told me about a girl he grew up with who he was very much in love with. And how she broke his heart." She watches me closely.

I can't help but feel guilty and a little uneasy under her scrutiny. "That would be me," I finally say."

Lesly smiles at me. "I know that, dear. He called and told me this morning that you would be here. I thought I'd have a little fun with you. He would want me to tell you."

I shake my head, laughing along with her. "He would."

"He did do that, though. Follow me around and talk to me. He's one of the sweetest clients I have. I did swear that I wasn't going to work for a rock star like him. I was worried about the mess, thinking I would be cleaning up a bunch of beer cans and condom wrappers. But he's not like that. He's an obsessively neat man. I like that about him. I appreciate how nice he keeps his last place and now this house."

"He was always very good at taking care of himself and his room when we were kids. He never had the typical messy room like other kids did."

"I can believe that." She smiles fondly at me.

"We didn't have houses like this growing up, so I can see why he keeps it so nice." She's no easy to talk to. I imagine that's why

Brent found it so easy to open up to her. "I'm sorry if I was rude when you first came in."

"You weren't, dear. I could see you were surprised I was here, but I'm not surprised that he didn't tell you I was coming. That's Brent for you, always looking to get a good rise out of someone like that. It's nice that you're here. He shouldn't be alone."

I nod. "Yeah, I agree."

"Well, I'm all wrapped up, so I'm going to get going. It was very nice to meet you, Blair."

"Thank you. It was nice meeting you too, Lesly."

"Take care of him," she calls as she shuts the door.

"You too," I say, though I'm not sure why. Do I feel like my place is temporary in his life? No…but I've come to find that you just never know. He might find that he doesn't like being in a relationship, even if it is with me.

I go back to reading on the couch, and then I fall asleep at some point. I wake up with a jolt and quickly scramble for my phone to check the time. *Shit*, I think to myself. He's going to be home soon. He texted twenty minutes ago saying he was on his way home.

Rising and stretching, I make my way into the kitchen to prepare him some dinner. I look in his fridge and see he has salmon and some vegetables and decide that's what he's getting for dinner tonight.

I'm in the process of marinating the fish when he walks in the door.

"Honey, I'm home," he calls.

"I'm in here," I call back, even though he can plainly see that with his open floor plan.

"Hey, darlin'. What are you up to?"

"I thought I would make us some dinner. Are you hungry?"

"I am." But the way he says it makes me think he isn't hungry for food.

I flush under his stare. "Wanna help?"

"Not particularly, but I'll sit here and keep you company," he tells me.

I shake my head. "Why don't you want to help?"

"Because I want to watch you do it. I want to watch you move all around my kitchen like I always dreamed you'd do."

The admission makes me still for a moment. "O-okay," I stammer out.

He chuckles and rises from the stool, confusing me. "Of course I'll help you." He goes to the sink and washes his hands. "Now tell me what to do, woman."

I swat him and shake my head. "You are so difficult."

"Yeah, I know."

"You look strong. Let's have you cut up the vegetables."

"Alright, which ones?" He looks lost in front of his own fridge. "I haven't really looked at what Lesley stocked me with."

I giggle. "Don't you give her a list?"

"Well, I've sort of told her you need healthy foods, so just to stock with that," he admits sheepishly.

"Oh, well, thank you." My cheeks flush at his words.

"I've noticed, by the way. That you only eat very healthy things—when you eat and if you eat at all. You realize you could probably put on a pound or two and it wouldn't kill you."

"Brent. Leave it," I tell him sternly.

He shrugs. "Okay, I just worry about you. I want to make sure you're okay. I want to make sure you're healthy, not just skinny."

"Being in a band is different than being a dancer. I have to look a certain way. I have my cheat days, sure. Just like everyone else. But you won't catch me eating too much junk," I explain, my tone giving a hint of finality so that he knows the topic is closed.

He seems to get it, because he makes a grab for the vegetables in the fridge and pulls out the zucchini, squash, and carrots. "I hope this mix is okay."

"It's perfect," I tell him, working on getting the fish laid out in the pan. "But you'll need to be starting that soon because this fish won't take too long."

He nods and does what he's told, carrying the vegetables outside so that he can cook them on the Blackstone grill. I remain inside and get things prepared and cleaned up in here. I grab for the bottle of open blush wine I've been working on for quite a while now and pour myself a glass.

"Well, if you're having some liquid courage, it appears I should too," he says, bringing the side back in on his grilling plate.

I giggle. "Go for it. There's some wine left."

"Nah, I'll take a beer."

We plate our food in silence, and then he moves to head back out to the patio. "I thought we'd have dinner by the pool. It's a really nice night and you might enjoy it."

"Sounds great." I follow out there with my own dinner and wine, and we lounge around and enjoy the view of the pool.

"Pretty soon we're going to need you to come to rehearsals. We're figuring out the logistics for how we'll handle the video when we're on tour. The band is thinking you should be there to dance when we play 'Love Drunk.'" He watches me and lets the words sink in for me.

"Okay, so I would be performing in front of all of your fans."

He nods.

"You are sure you want me to do that?" I ask.

He laughs. "Yeah, we want you to be there to show the fans what you can do."

"You play to sold-out stadiums," I stammer out, grabbing for a piece of his fish.

"We do."

"I can't do that."

"Sure, you can, and you're probably going to have to. It wasn't just our idea. Dale is set on it too. You'll do great."

I swallow another bite, thinking about it. "I suppose I'll have to get used to the idea.

Dancing in front of others in a recital or during a Broadway event or some ballet would be way different than this. Even if I was a backup dancer, there would be another dancer with me. This way, it's just me up there dancing.

"What does the setup look like?"

"Well, that's where we need you," he explains. "We need to show you what we're looking at for your stage and all that. You'll see it's gonna be great."

I nod. We finish our dinner in silence. It's like he knows that I need the time to just sit and think about what he's proposing. He picks up the plates and brings them into the kitchen.

"You'll rest, I'll clean," he tells me.

"I don't need to rest," I say, wanting to help him. Wanting to do something because he's letting me stay here and eat all his food. I feel guilty about it at times, but he seems perfectly fine to take care of me.

"Yeah, you do. This will only be a minute. There aren't many dishes."

He goes inside and it's not even ten minutes until he's back outside with me. He moves us over to the chaise lounge, and I enjoy more wine while he drinks a second beer. We lie together, my back resting against his chest, and he draws lazy circles around my inner thigh as we stare out over the water.

"You have such a beautiful home. I'm surprised that out of all the guys in the band, you're the one with the house."

"Well, Aiden is looking now, with the baby, but I always wanted a home. I wanted a nice piece of land I could retreat to and just be me in. I didn't want to have to see neighbors or worry about people camping out in front of my building. I'm here for the solitude not the convenience."

I nod. "I get that."

His hand moves lazily into the inside of my shorts. He's tentative at first as he circles the outside of my panty line. He taps it lightly, almost like he's asking for permission. I let out a low moan as he enters, running his hands through my slick folds as he readies me for his fingers. I grip his leg, trying to quell my cries.

"You can cry out, darlin'," he says lightly in my ear. "No one will hear you. We're far enough back."

With that, he slips a finger inside me, and that's when I do lose it. I can't hold it in any longer. A loud whimper escapes my lips as I hold on to his leg, digging my nails into him to keep myself from screaming.

"Oh, fuck," I cry out. I can feel the pressure building when he adds a second finger and fucks me harder. That's it. That's when he hits the spot that sends me over the edge. I cry out loudly in the back yard, and he tilts my head and swallows my cries with kisses.

"Hi," he says when I'm looking up at him lazily after he's broken the kiss.

I giggle and start a fierce make-out session that leads to more fun inside his bedroom.

CHAPTER THIRTY-ONE

My mail has been coming to Brent's house for a few weeks now, but I've never gotten anything interesting—until today. I come home from dance class to find Brent standing behind the kitchen island holding on to a letter.

"Whatcha got there, boss? Is that an eviction notice?" I laugh at my own joke, but he's not even cracking a smile. "What's going on?"

He sighs. "You got a letter."

"And what, is it from the president telling me how I've ruined my life and have no life prospects? Because the few places I dropped off job applications proved that enough for me."

"You don't need to work. I can take care of you until things kick off with your career. We'll win a VMA, and you will get to be dancing in all the places you've ever dreamed of."

"I hope you're right." I notice he's still holding on to the letter in his hand. "Okay, out with it. What are you looking at so intently? Is it paternity papers from a girl you knocked up?"

I mean it as joke, but I don't miss the hurt look that crosses his face. "Yeah, that was a low blow. Sorry about that. Seriously, tell me what you're holding on to over there."

Brent rubs the back of his neck and stares at me for a long time before saying, "Here."

I giggle and walk over to him and take it from his hand. I look at who it's addressed to and see it was sent to my old apartment. The return address says it's from the Georgia Department of Corrections. I know exactly who this letter is in reference to. I shudder and walk over to the couch, then lower myself down as I stare at the letter. I've gotten a letter like this before—the last time he was going to be considered for early release. He was released and then he screwed up again. This must be the letter from his latest chance at freedom. I don't move to open it; instead, I drop it onto the coffee table in front of me. Leaning back on the couch, I throw a pillow over my face and scream into it.

"Do you wanna fill me in? You're not wanted for murder or something and this is their way of contacting you?" Brent teases me.

If that were the case, there would be Marshalls at the door trying to collect me. I don't move or answer him. I just sit there with a pillow covering my face. "Do you want me to open it for you?"

"Nope."

"Okay, well, whenever you're ready then," he says. The couch dips beside me. He sits so close that his thigh brushes against mine. "Or I can read it for you if you would like me to."

"I don't need you to," I tell him through the pillow.

"Oh, can you read through the envelop? Because that is pretty fucking impressive."

I can't. I know he's just trying to make light of things, but it's not working. My stomach flips and churns with nerves. I've seen that letter before, and I've thrown it out. I don't know why they bother. I've rejected any form of communication from him for years.

"Nope, can't. Just know what it is. I've gotten it before."

"Want to tell me what the letter is about?"

"I do not."

"Alright, then. I'm gonna sit here with you until you're ready to talk to me." He places his hand on my thigh and gives it a gentle squeeze. "Just tell me when."

With the pillow still over my head, I murmur, "What if I just want to forget this is even a letter we received?"

"I guess I'd have to accept that because the letter is addressed to you. However, I do wish you'd talk to me about it. Clearly, it's upsetting to you, and that's what I'm here for." He shrugs beside me. The movement brushes my own shoulder, and the couch moves with his motion. "It'd be nice if we didn't have secrets from each other."

"How is this a secret that would affect us or our relationship?" I ask him.

"Well, because for all I know, it's a summons and you're required to be somewhere because you are in violation of your parole or are owed back to pay a debt." There's a light tone to his voice. He means it as a joke, but it doesn't feel like one right now.

I'm raw and angry from the letter that I'm currently clutching in my hand. I grip it harder and hear it start to crumble a bit.

"Or you could just rip it to shreds right there," he says.

"It's not a summons. Well, not for me. And I'm not going anywhere."

He sighs. "Okay, I'm trying to let you be here, Blair, I really am. But honestly, the thoughts going through my head are probably worse than what's in that envelope. I feel like it's something that might make you run on me again."

"I have a contract." As soon as the words are out of my mouth, I feel like an ass.

"Good to know you wouldn't screw over the band. But what about me?" There's a hint of anger in his voice, and I can't blame him. It was a shitty thing to say.

"It's not like I would just up and leave you."

He laughs bitterly. "Yeah, because you haven't done that before."

"And that traumatized you," I remark. "I'm sure you'll always wonder if I'm coming back to you when I leave or when things like this show up in the mail."

"I don't worry when you go to dance classes or job interviews, things like that. If you ever travel without me, the fear will be there. But if we keep in contact, it'll be fine. It's just hard, considering..."

A pit settles in my stomach. I'm making this letter bigger than it has to be, but at the same time, I'm glad it's making us say things. Even though I hate the reason this letter is in my hand and the man it relates to.

I remove the pillow from my face and look over at him. He looks like a lost little boy—wild brown eyes that keep searching between mine and the letter in my hand. The tension is written all over his face. Fuck it. I just need to tell him. It'll make it so much easier than *this* situation that I've created.

"This is a letter from the Department of Corrections in Georgia," I begin, but he jumps in.

"Yeah, I got that much."

"Just let me do this my way. You might hear some things you already know, but please just let me get it all out." I pause and look over at him. He simply nods. Taking a deep breath, I dive into my explanation. "The Department of Corrections has reached out to me before, when they were thinking of releasing my dad. His lawyer requested a character witness, and the DOC sent out the letters on his behalf. They do this because I've asked that no contact information of mine be shared with my dad. I don't want him to write me or to show up at my doorstep if they let him out. Otherwise, his lawyer would be the one reaching out." I take a breath before saying more.

Brent stops me by putting a hand on my thigh. "Do you want some water?"

I laugh. He always knows what I need. Time and years spent apart haven't changed that. "Yeah, that would be good.

Brent rises off the couch and gets me my water. I take a big gulp when he hands it to me, then put it on the coffee table and get ready to dive back into the explanation of the letter.

"This letter means that they're looking to release him again and he needs a character witness. I'm the only family still living, I think, or that might not be in prison themselves. I'm pretty sure my uncle is currently serving time as well, and my grandmother has since passed away. My mom's family never really had anything to do with us once she left. He found it best that way."

"So, the lawyer thinks you would make a good character witness for him? That's laughable." Brent snorts.

"Yeah, I don't know what he knows about my childhood, or if he's just grasping at straws."

"Why does he need character witnesses anyway? I mean, if you really think about it, he's in for nearly killing someone and he's been in and out before. Why would his character have anything to do with it? Doesn't the record speak for itself in this case?"

I'm not sure if he's talking to me or just saying these things out loud, but he keeps going.

"Goddamn, what the fuck is he thinking? Does the lawyer ask him, or is this just what he does?"

I let out a hollow laugh. "I don't know, I've only spoken to the lawyer once. I always just see the letters and throw them away. They never require a response. There is contact information for the lawyer, should I choose to reach out to him, but I never do. I don't want him to find a way to figure out where the call came from and track me down. I don't even want him knowing that I'm living in LA. The court does a good job keeping my location secret from him. I did do a check with a lawyer about that. He was able to confirm that my location would be secret."

"You really hired a lawyer to check in on this shit?" His head snaps in my direction. Out of all the things I've said right now, for some reason this gets the biggest reaction.

"Well, yeah. When the first letter came through, it scared the shit out of me. I had visions for weeks that I was seeing him all over the city. I knew I couldn't be, because he was still in prison. I looked him up so many times on the prison's website, just to be sure he was still listed as an inmate. But I knew he would be getting out, and that scared me more than anything. I needed to know that when he was released, he couldn't come and find me. For a hefty fee, the lawyer verified that. It was how I found peace of mind."

He pulls me into him and presses a kiss to my temple. "I am so sorry. I really wish I could take all of this away for you."

I shrug. "You can't. You couldn't back then, and you can't now," I remind him.

"I should have fucking killed him."

"No, you shouldn't have!" I exclaim. "Are you kidding me? As I told you and your mother, you would be rotting in jail right now."

Brent cringes when I bring up his mother. She's gone, but I'm not sure of the details. I shouldn't ask, at least not right now. But someday I do want to have that conversation. I saw the obituary, but it was all very vague. Any funeral donations went right to her church. I'm not sure if it was an accident or a disease. If it was a disease, seems like it must have been quick, because she died not even a year after I left him.

"Well, still. He shouldn't be asking you to do this."

"I know, but he does." I rip the envelope open and look at it. "Yeah, just as I thought. He has a parole hearing coming up in a few weeks. If I should choose to come, I need to notify them directly." I hold the letter out to him after a quick scan of it.

Brent reads it and shakes his head. "What are you going to do?"

"I'm going to ignore it. Throw the letter away and just pretend like I never received it."

"You don't think you should go and talk about the kind of man they're looking to let out into the wild?"

"Would it make a difference? Doesn't his criminal record and prison behavior stand for that?"

"Unless he was a model prisoner," Brent points out.

I sigh and shake my head. "You really think I should attend, don't you?"

Brent picks the letter back up that he discarded on the table in front of us and checks something on his phone against the letter. "We don't have any commitments that day for Crave. Not sure what your class schedule looks like. But it looks like a quick trip down and back is possible."

"Or we could just ignore it like I always do," I say with a shake of my head. I really don't want to go. I'm curious as to why he's pushing me so much. "Is there more to this than just showing them what kind of a person he is?"

"Maybe," he says with a shrug. He gets up and heads over to the wet bar by his kitchen and pours himself a fifth of whiskey. He gestures toward an empty glass, but I shake my head. After emptying his glass, he looks at me and says, "It's about you getting your day in court. You being able to tell another adult what happened to you. Someone should know about that. I always thought so, but it wasn't my place. Now I just feel like it would be a crime to pass this up."

"I told you no one needed to know. Who knows where they would have placed me? I didn't want to be a part of the system."

"Well, now that excuse doesn't hold up. No one can take you away from anyone. You're an adult. An adult who deserves for someone to know the full gravity of what you went through as a child. That's why it's important that you do this."

I stare at him for a moment. I hadn't really considered that before. He does make a good point. "But then I have to be in the same room as him," I remind him.

"Yeah, but he'll be in handcuffs and restrained. I'll be there to keep him from hurting you. Plus, I imagine they have armed guards in those rooms too. But you don't need them, because you'll have me." He comes over and gently kisses my lips, and I appreciate the sweet, simple gesture.

I keep turning it over and over in my mind. What would it be like to show up and derail all his plans of getting out early? A smile crosses my lips.

"What are you thinking?" Brent asks as he sits beside me. His hand finds my knee.

"I would love to be the one who makes him suffer just a little bit more," I reply. Dread fills me. "But I feel bad for thinking that. I mean, after all, he's still my father."

"That man was never your father. At least when I knew the two of you."

"Agreed. Your parents were more my parents than he ever was, at least after Mom..."

"So, we're going to Georgia?" He looks happy about the idea that we could screw over my father.

"Looks like we might be going to Georgia."

"I'll book it." He has a wide smile. "I'm so proud of you. It's great that you're going to do this."

I just smile and sit back on the couch. Brent seems to get that I'm tired of talking for the time being, so he switches on the TV. I don't really pay attention to *Law and Order*. Instead, I think of the new perspective Brent has given me about going to talk about my dad's character, or lack thereof. I don't think I considered this before—tell them what kind of a person he is and then maybe he'll stay in longer. It will sure stop the asks from his lawyer for me to come testify. Which, ultimately, might be reason enough to do it.

CHAPTER THIRTY-TWO

We're lying in bed enjoying a lazy Sunday together. Brent is tracing a slow line up and down my spine. He's watching me, but I get the feeling that he's not really here with me. His brown eyes aren't really focused on me; he's looking right through me.

"What's on your mind?" I finally get the courage up to ask him.

A smile breaks out across his face. "Nothing."

"Oh, there's something there. Come on, tell me what you're thinking."

He rolls onto his back, breaking our connection. "It's not something good."

"Is it ever with us?" I mean it as a tease, but I don't miss his grimace.

"What do you mean?" he asks me.

"We just always seem to be around one another when shit is going bad. Things were going so well, and then they weren't."

"Is this thing between us only something when you have the ugly things in your life? Is that what we are?"

I don't respond, and he eventually changes the subject.

"Have you given any more thought about what you'll say about your father?"

I have. Frankly, when I'm not with Brent, in class, or out looking for a second job, it's all I've thought about. I wonder if he can tell.

"Just stay it," he says, surprising me but not, all in the same breath. He always could read me so well.

"I have been thinking about it, but I'm not really sure what to say. Nothing I could say would be positive, and I feel bad for that. The man is my father. Shouldn't I have something nice to say about him?"

"It's more complicated than that, Blair. It's not always black and white. Yes, he is your father and there were some good things that happened between the two of you, but fuck, wasn't that when you were four? Can you honestly say that since then life with him was easy? Why else did you flee and leave me?"

He's right, and I don't miss the pain that crosses his eyes when he mentions that I left him. Will this ever go away? I hope so, with time. Or for as long as I'm here with him.

"You're right. I just feel guiltier than I thought for not having anything good to say."

"He's reached out to your before, right?"

"Yes, but I've never agreed to go before. But a wise man told me I need closure from all of this and that facing him one more time would help."

"Exactly. Do you trust me?"

"With my life," I reply quietly.

He leans over and brushes my lips with his. "Then let's go do this. I'll be with you every step of the way. We can fly in there, do the damn thing, and fly out. Easy peasy lemon squeezy." He punctuates every word of his last sentence by tapping my nose.

I laugh and shake him off. "Easy for you to say. You don't have to face him."

"Yes, I do. I'm going in that room with you. I'll have the hardest job of all."

"What's that?"

"Not getting myself arrested and ripping his face off for doing all the horrible things he's done to you." He shoots me a knowing grin. He's right. Brent has always wanted to go rounds with my father. Even as a teenager, he could have taken him; in size alone, Brent had him beat. But my dad is a drunk, always has been and always will be. So, there was no competition there.

"You will not get yourself arrested, honey. I can't you have you sharing a cell with the man," I remark with a smirk.

Brent laughs and shakes his head. "I don't think a judge in the country would convict me of anything. Sure, assaulting someone is wrong, but if I tell them all of the things he's done to you, they might even give me a medal."

My mind keeps turning over the words, *"What he's done to you."*

I sigh. "Can I ask you something?"

"Always," he replies, leaning in and kissing my cheek.

I smile lovingly at him. I hope this doesn't ruin the moment, but I've got to know. "Have you ever told anyone about all the things my dad did to me?"

"Why do you ask me that?"

"Who did you tell?" I ask him, sitting up and facing him.

"I might have mentioned it to Derek a time or two. I don't think Aiden knows."

I nod, processing the information. "Do you think he told Audrey?"

Brent shrugs. "I don't know. It was a while ago. We were drunk one night and talking. I was talking about you and some of the things just kinda spilled out."

I don't say anything for a while. I'm turning over the possibility that someone knows about some of the worst moments of my life. "Why did you tell him, though? Like, were you complaining about me? Or just talking about growing up?"

I know Derek had a shitty life with his mom before he finally got placed with his grandparents. Was he playing a game of whose life sucked more? I'm not sure if I would necessarily win, because who knows what Derek saw. That's the thing with addicts; the horrors of what they can do varies, but it's just as damaging.

"No, I wasn't complaining about you or anything. I was just explaining him why you stayed with me so much. I'm not sure that I told any specifics of what your dad did to you."

I nod again, trying to slowly put the pieces of all of this together.

"What are you worried about? That he'll look at you differently? Because he won't. He's been through some shit too. Out of anyone, he would understand."

"Yeah, I'm sure you're right. I just I don't know. I hate that it's a part of my past, and I hate it even more that other people know. It felt like when I came here, I could be just a normal girl and not the girl whose dad used to beat her."

"I hate that you were ever that girl." He pulls me into him and sighs into my neck. "I'm sorry I told Derek. Honestly, I never thought the two of you would meet."

"Really?" I ask, pulling back. "You never thought that we would find each other again?"

He shakes his head. "Nope, I just assumed you went somewhere else and wouldn't be contacting me or looking me up."

"What about dance?"

"Honestly, I always saw you in New York. I just assumed you would go there. I didn't think I'd ever run into you in LA, let alone that you'd star in my video."

I did almost go to New York, but I didn't want the cold. "I don't like the seasons there," I admit with a shrug.

"The cold," we both say at the same time.

He laughs. "Yeah, North Carolina has some chilly temperatures, and one time we even saw some snow. I was glad we relocated to LA. It's much warmer."

I nod. "Yep, it was a really long trip out here. The Jetta sure came in handy. As you can see, she's still running strong."

"I do see that, and I'm glad."

"Me too."

"I'm glad I made you get the VW. I told you it would serve you well."

I smile at him, remembering how we shopped for it together; his parents helped me buy it too. Sometimes I even left it parked at their house so that my dad couldn't sell it or try to drive it and wreck it.

"Well, thankfully our trip to Georgia will be right before the VMAs, so we'll have some time to take care of this and then come here and focus on happier things."

"That will definitely be a happier thing to focus on. I hope you know how proud of you I am for that song and the video. It's amazing."

"Thank you, but are you forgetting that you're a part of the video too? Without you on the stage shaking your ass, we wouldn't be anywhere."

"Gee, thanks. Don't give me too much credit." I wink at him. "But seriously, the music you write is amazing."

"Thanks. I wrote a lot of the songs Crave sings, actually. Well, not the words, but the beats. Derek is the one who writes the lyrics."

"You guys are so great. I followed you."

"What do you mean, you followed me?"

"This is embarrassing." I cover my face with my hands. I can't believe I'm about to admit this to him. "I Googled you a few times once I realized you were in Crave. I wanted to see how you were doing, if you were dating anyone, and where you might be located. I just wanted to know all the things about you, I guess. And I wanted to make sure you were doing well. I hated that I left you and hurt you. I was glad to see you were a success. Even if I wasn't, it still made me feel like I deserved to keep paying my dues while you were the one who was a success, considering how I hurt you."

"Oh, Blair, it's not karma. It's just that our path was a little easier than yours. Doesn't mean your dues aren't paid. Didn't you say the other day that you had an audition coming up?"

I nod. "I do. I'm excited for it. This could lead to something bigger, some more permeant jobs. It's for another video."

"Great. What genre?"

"Hip-hop. The ad was vague, so I'm not real sure who it is."

He nods. "I'm happy for you. But when we go on tour, I want you to come along. It would be good if you were there and danced when we played 'Love Drunk.'"

"Is that the only reason?"

He chuckles. "Are you looking for me to invite you on tour with us?"

I shrug. "I don't know, maybe. Would you?"

"I would love it if you came on tour with me."

"Really, it won't cramp your style?"

"What do you mean?" He looks confused, his eyes searching mine like they hold all the answers, and maybe they do.

"You like to have fun with girls on the road. Won't me being there stop that?"

"I only had fun with those girls because I was lonely. I won't be lonely, because I have what I was always wishing for."

"And what's that?" I ask him softly.

"You." He says it as if the answer is obvious.

"You're incredible."

"I mean it."

"And you're about to get so lucky," I tell him, pushing him back onto the bed so that I can climb on top of him.

"I should say nicer things to you more often."

We're both naked, so I can feel exactly when he's ready for me. I rub my hips over him, his tip playing with my center. Slowly, I move in small deliberate circles. He lets out a low moan, and I lean in to kiss his lips.

"You really should let me inside," he says when we part.

"Should I now?" I ask him, trailing kisses down his neck and chest.

"Yes," he says in a moan. "Oh God, Blair."

I roll my hips so that he slips inside, then make my movements torturously slow for him. I love watching him as his eyes roll back in his head. He's a strong and powerful man, and when I ride him, he turns into putty in my hands.

"Fuck, Blair, are you trying to kill me?"

"Maybe," I tease as he peers up at me through hooded eyes.

It's then I pick up the pace and ride him harder and faster. We're both breathless and panting, and Brent grabs my hips and helps guide my motions.

"Fuck, Brent. Fuck," I cry out. I might be riding him, but he still has the power to bring me to my knees. I can't hold back anymore; my orgasm takes over, and I milk his cock all while moaning his name.

"Jesus Christ," he moans.

I pick up the pace, trying to get him to come. One roll of my hips along with some quick strokes and he's falling apart beneath me. He grips my hips tightly, and I hiss out in pain, knowing I'll have marks in the morning. But I don't care. It's so worth it.

"You're amazing," he breathes out, holding me to his chest.

"You're not so bad yourself, honey."

He chuckles. "That's the second time you've called me that today. Are you trying out nicknames?"

"Something like that." I shoot him a lazy wink and lie flat on his chest.

"We gotta clean up or the sheets are going to be really messy."

"Yeah, well, we can always use my room."

He pinches my ass. "My room is your room."

CHAPTER THIRTY-THREE

The nominations are going to be announced for the Video Music Awards. I had no idea the simple fact of hearing the nominations was such a big deal. I understood how much it meant to these boys to be nominated; I've seen it in how hard they work—the rehearsals I've attended and the time I saw them play live. This is their whole world. A world they have such a large place in. The amount of respect they've garnered over the last few years is well deserved.

I'm so proud of Brent. Never in my wildest dreams did I imagine he would have a career like he does. I knew he wanted it, but so do a lot of people. I have firsthand knowledge of what it takes to make it in this business, and to have made it to this level is just incredible.

The band is all heading to Dale's office to listen to the nominations, which apparently means there will be more photo ops and even an Instagram live that will take place. Dale asked that we all dress nicely. I had hoped that I wouldn't be included, but that's not the case.

Brent opted to not have a car pick us up, so we are heading into the office in the Audi.

"Why not the bike?" I tease.

"Darlin', I would but that's a short dress you've got on there, and add to that the heels... Not the best combination for the bike." He shoots me a wink and gets into the Audi.

I do like the Audi; it's smooth and sleek, with its darkened windows making sure no one can see inside of it easily.

When I get in, I see the tint extends to the windshield as well. "Does LA allow a tinted windshield?" I ask him.

"Sure, we'll go with that," he says with a chuckle.

I just grumble at Brent. It's too early, which makes the ride to the studio quiet. It could be because of the hour. They announce the nominations at ten eastern standard time, so we are on the road before six in the morning.

"You're sure not a morning person," he comments.

"Nope, I'm not."

More laughter from Brent's side of the car. I just ignore him and focus on the stark streets of LA as they fly by. This is the only good thing about it being this early. Not much traffic.

"Should we stop at Starbucks?" Brent asks.

I wave the Red Bull at his face. "I have this."

"Oh, you're not playing today, huh?"

"I need my caffeine. It's like a food group to me," I tell him, earning more laughs from him. "Why are you in such a good mood this morning?"

"It's hard not to be. Look where I'm headed." He gestures toward the road ahead. "I'm on the way to my manager's office to hear if the band I'm in is nominated for a VMA, and I have the girl sitting by my side who I thought I lost a long time ago. Yeah, life is pretty good, wouldn't you say?"

"Yes, but I would be doing so much better if we were in New York and got to sleep in this morning," I grumble.

"Just drink your Red Bull, okay? It'll be fun. Maybe we'll even go out for a celebratory breakfast once we hear the nominations."

What will we do if they don't get nominated? Dale has only been talking like they *are* nominated. Or maybe he's done something to ensure that they will be. He's going to an awful lot of trouble to have the boys show up. The Instagram live has also been announced.

Even if Dale did do something, the nomination would be completely deserved. The video has earned some high marks from the critics and also from the fans. "Love Drunk" is flying up the charts, and the video has so many streams. It's incredible to be a part of this. I do love that I was brave enough to, knowing that Brent wouldn't like it, because it should do wonders for my career.

"Who would have thought videos were still a thing?" I tease him, reaching over and squeezing his thigh.

He chuckles in response. "Music videos are just used differently than when we were kids."

"They sure are. I can remember being kids and lying on your living room floor watching *Total Request Live*. Or when VH1 still had music videos."

"The world sure has changed since then, especially with the way we listen to our music."

"Sure has, Grandpa," I tease him.

"Look like your Red Bull has kicked in," he gives sass right back to me. "All right, here we are. Let's behave ourselves, little girl."

"Oh, you can only hope," I fire back. We park and head inside. While we wait for the elevator, I smooth out my black shift dress.

"You look beautiful," Brent says so softly I almost don't hear.

I pull at my long red hair, which I styled in a half-up, half-down style. My makeup was kept light and soft for the event. Honestly, it was all I felt like doing.

"Wish I had known that a T-shirt and jeans were acceptable, because I would have worn that," I say, a nod to his black jeans and tight gray T-shirt.

"When you're the drummer, no one gives a shit what you look like," he teases.

"Yeah, that's not the case here. Everyone is pretty much losing their shit over your beats and the arrangement you wrote. Just sayin'."

He motions for me to get into the elevator when it arrives. We ride up in silence, and the tension is palpable. I want to reach out to touch his hand, which is almost touching me. Almost. But I don't. I look over at him and open my mouth to speak, but the elevator door opens, and the rest of the guys are standing right there.

"No Audrey and Emma?" I ask them after we've all said our hellos.

"Emma is home with Jade," Aiden tells me.

"Too early for Audrey," Derek jokes.

"You're in the video. That's why you're here," Brent says from behind me. He's standing so close that his body is against mine.

I lean back a little bit and enjoy the comfort of his warmth. His arms come up and wrap around my waist, and he places a gentle kiss on my temple as we stand there.

"Aw, look at you two. So cute," Aiden jokes.

Brent lifts his finger and flips him the bird.

"Being here this time is a lot nicer than the last time I was here," Derek remarks, toeing the carpet with his boot.

"What happened the last time you were here?" The words are out of my mouth before I can stop myself.

"The last time I was here, Audrey and I got called into the principal's office because we were caught. That was when the world knew I was seeing his sister," he says, motioning at Aiden.

Aiden sighs. "Oh yeah, that's the last time we were here. And thank you for not saying that's when the world found out you were fucking."

Derek snickers. "I do love to get a rise out of you, but it's too early for that."

Aiden flips him off and gives him a gentle shove. It's then that Dale appears. He stops and looks at Brent and me.

"Ohhh, I thought something might eventually happen here."

He drums his fingers together like he's some kind of Austin Powers villain. "Can we use this?"

I hope Brent is about to shut him down. I can't see his expression because he's behind me, but I do feel him tense.

"No, you cannot," he grumbles out.

"We'll talk about it," Dale says, waving him off. "Now let's get you all set up for the announcements." He motions for us to follow him, and we do. We go down the hallway to a conference room at the end of the hall.

"Sorry, this is the same conference room I had to bring you into when I tried to end your relationship. But hey, it's the nicest one I've got."

Derek shakes his head. "Yeah, yeah, can we all stop giving me shit about that?"

The guys just chuckle as Dale tells everyone where he would like them to sit. He has us at the far end of the room. There are four stools set up behind a web cam I assume we're using for the live. The Crave logo is displayed boldly in the background.

"You all can sit in the comfortable chairs while they work their way through the announcements. No pictures for that, I don't think. But when we do the live, I'll want you on the stools," Dale explains.

I look over in the corner and see there's a spread of food and drinks available for us.

"And help yourselves to breakfast since this is happing at the fucking ass crack of dawn." He points in the corner to the spread I was previously eyeing.

The guys head over to get something, so I follow. They can eat all of the pastries and donuts that they want, but I can't. Well, I could, but I'll hate myself for doing it. When you're a dancer, your body is what helps you get jobs; sure, there's a body positivity movement happening, but it hasn't hit everywhere yet. I like that Dale has some fruit out that I can have. I reach for a grapple and place it in a small bowl. I also grab a water while the guys either take soda or juices.

We take our seats and begin mucking. Dale is going over the logistics of what will happen, basically saying the same things he was previously saying. He seems jittery today; not like I usually see him. I wonder if he's nervous,

"How much coffee have you had?" Brent finally asks him, taking a seat beside me. Aiden and Derek are on the other side of the table, while Dale is at the head, controlling the phone.

"Enough. I'm just excited for all of you," he replies. "Okay, the calls have started, and they will only call if we are nominated," he explains, reading the notifications that are coming into his phone. "Looks like it will be about thirty minutes until we hear something."

We all nod. This feels like a *long* thirty minutes. I can't even count the number of times everyone is looking at their watches and phones. Unfortunately, we don't get any notifications of the nominations as they are happening. We'll get the full list once it's complete.

"It would be nice to at least know who's receiving nominations," Aiden complains.

"It would but they stopped doing that when the televised version of this went by the wayside," Dale explains.

Brent begins drumming his fingers on the table, continuing to do it again and again.

"That a new beat, man?" Derek asks.

He scoffs. "Nope, just killing time."

"It's our category!" Dale exclaims.

We all straighten up and stare at Dale's cellphone, willing it to ring. It's only three minutes, but those are an agonizing three minutes.

The phone rings.

"Hello," Dale answers and places it on speaker. He looks just as nervously excited as the guys do.

"Good morning is this Dale?" the woman on the phone asks.

"It is, and I'm here with the band Crave."

"Awesome, I'm Amanda calling with the VMAs, and I

wanted to let you know that the video for 'Love Drunk' has been nominated for VMAs in Best Rock Video and Best Choreography. Congratulations, gentlemen."

The boys all look at each other eyes, shining with excitement.

"Thank you. Thank you so much," Derek says, speaking for the band. The rest of the guys nod. "This is such an honor. We appreciate the nomination."

"You're welcome. It was well deserved. Enjoy the rest of your day."

She clicks off the phone and Dale hangs up. It's that moment when they all jump up and start cheering. I get up slowly and take it all in. The boys are high-fiving and yelling. Brent comes over and picks up me, then spins me around.

The guys give me hugs, and I join in on their celebration. It's so easy to get excited with them. Their energy is contagious, and I'm so genuinely happy for them.

"You got nominated too!" Brent exclaims.

"I wasn't nominated," I tell him with a laugh. He looks at me like he's having trouble multiplying two large numbers. The confusion looks super cute on him, although everything does. "I didn't come up with that choreography. That was someone else. I just danced it."

"Yeah, but no one has to know that." He shoots me a wink.

I can't tell if he's kidding or not. Shaking my head, I tell him, "No, we don't want to do that. You wouldn't like it if someone else got the credit for the writing work that you did on 'Love Drunk,' right?"

"Yeah, but still, I want you to get one too."

I realize then that the VMA win will just be for the guys. "Well, that's okay. There's no video without you guys. And you did pay for everything, including me. This is the way it should be."

"Yeah, and Brent's really paying you," Derek teases. He lets out an *oomph* when Brent hits him in the arm.

"We can order her one when you win," Dale tells us.

"Yeah, we're doing that," Aiden says. "You worked just as hard on this video as we did. I want you to get an award too."

"Thank you, Aiden."

"Yeah, thanks, man," Brent says.

"We gotta get ready for the live," Dale says.

Clearly, he's in business mode, and the celebrating is on hold for right now. Although, the way Brent is looking at me right now tells me we're going to be celebrating late into the night.

CHAPTER THIRTY-FOUR

I've forgotten how stifling the Georgia heat can be. But here we are, walking toward the Central State Prison. It's a medium-security prison, which means he hasn't been in with too hard of criminals. I almost wish he had. I make a grunting noise, appreciating my own joke. Brent's head snaps in my direction.

"What?"

"I was just thinking that it's a shame he's not in a more maximum-security prison, then these men could have really done some damage to him," I say, trying to decide if he looks appalled or appreciates my twisted humor.

Thankfully, he's grinning back at me. "Yeah, that is a shame. But hopefully when you're done talking to them, he won't be getting out any time soon."

"I hope so."

I reach for his hand and give it a squeeze. He hasn't left my side since we got to the airport earlier this morning. A hand is always touching mine or resting on my leg. I appreciate it because I could use all of the support I can get.

"Are you sure he'll be restrained?" I ask for the hundredth time.

"Remember when we called them to let them know you were

coming? They promised that he wouldn't be able to touch you or even come near you. He's going to have handcuffs on and shackles on his legs. The man won't get anywhere near you. They're going to make sure of it. And since I'm here, I can say that with certainty, because I won't let him anywhere near you either."

I nod. "Thank you."

My phone dings. I look down and see it's a text from Audrey.

> Audrey: Thinking of you today, girl. You've got this and we love you.

"Aw, it's a text from Audrey." I show Brent the message, and he smiles and gives my shoulder a squeeze.

Another ding.

> Emma: Rooting for you. Put that son of a bitch away.

There's a heart emoji with Emma's message and then a picture of baby Jade. I smile widely and reply to both of them with the same message.

> Blair: I appreciate the support. Thank you, love you too!

I agonized over whether or not I wanted to tell them what we were doing. I was worried about what they would think of me. The guys kinda already knew because, apparently, when Brent told Derek, he blabbed to Aiden. to their credit, they didn't tell Emma or Audrey, but that meant I had to tell them something.

I kept the specifics to a minimum and just said that my father wasn't a nice man. That he beat me more times than I could count and that I hid away at Brent's house to get away from him, finally leaving and fleeing to LA so that I didn't have to deal with him anymore.

"I always thought he'd end up here," I say while we wait our turn to be searched.

"Yeah, well, I was always hoping it would be for the shit he did to you."

"I don't even think he could have," I reply, staring at me feet. My ballet flats make a slight squeaking sound when I move them back and forth. The guard who will be checking us looks up and glares in my direction. "The people here are so friendly," I tease.

"It's prison, dear. They're not supposed to be," Brent reminds me.

"But I didn't do anything."

He just chuckles and pushes me forward slightly so that I can be searched by the glaring guard. I end up getting wanded because of my belly ring. However, Brent gets through with flying colors. We're sent to a room where we're told we'll be waiting until my dad's hearing starts, which should only be in about twenty minutes, assuming they're running on time. I wanted to ask the guard who brought me in here, but he didn't look friendly either, so I kept my mouth shut.

"I hope this doesn't take too long," I complain.

"Relax, it shouldn't be too bad. And then we'll end up back at the airport on the evening flight out of this place."

"There's no one you want to visit while we're here?" I ask him for the millionth time.

"Nope. The only people I care to see are back in LA."

I nod. "Okay."

Truth be told, I don't want to see anyone here either. I just want to get this over with and get out of here.

"Think he'll try to talk to me?" I ask.

"No. I don't think he'll be able to, anyway. Don't worry, the hearing staff will be in here shortly to explain everything to us. We get this done and we're out of here."

I nod. *We're leaving when this is over*, I keep repeating over and over again in my head. I don't want to be here any longer than I have to be. The nerves are getting the better of me. I keep fidgeting and pacing around the room. Brent doesn't say anything, though. He just lets me do my thing, pacing back and forth until a woman wearing a police uniform enters the room.

"Hello, you must be Blair Masters, Mr. Master's daughter."

My whole-body tenses when she calls me his daughter. I don't know why, because that's exactly what I am. But that doesn't mean I like hearing it.

"I am," I confirm. "This is Brent Allen. He's here for moral support. Can he come along with me, please?" I throw in the please hoping she doesn't say he can't, especially if she sees how much I need him with me.

"Are you ready to head into the room? We like to bring the witnesses in first so that you're seated before we bring him in," she explains.

We both just nod and wait for her to take us to the room where we're supposed to see my father.

"Come on, we can go into the room now. Do you need anything before we head in there?" she asks.

I'm not sure what we could possibly need. I would imagine she wouldn't like it if I said I needed a gun. I might be here and sharing a cell with him.

She motions for us to leave the room, then we head out into the hallway and down a long hall. The walls are white and bare, while the floors are a stone concrete. The hallway is bit blinding as we make our way down it. I'm not sure what to expect when we get into the room, but I don't have to wait long.

"We're in here," she tells us.

We file in and I can see that the same walls and flooring are in here. The room is set up like a makeshift courtroom, but instead of one judge, there will be several. Five men are situated at the front of the room.

"Please sit in these chairs," she instructs us, pointing to a row of chairs on the right side of the room. To the left is a table with a door beside it, where I presume he'll come out. I tense at the sight of it. Brent reaches out and grabs a hold of my hand. I'm going to have to squeeze this hand a lot in the next few moments.

"Good afternoon. I'm Brad Smith, and I will be in charge of this hearing today. We're here to determine if Leonard Maxwell is able to be released from prison on early parole. He's requested a character witness to speak on his behalf, and for that we have Blair Masters, his daughter, here to do just that."

I want to snicker because he has no idea what's coming from me.

"Does anyone have any questions?" Brad asks.

Brent and I both shake our heads. My palms feel like they're going to start sweating any moment now. The door opens and I hear the clacking of shackles and metal. He's coming.

When my father enters the room, I tense all over. Even Brent's grip on my hand tenses.

He's a lot smaller than I remember him being. He's hunched over quite a bit. I can't be sure if it's because of the shackles or the fact that the years haven't been kind to him. At least that's how I hope they've been. His hair is gray, with all the brown gone. He looks tired and thinner than I remember. He looks up at me, and we make eye contact for a brief moment.

The fucker actually smiles at me.

I don't return it. Instead, I keep my face schooled, showing no emotion. I don't want him to see how he's affecting me as my insides scream that it's time to flee. That it's time to leave and never return to this fucking state again. Even though Georgia is quite pretty, the place will always be tainted for me because of the ugliness that he's caused.

"Please be seated, Mr. Masters," Brad states. "We're here to decide if you should be allowed out early for your crime of grand theft auto, which carried a sentence of eight to ten years. Because of the seriousness of this crime, you being released early will depend on the testimony of those present for you. I under-stand your daughter is here to do this for you?"

"Yes, sir, she is," his lawyer replies.

"Counselor, you can begin whenever you're ready," he states, signaling the beginning of the hearing.

I take a deep breath in and out, hoping that it gives me the courage to sit here for the entire time. I had a dream that I ran out of the hearing. It almost involved him chasing me, but clearly, he's restrained so that won't be possible.

He sits down and attempts to look in my direction. Brent is sitting closest to him, blocking my father's view of me. I love that he can't get a good look at me and that I won't be able to see his face when I give my character testimony.

"Miss Masters, you have been called here as a character witness for your father." His attorney has joined him at the table. He must have been one of the men in the back. Now he's up there speaking directly to me, but I refuse to look in either one of their directions. I instead focus on the five men who are in front of me. The only one who introduced himself to me is Brad. The rest just have name tags in front of them—Michael, Jeffrey, Adam, and Christopher. These are the men who will decide whether or not my father gets out of jail, though hopefully my testimony will make a difference, too.

"Can you please give us a statement about why we should be letting your father out on early release?" he asks me.

"Sure." I pull out the paper that has been tucked into my purse. I wrote something ahead of time because I was afraid I would be so crippled with fear that I wouldn't be able to do this. I clear my throat and begin.

"You asked me to be a character witness for my father, but you have no idea what you're asking me to do. You have no idea the type of character he had when I was growing up. My father, Leonard Masters, was not a good man. He did not take care of me the way a father should. When my mother left us, he changed. He began drinking and getting involved in some questionable things. The drinking would lead to him being violent a lot of the time, and being the only person at home with him, that violence was focused on me. While I never had him arrested for his crimes against me, they include a broken arm, dislocated shoulder, broken ankle, multiple bruised ribs, and other bruises and scars that I still bear today. I couldn't come here and lie to you all and tell you that my father is a good man, because he isn't. I fled my home state one night while he was passed out drunk so that I could live a life of freedom from his abuse.

"This might not be the testimony you felt you would be getting, but I couldn't come here and lie to you. I could not allow you to not know the man who I knew growing up. I realize this might seem an unorthodox testimony for a character witness, but again, you needed to hear the truth about Leonard Masters. So whatever decision you make, just understand that his character is not one that should be released early for good behavior. Because a once-scared six-year-old girl who was abused until she was eighteen was not released early or freed from her torment."

I finish the words with tears in my eyes.

"You!" my father growls, jumping to his feet.

But the guards are quick, and the men up at the front are yelling at him to stop.

"May I go?" I ask.

"You don't want to hear the verdict?" Michael asks me.

"No, I don't care to know the verdict. I just wanted you to know what his character truly is."

He nods. "You may go."

"Let's get out of here," I say, turning to Brent.

"Okay." He's smiling widely at me.

We walk out of the room and out of the prison, handing in our visitor badges as we go. When we reach the parking lot, he stops me and grabs me by the waist.

"I am so proud of you," he says, kissing me passionately.

When we break apart, I say, "I'm kind of proud of me too. Now let's go back home and never come back to this place again."

"You got it, darlin'."

CHAPTER THIRTY-FIVE

We return from Georgia to find the house full of Derek, Audrey, Aiden, Emma, and even baby Jade. There are hugs and hellos all around.

"We've been cooking," Emma announces.

It truly does smell amazing. With the only two-hour time difference, I'm surprised at how tired I am. I did nap a bit on the flight, but even though it was a four-hour flight, I didn't get a lot of sleep. I kept waking up and checking where I was. I had a dream that I woke up in prison with him. I jumped out of my skin and Brent was right there to hold me. He's been wonderful and hasn't left my side for a minute since we left the prison.

"I can see that. What are you making us?" I ask them.

"Lasagna. You like Italian, right?" Audrey is asking me. She's talking really fast, like she's either hopped up on coffee or nerves.

"Yeah, sure. Thanks," I reply.

"Listen, guys, I'm just going to say it one time, if that's okay?" My voice comes out timid. I'm afraid of coming off bitchy or ungrateful for the fact that they're all here and making us dinner.

"Of course. I'm sure it wasn't easy," Audrey says, stepping

forward and wrapping me in a hug. I take comfort in her arms being wrapped around me and sink into her.

"Thank you," I say, tears welling up in my eyes. I hate that I'm about to cry. I haven't cried since all of this started, but right now, I need to. Her arms are almost motherly, and they nearly bring me to a breaking point.

"Oh, honey, I'm so sorry. I didn't mean to make you cry," she says softly. "But we're here for you, no matter what."

"Thank you." I pull back, looking at her with tears in my eyes. "That means a lot."

"Oh sure, I tell you that and you only nod, but she says it and you cry," Brent says.

He makes me laugh, which is exactly what I need. He always has a way of knowing when I need to laugh. I love him for it. I stop and shake my head. No, I can't be thinking of love; I'm not sure that he is, but either way, we're not saying it yet.

"What?" he asks. He must have caught the weird look in my eye.

"Nothing," I say, taking the tissue that Emma holds out for me. I sigh. I just need to let them all know what happened.

"You good?" Brent pulls me in and whispers in my ear.

"Yeah, I'm good." I give him a quick peck on the lips and turn back toward everyone.

Brent takes the opportunity to haul me against his chest, his arms locking protectively around my waist.

"So, we went to Georgia so that I could testify as a character witness for my father," I recap.

"I just can't believe that asshole thought you would make a good witness," Derek says, rolling his eyes.

"Me neither. I don't think they were expecting what I had to say, because the counsel made it sound like he invited me there and the news would be good."

"You should have seen their faces when you started talking. No one was expecting what you said," Brent says from behind me. Everyone's smile grows. I can only imagine how big Brent's grin is.

"Well, as much as it sucked to do it, I'm glad that I did. I told them what he did to me in a Cliffs Notes version, but they got it. They understood he isn't a good man. No one asked me any questions, and he didn't get to speak to me. I just got to say my piece and then leave. Thankfully."

"What happened to him?" Aiden asks. He looks a bit confused that I wouldn't have stayed around long enough to hear what happened.

"I don't know. I'm sure I could look it up on the website or something, but I don't need to know. All that matters is that I went there. I told the board the type of man he was, or is, and I'm moving on with my life. It almost doesn't matter to me what happened to him, because he's not in my life anymore. I just hope that it helps stop the character witness invites and also paints a more accurate picture of the man they were considering letting out into society."

"I am so proud of you," Brent says again. He's been saying that a lot since we left the prison. In the airport, on the plane, and on the way back to the house while the driver was unloading our bags.

"You keep saying," I tease him, craning my neck so that I can see his face.

"Okay, I'll stop," he says, laughing lightly in my ear.

"I gotta say, I really love this." Audrey props a hip on the island and watches us.

"What do you love?" Brent asks her with a sigh.

She lets out a giggle and tells him, "I love that you have Blair now. It looks good on you, this little love that you're both creating. Was it like this when you were kids?"

"Yes," he says, but at the same time, I say, "No."

"Really?" Brent asks me.

"Right now, we're a little more mature with everything. Sure, back then, we knew that we cared for each other, but it wasn't like this. I would call it kids trying to figure it all out."

"Nah, I knew," he says, tickling at my ribs. "I knew way back then that you were it for me. But hey, it's okay if you didn't."

I still for a moment, wondering if he's going to bring up me leaving him, but he doesn't.

"Well, either way, I love that he has you. He was a miserable bastard before you," Audrey replies.

"That's just because he couldn't always find a good piece of ass," Aiden says with a laugh.

I don't laugh, though; I just still in his arms.

"Thanks for that, Aiden," Brent says. His hand comes up from my waist and flips Aiden the bird. "You could have kept that to yourself."

"Sorry, man," he replies with a laugh.

"It's okay, Brent. I knew the rumors about you and I'm still here," I say, trying to sound like I'm teasing him and hoping I keep the sting out of my voice.

"Well, I could have had some more fun or a more stable relationship if you two weren't so fucking busy screwing up and making me keep you all in line," he says. "You wouldn't believe the shit they got into. I had this one"—he gestures toward Derek — "starting a relationship with his bandmate's sister while he was supposed to be fake dating Serena, the princess of rock n' roll."

The way he says Serena's name and title makes me think that he didn't really care for her.

"Yeah, I was supposed to help soften her image and take down that demanding façade she was earning," Derek says, shaking his head. "But fuck, that wasn't an easy or appealing option. I hated that assignment."

I remember reading about all of that, dreaming of what she was really like. I remember thinking that she didn't seem very nice, but I didn't have a read on Derek. Crave wasn't in the media as much as they are now.

"And you, having her come down and announce that she was pregnant the first night of our tour," Brent says to Aiden. "Jesus, I had to go into crisis management the minute it all happened, making sure no one told the press what little Miss Emma was spewing out there."

Aiden chuckled and glanced over at Emma. "Yeah, we all sure kept you on your toes."

"And that was why it was easier to have hookups than relationships. I had to keep these two boneheads in line. No time for me," he tells me, looking over with a wink. "And now that we have a family man and one who's more settled, I can."

My body heats all over when he says the last line.

"Just wait until the media gets a hold of this," Derek tells us, laughing a bit about it. "They're going to have a field day with it."

"They'll know soon enough, when we go to the VMAs. I plan on walking the carpet with her."

My head whips in his direction. "You are?"

"Oh yeah, did I not mention that to you?" He chuckles, knowing damn well that he didn't mention that to me.

"But I don't have anything to wear." I say, looking at him with my mouth hanging open.

"Dale will take care of all of that for you," Audrey explains. "Well, the stylist will. He'll send someone over to talk to you and figure out what you like and don't like. They'll pull some looks and you'll chose."

"That part is actually fun," Emma says. "It's what comes next that will be difficult. I never get used to walking the carpet and having everyone stare at me like that."

I nod. "Okay."

"Relax, I'll be there the whole time," Brent says. "I'll hold your hand and keep you safe from them and all of their questions."

I nod again. "Sure, yeah, and I'm sure there'll be plenty of prep from Dale," I say, thinking of all the times he reminded me what I could and couldn't say.

"Sure will," Brent says, squeezing my shoulder.

"It's dinnertime, if anyone is hungry," Emma says, turning off the oven.

We gather around the table and begin digging in.

"Oh my god, this is amazing," I moan out as I take bite after bite of the lasagna.

"You're just really hungry," Brent says, looking at Emma and Audrey and laughing.

"Hey, this is my mom's recipe," Audrey replies.

"Don't be dissing on Mama Zaks," Derek says, coming to their defense. "Her food is the best."

Brent shakes his head and laughs. "It is amazing. Thank you, ladies."

"Yes, thank you. I really needed a homecooked meal today," I tell them.

"I would have cooked for you," Brent whines.

"Um, you were talking about ordering takeout as the driver was bringing us here."

"Sure, I might have been, but I would have cooked if you needed me too." He reaches over and squeezes my hand.

That earns us a lot of hoots and hollers.

"Oh, Brent has it so bad," Aiden teases him.

There's not more teasing during dinner, just the guys talking business and the girls chiming in here and there. I don't say much, though. I just keep his hand in mine and relax for the rest of the night.

CHAPTER THIRTY-SIX

I'm sitting at a Crave rehearsal watching the boys work. Dale rented out a smaller venue that they've played at before. It reminds me of the setup of The Black and Blue Bar. They're working some things out for tour. He also brought in a wooden base I'm supposed to be dancing on. It's bigger than I expected it to be.

"We just want to make sure you can do your moves on it," he explained, and that's what I've been working on since they showed it to me.

With a set of Air Pods in my ears, I'm listening to "Love Drunk" over and over again, dancing my section of it, and working through the sections that are giving me issues being on the box.

"So how is it?" Dale asks me when I'm taking a drink of water. "Think you'll be able to work with it?"

I nod. "I think some of the range of the combinations are going to have to come down, unless you can get me a bigger stage. Other than that, it should work."

"I don't know about that. See what you can do with that, and I'll try to work on something bigger. The hardest part is going to be traveling with it. We'll need to make sure we have room to haul it."

"Understood," I tell him.

Dale seems to dismiss me as he looks back at the platform I vacated, so I get back to it, working on the combinations and shortening the distance.

Brent taps me on the shoulder. "You doing okay?" he asks me. "Is this little idea of his going to work?"

I shrug. "I think it is. It would honestly be better if he could make it larger, but that's a challenge, so we'll see."

"Well, just be careful. He has this whole vision for it. I want to see it come true, but we all want you to be safe. The simulation he ran through with this earlier looked pretty cool."

I nod in agreement. But none of them knows what it will take to get these moves to work, and it's going to be some real tweaking of the choreography to make it happen. The choreographer is going to come back later to talk with me about it and help, which will be good. It will be nice to have someone who understands what I'm talking about and to be able to bounce some ideas off of.

My phone rings in my ear. It's my agent, Presley.

"I'm sorry, I need to get this," I explain to Brent. He just nods and heads back over to the guys.

"Hey, Presley. How are you?"

"Hey, Blair. I'm doing great! And you are about to love me oh, so much," she says with a giggle.

I find myself laughing along with her. "Why is that?"

"Well, because the press that you're getting from the Crave video is phenomenal, I have a job that would like to book you. They don't want you to come try out. They want you to just agree to this, which is a bit unorthodox. But it will be great."

"Okay," I say hesitantly. I'm bouncing on my toes thinking of what this could be and how it will jibe with the Crave schedule they have coming up for me. Granted, the tour isn't starting for another three months.

"So, it's for the American Ballet, here in LA, and it'll be The Nutcracker," she says excitedly.

"Which part?" I ask. I'm holding my breath, wondering if it's the lead. I'm sure it's not, but a girl can dream.

"It's for the Sugar Plum Fairy! They want you to be the Sugar Plum fairy!"

"Oh my god!" I shout, jumping up and down, not caring that I'm in the middle of this studio while the boys are performing and now staring at me. I've never been so excited. "Will this work with my schedule with Crave?"

"Well, I'll need to talk to Dale and see about that. But what do you think?"

"Oh my god, I'd love to do it. But yeah, we need to figure out those logistics and when the rehearsals for all of that would start."

"They've already been rehearsing. It's almost September, and they want to be sure they have a tight show when it starts just after Halloween."

"Okay," I say, thinking about the Crave schedule.

"And Blair, they want to pay you surprisingly well for this part. You should consider doing this. I mean, the video press has been great, and it's doing what we hoped, but we need you to take other opportunities too. This well help keep up that momentum. As someone who is solely looking out for *you*, I would say that you should do it."

I sigh. The band is watching me, and the looks they're giving one another is causing Dale to step forward as if he knows something is happening that might need his attention.

"I've gotta handle something right now, but I'll call you back." I can't have them hearing Presley talk to me or vice versa.

"Okay, but you have forty-eight hours to respond to this offer, so please don't make it go any longer."

"Understood." I disconnect the call and see four sets of eyes staring at me. Crap, they're going to take this good thing that's happening to me and make it ugly. And it's only going to be ugly because I'm not sure how I can swing this with Crave. My mind is racing with all of these thoughts, and I realize that I want to think about the logistics before we all have a conversation.

I hold my hand up and say, "I need to use the bathroom."

The guys look dumbfounded, but business-savvy Dale shoots me a knowing look; I haven't fooled him.

I head down the hallway and into one of the bathrooms, pulling my phone out after locking the door. I look at Crave's calendar on the website, trying to figure out if this is even possible. Right now, we're in the end of August, and the tour will be staring in November, the same time as the show. There's no flipping way. I can't do both. I suddenly question what my contract says. I have it in my email. I go to pull it up when I hear a knocking on the door.

"I can probably help with whatever is going through your mind right now." It's who I assumed it would be—Dale.

I open the door and look at him wearily. "How's that?"

"What job did you get offered?"

"How can you help?" I repeat.

"Tell me what job you got offered first, please," he replies, his charming, schmoozy smile is well in place. "I might be able to help you. I'm not always the bad guy."

There's no way around this—he has me backed into a corner. Is he right? Is he not always the bad guy? Well, there's only one way to find out.

"I got offered the job as the Sugar Plum Fairy in The Nutcracker here in LA," I say, and I smile because I still can't believe I got offered such an amazing opportunity.

"Huh. I had no idea you were a ballet dancer" is all he says—not that I expected a congratulations from him.

"Did you not read my resume?" I ask him, exasperated. Clearly, he didn't do much with it, because it was on there. Or maybe someone else reads those for him.

He shoots me a smile that answers my question for me. It must not be his job.

"So, when do they want you to start? The Nutcracker is a Christmas thing, right?"

"It is. They want me to start rehearsals soon because the performances begin just after Halloween. So, I'll have two months to learn everything," I tell him.

"I'm guessing someone quit or got injured? Is that the reason for the fast turnaround?"

"I'm not sure. It seems that way, though. In my experience, they usually have these parts cast way before this," I reply.

"Have you done one of these before?"

"No." My tone is curt. I'm not sure if he's asking because he doesn't know or if he's pointing out my lack of experience. Either way, I don't like it.

He chuckles at my rudeness. "Okay, well, when do you need to let them know?"

"I have forty-eight hours. Is this even doable?" I ask him. "What does my contract say?"

He sighs and pinches the bridge of his nose. "Well, I could let you do this as long as they didn't need you for rehearsals on the weekends, and we could just use you for the Friday, Saturday, and Sunday shows. That might work. But you'd be deadass tired on Monday. It would be a lot for you." He watches me like he's waiting to see how I'll react. "And it would mean you wouldn't be going on tour with your man there. You'd be leaving him largely alone. Would the two of you be alright with that?"

He's baiting me, trying to rile me up by pointing that out. "Yeah, that would mean I wouldn't be on the tour. Which might not the worst thing. That bus is going to be crowded," I say, attempting to make a joke.

"There's talk of getting Aiden and Emma something smaller so that they can have the baby on the bus and have some privacy, because, hell, the bus we used last time won't fit all that shit," he replies offhandedly.

"Well, that's awfully nice of you."

"You see, I can be nice," he remarks. "Now go tell your

man and his friends. He wants to know what's going on. I can figure out how this works if you really want it, but they might not be the happiest about it. You'll be missing shows and the on-the-road experience with them. Plus, your part of this song is an attraction to the fans, so ticket sales may plummet."

He walks away from me, his phone to his ear. I'm not sure who he's on the phone with. For all I know, he's called Presley himself to talk this through.

I head out and see that the band is talking quietly amongst themselves. I walk right over to all of them and get ready to spill the beans.

"Hey, guys," I say timidly. I'm not sure how they'll react and if any of them will be happy for me.

"What's going on?" Derek asks. He seems to take his lead singer role very seriously and speaks for the guys when given the chance. They don't seem to mind, and I know Brent hates being the center of attention, especially in front of the press.

I sigh and dive in. I tell them about Presley and the part I've earned in The Nutcracker. I wait with bated breath as they process the news.

"When? When do you need to be available for this?" Brent asks.

I don't miss that he hasn't said congratulations about the job. "I have to start rehearsing very soon. Probably next week. And then the shows begin after Halloween."

"Is that like a lead role?" Aiden asks.

"Yeah," I say quietly.

"The video helped you get it?" he asks again.

I nod, and I look to see that Dale is still on the phone, so he can't help explain the next part.

"Is that what Dale's trying to figure out?" Brent gestures toward where Dale is.

"I think so. He said I could be available for the weekend shows, but I would just miss the weekday ones, and I wouldn't be on tour with you. He's trying to see if all of this would work logistically."

"This is a big opportunity for you, huh?" Derek asks.

"It is. And one that I might not have gotten if not for the buzz from the video. I'm not going to just leave you high and dry. We'll figure this out. Or I won't do it."

"Yeah, we have contracts," Aiden says. He seems to be the one who is bothered by the news the most.

"I am proud of you for this," Brent finally says, but his tone and his eyes aren't matching his words. All I can see is the worry.

"Thank you," I say, but it comes out hollow.

"How will you manage both rehearsals?" Derek asks.

"I don't know. I don't have a schedule yet."

"Okay, well, I guess we wait and see then." Derek looks over at the guys. "Should we get back to it?"

"Yeah, probably should," Brent says, walking away.

I stare at his retreating form. I can't believe he's acting so cold. I look at Aiden, who seems just as pissed. "I'm not going to do anything that jeopardizes the band or my contract," I tell him.

Aiden just turns and walks away.

"Yeah, we know," Derek answers for him.

His unspoken words are that they have contracts that prevent that sort of shit, so what are they worried about? Just me trying to squeeze out of it? Or me not showing up at some of the shows and people being pissed that the part of the video they wanted to see isn't there? The whole almost four minutes of the goddamn show. That's partly what pisses me off. All this hoopla for something that only takes place for a small fraction of a ninety-minute show. Like what the fuck?

The anger propels me to walk over to Dale and calmly say, "I'm gonna get going. Choreography will be here later this week. I just really need to go."

"Okay. I'll be in touch about things, but don't go agreeing before we talk," he tells me.

"Gotcha." I walk out of the practice without so much as a backward glance.

Once I get home, I shower, eat, and climb into bed. It might not even be dinnertime, but this is where I'm staying for the rest of the night.

When Brent finally comes home, he doesn't come to check on me. I hear the TV in the main room, but he never checks in to see if I want dinner or anything. He must be pissed at me too. But I'm pretty pissed at him for not seeing what kind of an opportunity this is for me.

CHAPTER THIRTY-SEVEN

Brent has left for band practice or something, because when I finally leave my room the next morning, he's not home. I sigh and shake my head. He's worried about what this means for the band and the contract. I am too, but I wish he would be a little bit happy for me. This is a big deal. I've worked hard for many years for a break like this. And now that's finally here, I would like it if someone was happy for me.

I sigh and throw myself down on the couch. I think about sending him a text, but I don't. I'm not sure if he would even answer anyway. I did stay in my room longer than I normally do, and he never bothered to look in on me. He had to have known I wasn't sleeping. I flip the television on and try to get lost in some crappy TV, anything to take my mind off it. Some good ole crime shows should do the trick.

But all that is interrupted with a knock on the door. I look at the door, expecting it to pop open with Lesly even though it might not be time for her to come back. The knock occurs again, and then I hear the yelling.

"Hey, Blair, open up!" Emma's voice comes from the outside of the door. "Come on, bitch, this baby stuff is getting so heavy."

I laugh and get up and run over to the door. I fling it open and there stands Audrey, Emma, and the baby. Emma's hands are full of baby gear, while Audrey is holding what looks like a beach bag and baby Jade on her hip.

"Sorry, come in. I thought you were the cleaning lady." I move to the side and allow them entrance into Brent's home. I want to tell them that I haven't seen him yet today.

"I thought we would come over here and have a girls' day with you. I heard that one might be warranted," Audrey adds, pulling me into a side hug. "Jade wants to see you." She hands over the baby. "Let's all head back to the pool and get situated."

I help the girls get settled out by the pool. We place Jade in the shade the with huge umbrella Brent purchased just for her, and once she's sun screened and happy, I head into the house and put on my own suit. I also grab some bottles of water and snacks before heading out to the girls.

It will be nice to talk to someone about what's going on, but I'm not sure how freely I can speak to them because of who their significant others are.

"Cute suit, girl," Audrey says when I reach them.

I look down at the blue and yellow polka-dotted bikini. "Thanks." Once we're all settled and all of the lotions of have been applied, I ask, "So, did Derek and Aiden tell you about the offer I received? Is that why you all rushed over to here to hang out with me?" I swing my legs over the chaise and face them, with Audrey in the middle and Emma on the end.

Audrey smiles. "We wanted to hang out with you as well. This isn't just about that."

"But you know about it, huh?"

"Yeah, we know." The guilt is seeping into Audrey's tone. "The guys were all on a call last night for a long time talking about it," she admits.

"But *we* think it's amazing for you," Emma adds. "Please know that."

Audrey gets up and gives me a hug. "Congratulations. It's really awesome to be selected for this," she tells me.

Emma gets up and hugs me too. "Yes, congratulations. I'm really sorry the news isn't going as well as you had probably hoped. It should be met with more joy."

"Thanks," I say lamely. She's right, I would have liked someone to appear happy for me. The girls seem happy, but I'm sure some of their excitement for me is dampened by the fact that the guys spent a lot of time discussing this.

"So, they talked until late last night about this, huh?"

"They did," Audrey confirms. "Where were you?"

"I was sitting in my room. That's where I went when I got home. Brent never really came in to see me or talk to me, but then again, I never left the room."

Emma nods. "The guys told him to talk to you, but he didn't feel comfortable. Have you heard anymore from Dale? Aiden said he was going to be looking into your contract to see what they could, if anything."

If anything. If I can go have this experience and still keep my commitment to the band.

"Are you worried that you'll need somewhere new to stay?" Emma asks me.

"Honestly, that thought hadn't occurred to me." I swallow deeply, wondering if he would kick me out. "Do you think I'll need to find somewhere else if they let me out of my contract?"

"Well, yeah," Emma tells me. "If they let you out, you're breaking your commitment to the band. He's not going to want you here. They can't even reschedule the video shoot and get another dancer. It'll always be you in there. Now, they can do something with the tour, but you were the draw in the video, so it's a bad idea to do that." Her voice trails off in the end. She looks like she feels guilty for having all that information.

Clearly, they've been talking about it thoroughly.

"But what do you want to do?" Audrey asks me. "Has anyone bothered to ask you what you want? Do you want to do this if it means trouble with the band?"

I sigh. "I've thought a lot about it—" I don't get to finish my thoughts, because Emma jumps in.

"You're going to break the contract, aren't you? This isn't the type of dancing you normally do, and you're gonna leave them high and dry. I guess that means we can't hang out much more. The guys would be too pissed to learn we were still seeing you. At least at first," she rambles until Audrey calls her name.

"Emma!" She shakes her head and laughs. "Holy word vomit. Come on, let's not just jump to any conclusions. Let her answer us. Go on," she says, gesturing toward me.

I laugh and shake my head. "Well, it's good to know where you both would stand, not that I would blame you."

Audrey goes to say something, but I hold up my hand.

"I don't want to breach the contract with the band. I don't want to hurt anyone any more than I already have. I want to make sure that I can keep my commitments to Crave by being available when they need me, but I also want to see if this Nutcracker role will be possible, because these things don't just come along every day. And just because I'm offered it once doesn't mean that I just can just do it again. There might be a younger dancer or someone else who comes on the scene who is more talented. We just don't know."

Emma comes over and puts her arm around my shoulders. "You're really in between a rock and a hard place."

"Yeah, I feel like I am," I say with a shrug. "I've looked at the dates and I've compared them to practices. Even if they allow the comprise, I'll be dog-tired when it's time to go to rehearsal."

"Oh, Blair, I'm sorry." Audrey wraps me into a hug. "You need to follow your heart with this one."

"He'll never forgive me," I rasp out.

"If you hurt him again?" Audrey asks in low voice.

"Yeah. I mean, would you?"

The question hangs out there for a long time. So long that I know the answer. They don't think he would, and I doubt that either of them would either. Because I'll not just be hurting Brent. I'll be hurting Aiden and Derek too.

It's then that Jade lets out a wail. We all hurry over to see what it is she needs. Emma picks her up and coos at her, while Audrey and I just stand there. When it's obvious there's nothing for us to do, we take our seats. Emma feeds her and we go back to relaxing.

The silence is refreshing.

I lie there on my chaise and think about how he'll hate me if I choose this opportunity. He'll never forgive me. What's that they say? *Fool me once, shame on you. Fool me twice, shame on me.* That's what he'll think. If I do this to him a second time, shame on him. There would be no third chance. There would be no more motorcycle rides and dinners by the pool. The quiet nights in would disappear, and so would me loving him. He would hate me for the rest of my life.

A tear rolls down my cheek, and the sob bubbling up in my chest isn't going to stop. I need to get out of here, so no one hears me. I look at the water and remember that he keeps it pretty warm. I decide that if I'm going to cry, in the water might be the best place.

"I'm gonna take a dip," I rasp out.

Neither one says anything as I walk to the edge of the pool and dive right in. I let the warmish water wash over me, and I close my eyes and let the tears break through underneath the water. I swim and swim until I can't take it anymore. My lungs are burning, and I must come up for air. I'm by myself at this end of the pool, facing the house and looking at all he's managed to build—without me. Maybe he'll be okay if there is no him and I anymore.

I sniffle. I must look weird. I should be heading back down to the girls, but I don't want to. I lie on my back and do a few backstrokes and look up at the sun, almost wishing it would light me on fire and make me disappear so that I wouldn't have this problem. The success Crave could create for me is unimaginable;

hell, it's already happening. But why is it happening so close? Shouldn't The Nutcracker understand that I have a contract with Crave? Shouldn't my manager? Shouldn't someone be looking out for me? My hand hits a wall, and I realize I've made it to the other end of the pool. I stop and turn around, and he's there, standing at the end of the pool right in front of me.

"Darlin', do you think we've avoided each other long enough?"

I look over at the chairs and see that the girls are no longer here. It's just me and him. He's holding a towel for me.

"We need to talk this out right now." He drops the towel and heads over to the chaise lounge. He picks the one where I sat at when he fingered me. That might have been done on purpose, but I can't be sure.

"Come on," he urges. "We've got to hash this out."

CHAPTER THIRTY-EIGHT

I use the towel he gave me to dry my body off a bit, then I wrap it around my waist and walk slowly over to the chaise lounge. I sit facing him, with my legs over the side of the chaise.

"I don't like that we're not talking again," he starts off by saying. "I thought that maybe when I came home here this afternoon, you would be gone. I was shocked you weren't."

"Did you not know that the girls were coming?"

"Are they the only reason that you're still here? I have to know," he replies, ignoring my question altogether. "If they hadn't come over to swim with you, were you planning on leaving?"

"No, I wasn't going to be leaving."

"Had the thought crossed your mind?" His voice is low. Even though it's just us out here, he says it like he wants to make sure no one else can hear us.

"It had."

He sighs and pinches the bridge of his nose. "Great."

"I want to be honest with you. It doesn't do either of us any good if I lie to you about this stuff," I explain to him. "But it wasn't like I was going to be up and leaving LA. It was just me leaving your house because I wasn't sure that you wanted me to be here."

He nods, his wide brown eyes marred with confusion. "Why wouldn't I want you to be here?"

"Because you think I'm about to screw you and your band over, tearing down everything you've built and all the momentum of the ticket sales and downloads of the songs. The votes for the VMAs would be jeopardized if I started doing this with The Nutcracker, because you would have to announce that I would only be there for some shows. Like it or not, you hitched your wagon to mine and, unfortunately for you, you hitched it to someone who you really couldn't trust at first. I'd like to think I earned some of it back now."

He chuckles. "Look at you growing."

"I just wish you would grow a little with me," I tease him, bumping my leg with his.

"What, I'm not showing you enough growth? Because, darlin', I can pull my pants—" Before he can finish those words, I smack him on the thigh. "Ow!"

We both laugh and I shake my head. "I haven't signed up for anything yet. If you would have talked to me, you would have known that."

"You could have come out and told me that too," he points out.

"Yeah, I could have, but I wasn't sure that you would want me to do that. I thought maybe you were doing that girl thing where you need your space."

I shake my head. "Nope. I didn't necessarily want space from you. I was scared, though."

"What are you scared of?"

I want to tell them that it's losing him, but I'm not sure how well that will go over. So instead, I say, "Well, I was scared that you would scream at me and name all the ways I was wrecking your dreams."

"You were afraid I would yell?" he asks me.

"Well, yeah, the little abused girl inside of me doesn't like it when people yell at her, and that's where it starts."

"Have I ever yelled at you?"

I sigh. "Well, kinda. When you saw me for the first time again," I point out. "I believe there was some yelling that day."

He chuckles. "You were a surprise. I was pissed that Dale didn't warn me ahead of time. I thought he owed me that much."

"In hindsight, I can see where he went wrong."

"We've come a long way since then," Brent says.

"We sure have. And now I even live with you."

He chuckles. "Yeah, you even live with me. Do you still?"

"I'm here, aren't I?"

"That you are. But are you here because the girls stopped you from leaving or because you want to be here?" he asks me.

I stare at him for a while. All of my thoughts from the last twenty-four hours are running through my mind, and the longer I don't talk to him, the more concerned he looks.

"You would have left," he finally says when I don't say a word.

"That's not what I'm saying," I tell him. "Sorry, there's a lot going through my head right now. I'm just worried about so many things."

"Like?"

"Hurting you, for one thing." I put it out there and watch a hint of a smile appear on his lips. "I don't want to hurt you. I don't want us to be in a position where I'm choosing you or something else. Or where I'm screwing you over again. We just got on firm ground, and I hate that the rug may be pulled out from under us again."

"But this is a big chance for you. I understand that. I don't want you to say no out of some kind of obligation."

"I don't see you as an obligation. I really don't. This is a great opportunity that you've provided me with. Just because I turn this down doesn't mean that I wouldn't get something better or something similar later down the road."

"Does that mean you're not taking it?"

I love how hopeful he sounds. "I don't think that I am. It's a great opportunity, if I'm being honest. But I can't do this if it's going to hurt you and the band. You believed in me and took a chance on me when no one else did. How can I just walk away from all of that?"

"You are an incredible dancer, and according to Dale, everyone dreams of being in The Nutcracker."

I giggle. "You talked to Dale about all this?"

"Yeah, he came to rehearsal today to go over some things with us. One of those things being you and what we would do if you decided that you wanted to pull out of your contract or if we were sharing you with The Nutcracker."

"Crave would actually share me with them?"

"We would. Dale talked to you before he had a chance to talk with us, and while we weren't thrilled with our options, we would allow it because, honestly, we just want you to be happy."

"All of you?"

"Yeah, all of us. Come on, Crave is a like a family. We don't want to be the ones holding you back, but we also want to make sure that we're taken care of too. If we can be a little selfish there."

"I don't think you're being selfish at all. You're looking out for yourselves. Thank you for being so understanding." I lunge forward and hug me, and he lets out a grunting noise. I'm not sure he was ready for me.

"For you, there's not a lot that I wouldn't do," he admits sheepishly into my hair.

I pull back. "You are nothing short of amazing, and you are so understanding. I'm not sure I deserve someone like you."

He shakes his head. "You do. And I'm going to figure out a way to make you feel like you do. Because, honey, someone has got to make you feel worthy. And if it's the last thing I do, I will be that someone."

I lean in and kiss him. "Oh, Brent, you old rock-and-roll softy."

It's then that Dale makes his presence known. I had no idea he was here, so I jump. Brent just chuckles and pulls me close.

"Sorry, I guess I should have mentioned that our meeting with Dale followed us here."

"Hey, guys, sorry to interrupt, but I wanted to know if we have any resolutions? What are we doing? Are we picking door number one, where she leaves us and dances in The Nutcracker? Or door number two, where we share her?"

"We actually haven't come to any firm decisions. But we're okay," Brent admits with a shrug.

"Well, that's really all that matters," Dale replies, and I can't decipher if he's being sarcastic or if he's trying to hide the fact that he couldn't give a shit about us. "Any closer to a decision?" he asks me.

"I can't leave Crave," I tell him. "I can't do that to Brent and the band. I won't make you share me, and I want to honor my commitment. It's not fair to these boys to jump on the first opportunity that sparks up. What would that say about me as a dancer or even an employee? The Nutcracker shouldn't want me if I'm the type of person who would do that."

Brent beams, standing up and dragging me with him. He swings me around, whooping and hollering. "I get to keep my girl!" he calls out as we spin around.

"I'm your girl?" I ask him, grinning widely.

"Oh, Blair, you've always been my girl. You might have left me for a bit, but I was always yours and you were always mine. It's about time we figured all this shit out and stopped making it so damn hard all the time!"

I laugh. "Yeah, I agree. I love you. More than you'll ever know."

The lust that fills those brown eyes is enough to make me want to take him right here, Dale present or not. "I love you too. More than anything in this world," he replies.

We kiss and I hear Dale clear his throat. "Uh, guys. I hate to step on this wonderful moment in your relationship, but there are more things to iron out here."

"Like what?" Brent asks him.

"Like, have you told The Nutcracker people yet?"

I sigh. "No, I just figured it out."

"Okay, well, you should go tell your agent that, because Presley is blowing up my phone, and fuck, is she annoying."

"She's kind of like you," I admit with a grin.

"Funny. But I'm not that bad."

Brent's motioning for someone to come out of the house, waving wildly at them. It's then that Derek, Aiden, Audrey, and Emma join us on the back deck.

"She's staying with us!" he yells to them. "She chose us!"

"Hell freaking yeah!" Derek says. "I knew I liked this girl."

I laugh when he picks me up and gives me a hug.

Aiden gives me a fist bump. "So happy you're staying with us. Thank you."

"No, thank you," I tell him. "Thank you all. Thank you all for making me a part of this family. I've never had anything like this before, and I'm just amazed at how quickly you all invited me in. I couldn't ask for better friends or a better band to do this with."

"We love you too!" Emma and Audrey squeal, pulling me into a hug.

There are more hugs and questions from the guys, but most of it's for Brent, so I just stand there grinning and taking it all in.

Aiden pulls me in for a side hug. "Thank you for choosing us. Really, thank you. You're not just saving us. You're saving him too. I've seen the way he goes through girls, and I knew it was just a reaction to the hurt he kept inside. He was just trying to screw the pain away. With you back and you guys doing so well, he's healing. So, thank you for that."

Emma looks up at him and says, "Aw, look at you being a romantic."

"Well, I do write love songs from time to time," he teases her.

I slowly back away from the group so that I can call Presley and give her the word. Brent begins to come toward me, but I hold my phone up and mouth, "Agent." He just nods.

"Hello, this is Presley," she says when she answers.

"Hey, Presley." I decide I'm going to rip the Band-Aid off. "I can't do it. I'm sorry, but I'm turning down The Nutcracker. It's not right to do this to the band."

"Does this have anything to do with a certain bald member of Crave?" she asks me. She does not sound happy with me.

"It might," I admit.

She sighs. "This is a mistake."

"It might be, but I have to honor my commitment." I repeat the same thing I told the guys. "The Nutcracker should want better than someone who bails for something better. Hell, I want to be better than that."

"Okay, well, I respect that. I'll keep looking for things for you, but I'll send you things that work with the availability of Crave."

"Thanks, Pres, I really appreciate that."

"Of course. Anything for you."

We click off and I walk back over, where Brent wraps his arms around me. Leaning in, he gives me a tender kiss. "I love you."

"Love you too."

CHAPTER THIRTY-NINE

It's the night of the VMAs, and I don't think I've ever been this nervous.

"I've never walked a red carpet before," I tell Brent. "I mean, we've been working on press, but I feel like this is so much more than that. More people and more cameras."

Brent lifts my chin so that he can see my eyes. He places a gentle kiss on my lips. "You're going to be just fine. I will be there the whole time, and I won't let anything happen to you, okay?"

I nod and he continues.

"And you've gotta remember that we're not the only band who will be there, so attention will only be on us for a bit. They'll also want to see the other stars."

I giggle. "True, sorry. I'm just so nervous!"

"You'll be fine. I promise you," he says again.

I love this man. He does so much to make sure I feel comfortable and loved something I haven't had in a long time.

Dale decided he was going to dress the band alike, and they are all in black tuxes. Brent looks incredibly sexy in his. Since the band's logo is a deep, vampire red, they have me in a long, flowy backless red dress. The dip stops just at the top of my ass, with a nice sweetheart cutout that accents my breasts. If I bend over too much, my ass will be out.

"Fucking amazing," Brent said when he first saw me.

I adjust his tie for a bit. The moment feels very domestic, almost like a bride-and-groom moment.

"You are so handsome and incredibly sexy in this tux. I love the all-black look on you."

"'Thank you," he says before giving me a quick kiss.

"Stop kissing me. You gotta watch the lipstick. Every once a while is fine, but you just keep doing it!"

He laughs. "I keep forgetting about that."

"Sure, you do." I give him a wink.

"We should head out and see if the rest of the group is ready to go, even if I want to stay in here and keep you all to myself all night long."

I giggle. "I guess." I wouldn't mind having him all to myself tonight, without all the crowds and sharing him with the press.

Dale has set us all up with suites near the hotel. Even though the awards show is held in LA, this allows us to not have to worry so much about the traffic. Our limo ride will be short, and the hair and makeup staff only needed to come to one spot and get me, Audrey, and Emma ready for tonight. I haven't seen them dressed yet, but they coordinated with wearing navy dresses. Their cuts are similar to mine; mine is just a bit more daring in the back than theirs.

We walk out into the hallway, and everyone is ready to go.

"Oh, ladies, you look stunning," I say to Emma and Audrey.

"Thank you, but look at you, girl," Emma tells me. "You are beautiful."

"Thank you!" I reply.

I notice that all of our heels are the same—black patent leather. Thankfully, they don't make me taller than Brent; we're just eye to eye.

"Ladies, if you're ready..." a man from the security team states. He's motioning for us to follow him to the elevator. "The limo is waiting downstairs, and we can't stay parked there for long."

We all nod and hurry along. Everyone is quietly talking, and I look in Brent's direction.

He beams at me brightly. "You're going to do just fine, darlin'. Don't worry, we've all got you."

I nod. "I'm so excited for you."

There was some discussion about me going up on stage with them if they received the award. Brent felt I should be there too, but I don't want to get in the way. A dancer has never been brought up for this before, and I wouldn't want to do anything that draws attention away from the guys. They've earned this moment; this is something they should experience without me. Dale was glad I was staying out of it.

We pull into the line of limos waiting to head to the VMAs. My stomach does a flip-flop at the thought of walking the red carpet.

"You'll do just fine," Audrey tells me, reaching across the limo and squeezing my hand. "I was a mess my first time too, but the only thing you need to do is hold Brent's hand and glide along. I'd like to say these get better, but they never really do."

"Okay, guys," the security guy states, "you have about fifteen minutes until we're at the front."

Derek is already grabbing for a bottle of tequila. "This is a ritual," he tells me. "Everyone gets a little bit of liquid courage before going in, and then we all eat a mint." He chuckles at the last part. "That way, we don't smell too bad, but we can manage to get through it all," he says, looking directly at me.

I nod and wait for the glass to be handed to me. I assume there's a toast, because everyone is waiting to take their shot.

"The most important thing isn't whether we win or lose," Derek begins. "It's that we are all here together and we're a family. We've gotten this far, and we've gained a lot of new followers and have put out some quality music. So, let's fucking go there with our heads held high. Be proud of yourselves and this band."

Brent and Aiden cheer and holler, raising up their glasses, and the girls do the same. I join in and take down the shot of tequila. I've never been much of a tequila drinker, but I take the shot all of the same. It burns as it goes down, and I hope the bit of liquid courage I get is enough to propel me through the night.

Soon, the limo slows, and Brent turns to me, wagging his eyebrows. "It's go time, darlin'."

I sigh and nod. *It's going to be okay. It's going to be okay*; I keep repeating in my head. Before I exit the limo, Brent leans over and captures my lips with his. He kisses me until I'm breathless; I can barely keep up with the way his mouth is working against mine. The sheer amount of passion he's putting into this kiss is making my head dizzier than the alcohol did. We pull apart and I'm panting.

"Let's do this," he says, pulling me out of the limo.

From behind me, I hear Aiden say, "He stole that trick from me."

It makes me laugh and ensures my smile is genuine when we leave the limo. Down the red carpet we go, cameras flashing all around us. It's so much brighter on the carpet than I thought it would be. Brent holds on to me tightly, and I squeeze his hand a few times. There are so many stars on the carpet who I'd like to see in person, but I can't even look in their direction. I'm too busy walking and making sure I don't fall.

I hear a couple of folks on the carpet screaming and calling me the "girl from the video." It makes my smile wider and makes me happier that I chose this path with this man and this band. He squeezes my hand, and we keep on moving down. The reporters are coming closer and closer. I take a deep breath and listen as the questions begin with Derek about how the song writing process was and why he's been absent from press. I don't listen to the answers, though; I'm too busy counting to ten and trying to keep myself calm.

My anxiety is really starting to prickle up, and my palms are beginning to sweat. I move to pull my hand back from Brent, but he holds it tighter. I'm sure he can see the fear in my eyes, like I wanna flee at any second. My heart is hammering in my chest as I take a step away from him, but I'm jerked forward.

I find myself in his arms as he pulls me close and places his lips on mine. He kisses me gently. It's not as fiery as it was in the limo, but it's a close second. I whimper under his touch and can hear the applause from all around his. Brent pulls back, and both of our faces are red.

"Damn, man," Aiden says. "What was that for?"

Brent just shrugs and looks at me. "Are you good now?"

I smile brightly at him. "Yeah, I'm good."

"Brent! Come here, dear, come here," a reporter is saying to him. "Are you dating the dancer in the video?"

He chuckles. "Well, if I'm not, then it looks weird for me to have kissed her, huh? Her name is Blair, by the way."

"Blair, it's so nice to meet you," she says, turning her attention to me. "Your moves in the video are amazing. I just wanted you to know that you *made* that video."

"She did. She really did," Brent says, giving me a squeeze.

"Well, thank you. That's so sweet of you to say. The beats Brent laid down are just incredible and made it so easy and effortless to dance to."

"You two are adorable. Congratulations, both of you, on the nomination," she says, and we move on.

Once inside, the guys are watching Brent with wide smiles.

"Did Dale know you were going to do that?" Aiden chuckles.

"I'll text him." Brent laughs along with him.

"You did great, Blair," Audrey replies, giving my arm a squeeze.

"Thanks, you too."

"I hate this part of it so much. I'm not sure how the guys can just walk the carpet like it's no big deal. But they do it."

We both laugh and look over at where they're talking about

something or someone, judging by the way they're looking around the room. When it's time to move in and take our seats, we all file into our row and wait for their category to be announced. Crave isn't performing this year, but Brent said the nomination is enough for him.

Finally, it's time. It's their category.

The announcer shares all the nominations for the award, but it's all a blur and happens so fast. The winner is announced and Crave wins!

The band is up and hugging one another. Before I know it, they're on the stage, thanking the world and everyone who made it possible.

Brent then takes the mic and says, "We would also like to thank one very special person. Blair, you took those moves and made them your own. Thank you for helping us get here and for making 'Love Drunk' the success that it is. Good night, everyone!"

Everyone jumps to their feet, and we applaud them as they're led off the stage. Audrey, Emma, and I hug one another. I'm so proud of him and this band. Brent has seriously blossomed and turned out be a wonderful man, not that he wasn't already, but he's just taken his music to a whole other level. I'm so glad I get to be here to see it all.

CHAPTER FORTY

It's about a half hour before we actually find them again. They text and say that they won't be back to their seats, and we should come and find them backstage, where there's food and booze. Which is great because I'm starving. We head on back there, and I immediately attack Brent's lips.

Throwing my hand around his neck, I pull him to me quickly. My lips find his hungrily. Our kiss is anything but PG. Our tongues are dancing with each other, and hands are roaming. I don't care that we're giving everyone a show. It's a private room only for the musicians and their dates to hang out in, so no press is able to see what we're doing. I almost don't care if they could, but Dale would have a field day with all of this. I'm not very comfortable with attention, so I don't want to bring any more to me than I normally would.

Derek holds out an award to me. "This is for you," he says, his voice full of emotion. "You helped us win this award, so I had them put one together for you as well. Well, Dale did before the show, on the off chance that we would win. You helped us with this just as much, if not more, with all the press tours and interviews. It was only right that you got a trophy too."

"Wow, I don't know what to say." A lump forms in my throat,

which I force down. "Thank you. Thank you so much for picking me and letting me stay after you heard he hated me. Thank you…just thank you for everything," I tell them all.

Each of the guys takes a turn giving me a hug, then Audrey takes the trophy they handed me and admires it. "This is so beautiful. It's really wonderful that you get one too."

"It really is," I say, dabbing at my tears. "I can't believe they did this."

"I can." Emma smiles knowingly at them. "These boys might be rock stars and sing some hard rock from time to time, but they're old softies. Their bark is a lot bigger than their bite. Plus, Jade has softened them all a lot too."

We all giggle at that.

"Hey, I'm still a badass," Aiden says, pulling in his wife for a kiss.

"Sure, you are honey," Emma says when they break apart. "Who cried at a Disney movie the other night?"

"Anna and Elsa's parents died. How could I not?" he asks her.

I laugh and shake my head. "That is a very sad part."

"See, she gets it," Aiden tells Emma.

"Please don't encourage him."

We never do make it back to our seats. We stay backstage and eat and have a few drinks. The limo is quickly called for, and we're off, leaving for an afterparty.

"Yes, we're going dancing!" Audrey exclaims. "You think you can manage in your heels, girl?"

"Oh, look who you're asking," Emma says, winking at me.

"I'll be fine," I tell her.

I recognize a couple of people from the awards show at the club, and even some other famous people who weren't at the VMAs.

"Holy shit," I say when I've spotted a famous actor standing over by the bar.

"Keep your pants on. You're here with me," Brent whispers in my ear. "Get used to it, kiddo. You're going to be noticed, and you're going to notice a lot more famous people around you. I'm going to help make all of your dreams come true. That little job you gave up for us is going to look like chump change when it's all said and done."

"I don't regret a single minute of turning down that job, Brent. This is where I belong. Where you go, I go. Remember?"

His eyes shine with love.

"Yeah, I remember the promise you used to make to me when we were kids," I admit with a shrug. "I just didn't always know how to follow it. But I do now."

He smiles back at me. He gets ready to say something, but Audrey jumps in.

"Let's get your ass to the dance floor so we can shake our groove things."

And that's what we do. We all head out to the dance floor and begin dancing together. I'm too busy getting lost in Brent to notice that anyone else is on the dance floor. He puts his hands on my waist, and at first, it's like he's trying to guide my hips. I look up at him and shake my head, then I move them for both of us. I work to get his pace to match mine. For being such a tall man, Brent is a good dancer. Although he is a drummer, so it shouldn't surprise me. The Brent I knew all those years ago wouldn't have been dancing like this. He would have stayed on the wall. But this Brent is moving along with me.

I spin around and grind my ass into his hips, and he responds by growling in my ear.

"You might want to stop doing that," he tells me.

"Why is that?" I whisper back to him, batting my eyes just bit.

"Because I'm going to try to take you right here on this dance floor."

"I'm really not seeing the problem," I fire back.

He just chuckles in my ear and sucks on it. It's enough to make me throw my head back and moan. The song ends and he pulls me off the dance floor.

"Let's see if we can get something to cool you down just a bit," he says. We head over to the bar, and he orders us some mixed cocktails that are the special of the night. "There's some food over there if you're hungry."

"I'm only hungry for one thing," I tell him, licking my lips and spinning my cocktail straw in between my lips.

"Be nice, dirty girl, and I won't be when we get home," he teases me.

"Should we wait until we get into the limo? Might be easier and more convenient," I tease him right back. I'm hoping to raise the bar enough so that he lets us go home.

"We'll go in a bit." He chuckles. "But I'm not doing anything with you in the limo. We're not going to be a cliché."

"Didn't Derek and Audrey fuck in the limo once on the way home from an awards ceremony?"

"Yes, and we're not doing that."

I just laugh and I look out on the dance floor where Audrey and Derek are practically having sex while they dance. Emma and Aiden are making their way over to us.

"We're gonna take off now," Emma explains. "I wanna get home to little Miss Jade."

"Have a good night, guys," I say. We all hug, and Emma and Aiden are soon gone.

"Are they only going home for that reason?" I say with a giggle.

"Well, they could be. They really are gaga over that kid. But it could also be a great excuse to leave early."

"Should we tell them we're leaving too?" I gesture to Audrey and Derek.

"I don't think they'll miss us," he says. "You ready to go home?"

"I am. But the good thing is, we don't have a baby waiting for us at home," I tease.

He chuckles. "Well, not yet."

I just smile and wink at him. He leads me out of the club,

and the limo is racing through the streets to get us back to our house so that I can ravish Brent.

When we get to the house and inside, I can tell he has the same thing on his mind. His eyes are wild, and his gaze is traveling all over my body.

"Should we go into your room or mine?" I ask him in a low voice.

"Do we really have to go into a bedroom? We could just do things here." He walks over to me, then picks up one of the thin straps and starts pulling it down my arm. When it doesn't go easy, he unzips the back of my dress, causing the straps and the dress to fall down and pool at my feet.

"What are you doing to do with me now that you have me naked?" I ask him, my tone low and husky.

"How am I only learning now that you weren't wearing any underwear under this?"

"I didn't want lines," I tell him like it isn't a big deal. Like, I can't see his eyes turning a molten chocolate brown at the sight of me. "Did you not go commando?"

"I did not," he says before clearing his throat. He moves forward and pulls me to him, capturing my lips with his. His hands roam up and down my body, but they avoid all the places I need him to be. My sex is throbbing at the thought of him touching me there.

"Brent, please," I beg him.

"Please what, sweetheart? What is it that you need?" He begins removing his jacket and unbuttoning his shirt.

"Don't I get to do any of that?" I whimper out at the sight of his bare chest.

"No, I'll do all of this. I want to save your energy for other things. What do you think about that?" he asks me in husky voice.

"What would I need that energy for?" I ask him.

"Oh, you're going to need to hold yourself up. Turn around for me and stick your ass out."

I swallow with anticipation and do as he asks. I wiggle my ass at him before I stick it out. His hand comes down and spanks it. It stings just a bit, but I love it. I moan at the feeling of the pain. I enjoy this side of Brent. So, I shake it again and hope that he spanks me again. Thankfully, he does.

"Do you like that, you dirty girl?" he husks out. "I had no idea you had this side to you. We'll have to experiment with this later tonight. But right now, I need to feel you. We'll have time for that later on."

I nod and whimper. "Please, Brent," I beg again. "Just touch me."

His arm comes around me, and he runs a hand through my slick folds. "You're dripping, darlin'. You seem like you're hurting. Do you need me to stick my fingers inside you?" He slips two fingers inside me, and my hips buck forward.

"Fuck!" I cry out while he pumps his fingers in and out of me. "So good, so good," I keep repeating.

"Oh, this is going to be so much fun," he says in my ear, pulling his fingers from my pussy. I cry out at the loss of him. "Don't worry, baby. I'm going to give you something else."

I hear the unzipping of his pants, and I wiggle my ass at him some more.

"I'm coming, sweetheart." He roughly grab my hips and enters me forcefully. It's a delicious dance between pleasure and pain and I love it.

I push back up against him, hoping for more. More friction, more something. And he gives it to me. He pumps in and out of me, using my hips to hold onto me and give himself some leverage to keep driving in and out. He's grunting and we're both a mess of moans and whimpers that are coming from me.

"Fuck, Brent, you feel so fucking unbelievable. Fuck, I love you."

"I love you too," he says, punctuating each of his words with a thrust.

"I am so, so close," I moan.

He pushes farther and faster inside me, so much that it feels like he's trying to split me in half. I cry out in pleasure, and it's enough to send me over the edge. Brent soon follows.

"Are you okay?" he asks me. I'm lying over the couch and he's resting against me. "I wasn't exactly gentle."

"That was amazing. I meant what I said, it was amazing. You were amazing."

He kisses my shoulder and pulls out of me. "Let's get you cleaned up so that we can go again."

And that's what he does. He carries me back to the bedroom, lays me down, and takes care of me three more times before the night is over. Thankfully, tomorrow is a whole day off for the both of us, because I don't think I'll be able to walk once it's all over.

CHAPTER FORTY-ONE

I love the new level of normalcy we've developed. I go to dance classes and practice for the tours. Dale has even added me to the regular Crave payroll so that I can keep the job and not have to look for some part-time work. Although Brent would love it if I could just stay unemployed so that I could never leave.

I told him that I wouldn't leave if he kept feeding me. The man may not like to admit it, but he sure can cook and grill up a mean piece of chicken. And when I let him, steak. I just feel bad that I'm not contributing, but he refuses to let me. He wants to take care of me. Every time I offer to pay rent or buy groceries, I get the same answer: "I want to take care of you the way everyone else in your life always should have."

I can't argue with that, as much as I would like to. I do find ways to pay him back, though, and not just in the bedroom. There are times when I cook for him and even bake. He enjoys the sweet treats I can make. He even devours my homemade granola bars. I have to hide them so that I have one or two.

Brent is still afraid that I'll leave him one day and won't come back. Like I did before. So, if me living in another apartment means I might be able to sneak away and he won't know it, then he doesn't want it. We're working on that one, too. I told him that living with him was never supposed to be permanent, but so far it has been. And with us going on tour soon, is there really a need to go look for a place to live? We leave in October, come back for Thanksgiving and Christmas, and then once the New Year is over, we'll be back out on the road again until March. I'm excited to experience life on the road. I like the idea of seeing the world with him, and I like that I'll be there with him.

Right now, we're getting ready to have a barbecue and spend some time with our little family. That's what I've come to know them as; they aren't the band and their girlfriends. They never really were, but they've become like my family too, and I love them for that. They've been my greatest supports, and I couldn't thank Brent enough for bringing them into my life.

It's comical how much they're here. Aiden and Emma are even looking at getting a house in the area. They want baby Jade to have a house with a yard, even though Uncle Brent is glad to share his yard with her. I would like it if they all moved near us. Brent says I'm crazy, like I desire some weird Real World scenario, but I just like having them around. I've never had family like this before.

I ready the vegetable plates and fruit platters while Brent is out on the grill. Everyone should be arriving here soon. It's just when I put the platters out on the dining table on the patio that I hear the cars pulling in.

"Someone's here," I call to Brent.

He walks over and kisses my lips gently. "Okay, good. The sooner they get here, the sooner they will leave, and I won't have to share you anymore."

I giggle, kissing him again. "Yeah, well, guests being here haven't stopped you from grabbing my ass or my boobs or making out with me fiercely. So yeah, not buying it."

"You never complained," he says, then shrugs. "Too loudly."

"Because I like it when you touch me," I admit, kissing him again. Although, I doubt I'm telling him anything he doesn't already know. I let him touch me many times last night, and I'm pretty sure he's gearing up for another round tonight.

"Stop it, guys. You have to give up the honeymoon phase eventually," Aiden teases as he walks into the door.

"We will when you will." Brent winks at him.

He laughs. "I'm not sure what you're referring to." With that, he gives Emma's ass a slap.

Derek and Audrey are coming in behind them. "Hey all," Audrey says. She's got her arm around Derek and looks like she has no intentions of letting him go.

"See, look at those two," Aiden points out. "They aren't even married yet and look at how attached they still are to each other."

"You wouldn't want me to be any other way with your sister," Derek says with a laugh.

"Yeah, but I could go for less of seeing you stick your tongue down my sister's throat," Aiden says with a roll of his eyes.

"I like it though," Audrey whines.

"Yeah, she does," Derek says, leaning over and kissing her.

"How soon until dinner is ready?" I ask Brent.

"Aw, look at you two all domesticated and shit," Derek says.

"We have been for a while, and you can stop eating all of my food," Brent says, pretending to punch him. But Derek just ends up pulling him into a hug.

"Look at this cute little family gathering," Dale says, entering the fence from the side of the house. "I'm sorry to bother you all on your day off, but I have some exciting news that I had to come over and share with you."

"It's cool, man. Do you want a beer?" Brent asks him.

"Nah, the wife is going to want me home," Dale says.

"I still can't get over the fact that you have a wife," Audrey says and then slams her hand against her face. "I'm sorry."

We all chuckle.

"No, it's okay. I look like the type of man who's going to be snatching your children at night or some shit like that," Dale says, laughing at his own joke.

"Well, no, not snatching children at night, but selling them if it would make a quick buck," Aiden corrects him.

"What's your good news, man?" Derek asks.

"Audrey and Blair, come here, ladies," he says. "I have some exciting news to tell you. Well, if you want it, that is."

I walk toward him and so does Audrey. We exchange a confused glance, and I shrug in her direction.

"I stumbled upon an interesting opportunity for you both, and you're really going to like it," Dale continues. "I was approached by Lululemon, and they would like for you two to be their spokeswomen. Be influencers and post their apparel on your social media accounts, and they'll give you free stuff for it. You'll also earn a handsome sponsorship fee for this, too. You have to agree to exclusively wear this workout brand."

I look over at Audrey and then at Brent. I'm sure my mouth is hanging open right now. I've heard of these types of partnerships, but I never thought I would be on the receiving end of one.

"Are you serious? They really want me?" I reply. "I mean, Audrey, I can see. She has that whole Beachbody thing happening. But me, I'm just a dancer."

"You're the dancer for Crave. I've told this one to work on some more beats for you to dance to so that we can keep this momentum with you and the band going," Dales says, coming closer to me. "Look, this could be a really great deal for both of you. But if you're not in, then that's fine. They'll take just one of you, but they do want both of you."

I'm still processing this. I look over and see that Audrey is bouncing up and down. "I'm not sure I can do this with Beachbody. Do they allow that kind of thing?"

"They'll let you. I called over there and spoke to the PR lady I had to work with when you two got into trouble," he says, winking in Derek's direction. "She was all for it. Totally on board with the whole thing. But they want to talk to you and make sure that you're comfortable with it."

"But they have their own line of stuff," she reminds him.

"Yeah, but she said you never wear it. She said you always wear Nike and other brands like that. She even has footage of you in Lululemon, which really helped seal this deal. So, what do you think, Miss Audrey? Do we have a deal?"

"Why do I always feel like you should be sitting behind a big desk tapping your fingers together?" she asks him. "Or sitting with a cat in your lap, stroking it as you laugh wickedly?"

"That was oddly specific," he says with a laugh. "Blair, thoughts? You've been quiet."

"This sounds amazing. I'm in," I say. I smile and look over at Brent. "What do you think? This seems good. I mean, I need to see the specifics and run it by Presley, but if she's good, I'm good."

Brent smiles. "She'll be pleased, but yes, we do need to do that. Aud?" he asks her.

"Let's do it. I mean, let's check into this some more. That's what we're giving permission for, not signing our lives away or making some kind of a deal with the devil."

Derek chuckles. "She's got your number."

Dale laughs. "She might, but I just want to do good things for you—all of you. But yeah, I'll get the specifics nailed down. If I'm right about this, it's going to be particularly lucrative for all of you. Okay, now get back to your family dinner and I'll see you later."

"Thank you, Dale," I tell him. "I appreciate all you're doing for me."

"You're welcome, kiddo."

"Yeah, thanks," Audrey adds in. "I do like to tease you, but man, do you ever look out for all of us."

"That's what I'm here for, babe," he says before saying goodbye to the band and leaving.

When he closes the fence, Audrey and I jump up and down, hugging.

"This is so awesome!" I yell.

"We're gonna be in Lululemon! Can you believe it?" Audrey squeals.

"It's what I do," Dale yells from the other side of the fence. "I make dreams happen."

"Thank you, Dale," we both call out.

Brent walks over to me and pulls me into a hug. "I am so proud of you."

"For what? Looking so hot in athletic wear that they want to hire me to wear it and take my picture in it?" I tease him.

"Don't do that. Don't minimize your accomplishments. You are an amazing woman and look at all of the amazing things that are happening as a result," he says, giving my forehead a quick kiss.

"That's one way to look at it."

"What's the other way?" He looks at me confused. The man is so handsome when he's all confused, with a furrowed brow and sun shining off his bald head. He's the sexiest, tamest rock star I've ever seen.

"None of these amazing things would have happened to me if it wasn't for you. *You* had so much to do with all of this," I reply. "And I am forever grateful for it and to have you back in my life."

It's me who cleans up and kisses him this time. "I love you."

"I love you too," he says, giving me one of his giant bear hugs. There's nothing better than one of his hugs, and there's nothing better than being with him. He's given me so much since he's been back in my life.

"But you gotta remember, it was your amazing moves that started all of this." He taps my nose.

"To your amazing beats," I remind him.

"You two make me wanna gag," Derek says, bringing us back to the group.

Brent leans in and gives me a quick kiss before heading back to the grill. "I gotta go check on my meat."

"Blair, don't you have to go with him?" Aiden teases.

Brent shoots him the middle finger as he walks away, but the guys are the ones who follow him to the grill to have their beers and chitchat. I stay with Emma, Audrey, and Jade so that we can have girl talk. I glance over and see Brent having a great time with the guys. He catches me watching and gives me the slightest nod, and I give him one right back. That man of mine—he's more than I could have wished for, and he's all I'll ever crave.

Life with him and this band is certainly good.

Thank you for reading *Wish*. I hope you loved this rock star romance and enemies to lovers romance.

This concludes the *Crave Series*. I hope you enjoyed spending time with them as much as I did writing these hot rockers.

And be sure to check out , *Sinning with You*, which has the same steam, spice and second chance as Wish For.

And you can sign up for my newsletter here:

https://dashboard.mailerlite.com/forms/543405/9642250996285669/share

ABOUT THE AUTHOR

J.L. Stray has always enjoyed reading books and writing stories. Finally, she gathered up enough courage to publish one herself. A former Policy Specialist and current Consultant, she spends any extra moment she has writing, outlining and scheming her next book. https://www.example.com

Raised in a small town in Pennsylvania, she graduated from Penn State University with a bachelor's degree in Criminal Justice and Public Policy. Most days she uses one of those degrees in either her career or dealing with her children.

ALSO BY J.L. STRAY

The Broken Series

Irreversibly Broken, The Broken Series Book 1

Fixing the Broken, The Broken Series Book 2

No Longer Broken, The Broken Series Book 3

The Crave Series

Lust For

Long For

Wish For

Standalone Novels

Tis the Damn Season

Sinning with You